Crime and Paradise

by

Julie Howard

Wild Crime Series

This is a work of fiction. Names, characters, places, and incidents are either the product of the author's imagination or are used fictitiously, and any resemblance to actual persons living or dead, business establishments, events, or locales, is entirely coincidental.

Crime and Paradise

Contact Information: info@thewildrosepress.com

Cover Art by *Kristian Norris*

The Wild Rose Press, Inc.
PO Box 708
Adams Basin, NY 14410-0708
Visit us at www.thewildrosepress.com

Publishing History
First Crimson Rose Edition, 2017
Print ISBN 978-1-5092-1645-1
Digital ISBN 978-1-5092-1646-8

Wild Crime Series
Published in the United States of America

Alarmed, she peered into the darkness, nothing but blackness at the end of the headlights. Just a single dot of light before them, off in the distance, never coming closer no matter how long they drove toward it. Meredith looked over at Brian, wondering at this strange joke. They were nowhere. Why was he taking his family to the middle of nowhere, in the snow, at night? A shiver of apprehension went through her.

"You're going to love it here." The words raced out of Brian. "No worries about the kids. No traffic or smog. People are real in Idaho. They don't put on a show, you know? It's paradise on earth out here. Paradise on earth."

Meredith stared at the dot of light, terrified now that the lonely outpost was their home. *I won't do this.* She sat up straighter in her seat, ready to confront Brian, no matter the consequences. *He can't make me do this.*

The truck's tires slid on the icy road and Meredith braced her arms against the dashboard as Brian turned the steering wheel from side to side, gaining control. She bit her lip, readying her words, when Brian slowed the truck and turned them away from the light. In front of them, a gray shape emerged from the darkness and Meredith realized they were in a long driveway. At the end, the truck's headlights illuminated a boxy one-story house. They bumped and slid into the rutted icy driveway and then Brian cut the engine. Meredith's words faded from her mind. They sat there, unmoving.

"We're home," he said.

Dedication

To Kelsey and Lake,
first readers who kept my heroine on the right path.

Part 1

If you're married, you need to know this—your spouse has thought about killing you.

It may be a flash of an idea in the heat of an argument and something they would never, ever follow through on. It may be a lingering wish for freedom, one that goes on for decades.

Your husband is cleaning his hunting rifle and you walk by. The idea flickers through his mind; he can end his misery with one shot. Your wife pours the coffee, contemplating how easy it would be to add a little antifreeze. But that's just thinking, not doing.

Despite the deluge of TV crime shows stirring up our basest instincts, most people don't act on these impulses. Your neighbor, your boss, your favorite barista—and frankly, you—all harbor murder-ish inclinations, but are all statistically unlikely to commit murder.

And for all you married people, calm down. 99.9% of spouses never plan out a murder, let alone follow through with it.

Of course, sometimes, things go wrong.

Chapter 1

Atticus had been crying for an hour before his eight-month-old voice faded to a gasping whimper. Meredith was nearly in tears herself, trapped in the truck with a distressed baby, a cranky four-year-old, and a silent husband.

"When—" she started tentatively.

"Don't ask me again how much longer," Brian snapped. "We'll get there when we get there. I told you, it's a long drive."

Meredith turned away from him and stared back out at the window. The landscape hadn't changed in three hours. Mountains to the right, mountains to the left, mountains in front of them. They'd drive up one stark hill and down the other side just to be confronted with its clone. No people, no houses, no billboards to read to relieve the boredom of the drive. And no signs to tell her how much farther they had to go before they reached their destination.

I can do this, Meredith thought. *But what exactly are we doing?*

"Mommy, I have to make a pee," announced Jamie from the backseat.

Meredith turned back more authoritatively toward her husband. He would have to stop now. Even if Brian wouldn't listen to her, he always listened to Jamie. He loved his little girl, the one female in his household who still adored him and believed every word he uttered.

"Brian."

"I know." Her husband was annoyed and cut her off again. "She's gonna have to pee by the side of the road. Geez," he added, "we're never going to get there if we keep stopping like this."

Meredith didn't remind him they didn't "keep stopping," that they had been in Brian's rumbling truck for ten hours with only two stops for gas and food. With windows closed, the truck was stuffy with the odors of crayons, sweaty children, and the last change of Atticus's dirty diaper. Brian swung the truck to the side of the empty highway, pulling off to the dirt shoulder.

A cold wind gusted across the empty prairie, rippling through the low sagebrush dotting the landscape. No trees or tall bushes for privacy. Meredith looked around quickly and then helped Jamie squat next to the car.

"Watch your shoes," cautioned Meredith, brushing back the strands of light brown hair blowing loose from her ponytail and across her face. "Don't pee on yourself."

Jamie looked down, bending forward and watching the yellow stream puddle into the dirt and widen toward her feet. Meredith shivered.

"Mommy, it's going to get on me," Jamie whimpered, scooting her feet wider and losing her balance.

Meredith caught her just in time, but stepped in her daughter's puddle herself.

"Mommy stepped in my pee!" Jamie squealed in delight. "Daddy, Mommy stepped in my pee!"

"Stay still." Meredith realized too late she didn't have anything to wipe her daughter. She swept Jamie up in her arms and leaned into the car looking for a tissue, feeling wetness against her middle as Jamie leaned into her. She sighed, pulled up her daughter's pants and then looked at the damp spot on her own waist.

This sort of summed up her day.

Their move was unexpected. It was to her, in any case. Yesterday, she lived in a somewhat shabby, but loveable apartment in Oakland, California. One quick train ride away from the deep blue of the Pacific Ocean. She knew the neighbors; which ones were always up for a chat and which ones to avoid. There was a small, vegan grocery store at one end of the block only open a few hours in the evenings when the owner got off his paying job, and an always-crowded laundromat on the other corner. A place selling deli sandwiches had been next door, but it closed after being robbed twice in one week. It was a neighborhood where you didn't walk around at night, but she didn't need to go out then anyway. There were rules to living in the city, same as anywhere, and as long as you understood the rules, things were fine. Keep your head down, mind your own business, and keep your doors locked. No different from anywhere else.

Then, Brian had pulled up in front of their building that morning with a trailer behind his truck and announced he bought a house in Idaho, a state somewhere "up north." He told her they were moving and to pack. She stood there stunned, still in the sweat pants she'd slept in at night and wearing a faded red jersey with "*Stanford*" written on the front.

She hadn't attended Stanford, of course; had in fact dropped out of her junior college after one semester. Pregnant with Jamie, thrilled Brian had immediately dropped to one knee and proposed, she didn't think twice about quitting. Her life was starting. Except, five years later, with two children who took all of her waking time and a husband who'd gotten increasingly testy, why did it seem her life had never started at all?

Meredith tried to talk to Brian as he and two strangers, men drinking from a case of beer at seven thirty in the morning, lifted her couch, her dining table, the chairs, and her bed and carried them downstairs to the enclosed trailer behind Brian's truck.

"Iowa? What?" she asked.

"*Idaho.*" Brian enunciated it as though she were a child. "It's a state. Anyway, I got us a house. You can raise your chickens. You'll have your own yard."

She had never lived in a house; apartments, mobile homes, motels, two cars, and for three months, in a tent next to a river. She was never in the same place for more than a year, for her entire life. Since she met Brian, life had been mostly steady and predictable.

"We can't afford a house." Doubt filled her voice.

"In Idaho, we can. That's why we're going there."

"How…" she started.

"Dishes," he interrupted, making a face and pointing to the kitchen. "Are you going to pack them? Or are you leaving them? We need to get a move on."

He turned away. Was this the full extent of their discussion on picking up their lives and moving to another state? She watched as he walked out the door, and a moment later heard him laughing loudly, deeply, in the stairwell with the other men. She turned to the kitchen, numb of all emotion.

Life is messy; it's all about how you handle it. Her mother's favorite saying echoed in her mind. Those words kept her mother afloat far longer than they should have.

This must be one of those messy times. I can either fight this, and surely lose anyway, or get on board. Not that there was any fighting with Brian. He made the decisions and that was that. The end. Lower the curtain. Finis.

When Brian came back into the apartment, the kids were dressed and Meredith had made a game out of giving them their breakfast on the floor where the dining table once stood.

"We're having a picky nick," Jamie cried out to Brian from where she sat cross-legged on the linoleum, spooning cereal to her mouth. Atticus was on his back sucking at his bottle, rocking rhythmically side to side.

Meredith had all their mismatched, thrift store dishes out on the counter. Jamie's princess mug and an assortment of plastic sippy cups lay in a tumble, and her own ceramic plate, the one she made in the fourth grade, glazed a shiny purple and not quite round, not quite oval, not quite level. Still, her teacher praised her for its artistic merit, a compliment she hugged to herself, even now. The purple plate came out at nearly every meal, holding bread or butter, or just serving as a spoon rest for Atticus's baby food.

The questions crowding Meredith's mind wanted to bubble out at her husband. The main one, of course, was *Why didn't you talk to me about this?* That was closely followed by *When did you buy a house? Where did the money come from? How long have you been planning this?* She had been married long enough to know better. Brian didn't like questions.

Instead, Meredith forced the corners of her mouth to turn up. Brian came over to her in an instant and hugged her tightly against his chest. Heat radiated off him from the effort of lugging furniture down the stairs, and he breathed the malty odor of beer down at her as he bent over to kiss her forehead.

"I knew you'd be a good sport," he growled into her ear. "I'm doing this for you and the kids, you know. It's gotten so you can't breathe here in California. Time to get out."

****

The two other men left once the furniture was loaded, and Brian helped Meredith throw the remainder of their belongings into boxes. Jamie ran shouting through the empty rooms, laughing at the echoes which bounced off the walls and ceiling. They left by eleven, the apartment stripped bare.

Exhausted by the morning rush, Meredith watched out the window numbly as the California cities flickered by, one after another. They headed east, up and over the towering, snow-covered Sierra Nevada range, and then dropped, driving past the casinos of Reno. Brian turned the truck north and the terrain grew drier. They began the long trek across the vast desert land toward Idaho.

Jordan Valley, Rome, Marsing, Caldwell, and Nampa. These sounded like places with substance, but as quick as they came, they disappeared in the rearview mirror, with so much empty space in between. They headed east again. Treeless mountains with rocky peaks dipped down into grassy valleys, then up again and then down into a long open valley. Idaho's tiny towns and cities were small islets lost in oceans of farmland and range.

Evening dropped on them suddenly as they stopped at a fast food restaurant off the side of the highway in Nampa for a bathroom break and took their dinner away in to-go bags. The highway took them through Boise where Brian became animated for the first time during their trip. He told her in an important tone how Boise was the state's capital and its largest city, but it disappeared behind them quickly, too.

That is the biggest city in the entire state, Meredith realized with alarm. In the dim light along the freeway, she had discerned nothing but industrial yards and the airport runway. From what she could make out, the biggest city in the state wasn't much at all. In the distance, a chain of mountains backstopped the spread of city lights and Boise appeared a place trapped and huddled in a dismal spot. *At least we're not stopping here*, she encouraged herself.

The day dissolved into full darkness and Jamie and Atticus grew silent in the backseat. Meredith became hopeful when the lights of a city appeared in the distance, but was grateful when they passed to the edge of Mountain Home, another place hardly worth a dot on a map, and kept going. They turned north again onto a narrow two-lane road. It wound through mountains that grew steeper and higher, and their headlights illuminated patches of snow by the sides of the road.

A chill seeped into the car and Meredith glanced back at her sleeping children. Atticus's head was tilted to one side and his long eyelashes dipped down toward his cheeks, a contented look on his face. Jamie had curled up on the seat, one hand clenched in a fist, the other tucked underneath her. Her mouth was open and moving slightly in a dream. Meredith wished she could set her own worry aside enough so sleep would come. Maybe she'd wake up in her own bed, back in Oakland, with all this just a weird dream brought on by fatigue, caffeine, and taking one of Brian's sleeping pills.

How much longer, she wondered, but didn't have the nerve to ask her husband one more time. They crested a hill and started on a gentle slope down before leveling out onto a high prairie cloaked with snow. A dot of light cut the darkness in the far distance, otherwise the darkness was complete.

"Who lives out here?" she asked with a short laugh, glancing sideways at Brian. *Talk to me. Tell me how much longer. Tell me about the house, the neighborhood, how you found it, when you decided to do this, anything. Talk to me.*

"Huh," he grunted.

Just short of the dot of light, Brian turned the truck onto a thin lane and the tires crunched over the hard-packed snow.

"Brian," she risked, one fear trumping the other. "Is this right?"

"Almost there."

Alarmed, she peered into the darkness, nothing but blackness at the end of the headlights. Just a single dot of light before them, off in the distance, never coming closer no matter how long they drove toward it. Meredith looked over at Brian, wondering at this strange joke. They were nowhere. Why was he taking his family to the middle of nowhere, in the snow, at night? A shiver of apprehension went through her.

"You're going to love it here." The words raced out of Brian. "No worries about the kids. No traffic or smog. People are real in Idaho. They don't put on a show, you know? It's paradise on earth out here. Paradise on earth."

Meredith stared at the dot of light, terrified now that the lonely outpost was their home. *I won't do this.* She sat up straighter in her seat, ready to confront Brian, no matter the consequences. *He can't make me do this.*

The truck's tires slid on the icy road and Meredith braced her arms against the dashboard as Brian turned the steering wheel from side to side, gaining control. She bit her lip, readying her words, when Brian slowed the truck and turned them away from the light. In front of them, a gray shape emerged from the darkness and Meredith realized they were in a long driveway. At the end, the truck's headlights illuminated a boxy one-story house. They bumped and slid into the rutted icy driveway and then Brian cut the engine. Meredith's words faded from her mind. They sat there, unmoving.

"We're home," he said.

Chapter 2

She woke up cold.

At some point during the night, Jamie climbed in bed between the two of them and heat rippled off her daughter's body. She considered moving closer to Jamie and taking advantage of her warmth for a few more moments of sleep, but she realized Atticus might have gotten cold during the night.

She edged out of the bed, trying not to disturb Jamie and Brian as she pulled one and then two sweaters over her head, adding to the sweatpants she had gone to sleep in. She grabbed socks from her open suitcase and slipped them on quickly before going down the hall to the room where they set up Atticus's crib the night before.

A miracle child if ever there was one, Atticus had slept through the night after three months. He was happy, uncomplaining, and easygoing. If all children could be like him, she would have ten. But if they were all like Jamie, who sometimes seemed to have a personal vendetta against the world…well, that was playing with fire.

Atticus was awake and standing in his crib, looking around wide-eyed but unafraid at his new surroundings. There were full boxes heaped in a corner and several more open in the middle of the floor, partially and haphazardly unpacked. When he spied Meredith, he smiled and held out his arms to be picked up.

"Home sweet home, huh kiddo?" Meredith lifted him and his diaper sagged heavily. She laid him on the floor and grabbed a fresh diaper and wipes from under the crib.

The house had been a shock the night before, and wasn't much better in the morning. She carried Atticus silently through the rooms, fighting down a rising panic as she assessed their new home. Walls were dirty with smudges and marks, mismatched carpets torn and worn, linoleum faded. The master bedroom smelled faintly of smoke and part of the carpet had been cut away, revealing burn marks on the old wood floor. There was one bathroom with a bathtub streaked black in the bottom and a toilet with deep yellow stains. Black mold had settled in where grout was missing around the tub, along the edges of the bathroom floor and in the ceiling corners. She could smell and sense the dampness seeping into the walls, floors, and ceiling.

How is this place still standing? she wondered.

The kitchen looked reasonably clean at first glance and somewhat charming in a dated fashion, with its yellow linoleum counters and pink metal cabinets. Her spirits rose somewhat until she inventoried the drawers and found mouse droppings. It went downhill from there as she discovered rodent holes chewed in the panels under the sink and water stains on the floor by the refrigerator. She wondered what possessed Brian to buy this house without even a hint to her in advance.

"How's my little man today?" Brian came into the kitchen and lifted Atticus from Meredith's arms.

He noticed the look on her face and spoke quickly before she had a chance to say anything, "It'll take a little work, but it has good bones, as they say. It's a good investment."

She nodded, but she didn't believe it. Meredith knew people in California could fix up a house and make lots of money from it, but surely not way out here. Even *she* knew value came from location. She didn't even know how much they were paying for this house or where the money came from. Brian wouldn't talk about it to her, though she overheard him talking to the men who helped them move, saying he had worked a deal with a "business buddy."

"Geez, this cold gets you up and going, doesn't it?" He headed into the living room with Atticus, calling back over his shoulder, "Find the coffee pot yet? I could use a cup."

Meredith looked around. They had stacked a few boxes on the kitchen floor, but who knew whether these contained the coffee pot or if it was still out in the trailer. Exhausted from the long day, they had hauled some boxes out of the trailer in the dark the night before to get at Atticus's crib and mattresses for them to sleep on. Jamie crawled immediately onto her own mattress and fell into a deep, unmoving sleep. Meredith barely had a chance to look around before her own weariness led her to lie down too, piling blankets on top.

"I don't know where anything is." She was tired and in no mood to search through their boxes. She needed to clean before they unpacked and they had no cleaning supplies up to the task.

"I need to go to the store," she called out. "Let's get some coffee in town."

Brian came back into the kitchen and leaned

against the wall.

"What town are you talking about?" he asked, smiling.

"The *town*. The *city*. Hay *City*, right?"

"That's what it's called, yeah. But I wouldn't call it a city, necessarily. Or a town. You can get groceries there. Gas. Not much more out here."

She nodded slowly. There had been no lights of a city the night before. No stoplights or streetlights. Only a rare oncoming car and one lone, tiny light coming from somewhere off in the distance.

"What's the next town, then? The next *real* town."

Brian wrinkled his nose.

"Mountain Home maybe, about an hour and a half away. We went by there yesterday but you probably didn't notice it."

Mountain Home, she thought miserably. She did remember passing by its city limits sign and not recognizing anything resembling a city. *Oh god.* She fought the panic rising inside. *I want to go home.* This was too much to take in this early in the morning. She was tired, cold, hungry, and under-caffeinated.

Brian was standing there, and she knew he was assessing her, waiting for her response. She wanted to ask why this place, how he found it, when he bought it. Instead, she kept her face and tone impassive.

"Well, this place needs cleaning up." She looked around at the piles of boxes, not meeting his eyes. "I don't know where anything is and the kids are going to be hungry."

They stood there a moment.

"There's no coffee." She walked by him, off to the bathroom.

****

After dressing, she brushed her teeth and washed her face, helped Jamie get up and dressed, dug out cold cereal, eaten straight from the box since she couldn't locate the dishes, and fed Atticus strained pears and cereal out of jars. With the kids taken care of, she stepped outside to get another look at the place.

Despite her layers of clothing, she began shivering instantly as a frigid wind brushed over the snow-covered yard and made her gasp. Long ash-brown strands of hair blew across her face, momentarily blinding her. She pulled it back and knotted it at her neck, then assessed her new home. If the inside had been bad, the outside was worse. Old, dirty-white paint was peeling from the wood, and the black window frames were cracked. Rotted wood shingles melted into the roofline.

Around the house, as far as she could see, was white. More white than she had ever seen. White flat prairie, white jagged peaks looming on all sides, and white lumps of varying sizes scattered about in what she assumed was her front yard. Even the sky was a dull white, melting into the mountains, merging into the landscape, giving the impression the world had been erased.

Her new home looked like an ugly gray smudge on a blank landscape.

Bleak. There's no other word to describe this.

"I have a surprise for you." Brian had come up behind her.

She turned and raised her eyebrows skeptically and he smiled.

"A good one." His tone was jovial, proud. "I

promise."

He led the way around the side of the house where a wide, rusted metal shed stood, the doors padlocked shut. One look at the shed made her doubtful anything good could be inside, especially when Brian struggled to open the padlock.

"Damn it all to hell," he growled, twisting a key in the lock and then yanking at it over and over without success.

Worry bubbled up inside Meredith. Her husband had been in a good mood, happy at showing her whatever surprise was inside the shed and now it was spoiled. Suddenly, Brian took a step back and aimed a sharp kick at the lock, making Meredith jump.

Please open, she begged silently. As though heeding her plea, the lock released with a click and hung loosely on the latch.

"Sometimes things just need a good swift kick, ya know?" Brian laughed, glancing back at her.

She didn't say anything, but waited until he slid open one of the double doors and gestured for her to come inside.

"I negotiated this with the house. For you." She came up to stand beside him as he spoke. "It might not get you far, but it'll take you to the store and back."

The car was a good match for the house. Chipped paint on the hood and one door dented deeply and painted a different color. The windshield had a network of cracks spider-webbing their way across the passenger side.

"They always say you remember your first car." Meredith chose her words with care.

Brian looked over at her, judging her reaction.

Meredith felt his eyes on her and there was a tense silence.

"It has personality, right?" she added in an approving tone, and then held out a hand. "Where are the keys?"

He dropped them into her hand and she stepped into the shed and opened the driver's side. She caught a whiff of cat urine, mold, and decay from inside and was about to make a comment, but reconsidered. It was a car. It had an engine and wheels. He was trying to be nice. She turned the ignition. Nothing.

"Try again," Brian ordered.

Nothing.

"Damn, it's supposed to work." He scowled. "Wait here."

He ran across the yard to his truck, slipping a bit on the snow. Meredith waited, wondering about the kids alone inside the house, but knew she had to wait for Brian. She twisted in her seat to look around, taking in the stained and torn backseat and cigarette burns in the car roof, and wondered what kind of 'deal' Brian had gotten.

"Pop the hood." Brian was back in the shed with a box in his hands.

His confidence he could do anything, that he was in charge of his life, was part of what attracted Meredith to him in the beginning. They met when he sat down next to her in the campus quad her second week at junior college. She was sitting there, amazed she was actually a college student, something she never believed could happen. But the scholarship had come through, enough to pay the fees and books, and the shelter offered to let her stay as long as she was going to classes.

"Let me guess. Math."

She had looked over at him, startled.

"What?"

"Your major. It must be something smart. Okay, not math then. Biology."

She smiled. This man was flirting with her, and he must be a professor, at his age. It was like what ordinary people did, on campuses all across the country. Meredith felt so normal in that moment her spirits soared.

It turned out Brian was a student, too, taking a class in accounting. He was going to own his own business someday. He was stocky, with large hands and jet-black hair. The corners of his eyes curved upward when he laughed and his voice boomed right through her. They'd had lunch together, and arranged to meet the next day. He was interested in her life, her interests, and her mind. They talked for hours, meeting day after day. He kissed her, and one day in the library, when she whispered a confession that she was living at a shelter, afraid her disclosure would be the end, he had taken her in his arms and told her he wanted to take care of her. Right before finals, she found out she was pregnant.

Terrified he would leave her, she told him.

"Marry me," he said.

She had shaken her head. She didn't want to marry for the wrong reason.

"Isn't love the right reason?" he asked, then actually dropped to one knee. "Marry me. Please." It was a plea.

The "please" dissolved any reluctance on her part. Did she love him? She thought she did. This was a man who would never let her slip through the cracks of life again, and he hadn't. He took care of her, paid the bills, and, even if they couldn't afford luxuries, made sure there was always enough food.

But there was something wrong in her marriage, something unsettling about the way Brian watched her at times, his eyes assessing her. There was his volatile temper lashing out abruptly, occurrences happening more and more as time went on. He had never struck her, but he had a cruel streak occasionally aimed at her. After five years and two kids, she was becoming increasingly aware of the fear she had of her husband.

A rap at her window startled her out of her musings. Brian stood there holding a wrench. He waved it at her and she obediently turned the ignition key.

This time the car sputtered to life, coughing up a cloud of black smoke into the shed. Brian dropped the hood shut with a bang and climbed into the passenger seat with one hand over his nose. Meredith snorted out a laugh.

"You sure it's legal to drive this thing on the road?" She smiled wryly at him.

He chuckled good-naturedly and patted her leg.

"Just keep it under fifty-five, I'd think."

She revved the engine, blowing more smoke into the shed and then played with the different controls on the dashboard.

"What do I do if it doesn't start while you're gone?" she asked.

He waved her concern away.

"It's just been sitting here awhile. It'll be fine now. You'd be surprised how long these old cars can go. You'll probably have this one for a long time."

Her heart sank at the possibility, but then instantly chastised herself. *He gave me a car. Isn't that enough?* She turned the engine off and smiled at him.

They walked back across the yard together in silence. Meredith breathed in the cold air, feeling it sting her nose and make her lungs ache. Her tennis shoes were wet from stepping through the snow and her toes had gone numb. On the horizon, far from them, she noticed a lonely house tucked into the shadow of the mountain.

"Who lives in places like this?" She tucked her hands under her armpits for warmth and shook her head sadly.

Brian glanced over at her.

"We do."

****

The TV came in first. Brian set it on the floor and then they dug through boxes looking for Jamie's DVDs. Two hours later with no movie or player, Jamie was in full meltdown.

"You left it. *You left it*!" she shrieked. "Take me home. Now!"

"F' Chrissakes, Merry," Brian said disgustedly.

"She wants to watch *Ice Land*," Meredith explained. "I'm taking her outside. You watch Atticus, right?"

Jamie sniffled as Meredith explained they would build a Lafayette snowman, just like in the movie.

"Out of snow?"

Meredith realized her daughter didn't know there was nothing *but* snow outside.

"Lots of snow," she assured her.

Jamie looked at her doubtfully and didn't budge.

"Daddy will find your movie while we're outside." Meredith was annoyed at the pleading in her tone. This was a four-year-old she was dealing with, after all. She put out a hand firmly.

"Let's go," she ordered, trying to sound authoritative.

Jamie stomped to the door and then protested loudly as Meredith led her to the bedroom to find warmer clothing. Oakland's temperature was hovering at fifty degrees, now on the verge of spring, with daffodils blooming and trees budding everywhere. The outskirts of Hay City, Idaho were still stuck in winter, somewhere below freezing, punctuated by snow and wind. Meredith pulled two sweaters over Jamie's head and then zipped her into a jacket that was little more than a windbreaker.

"I don't like it here," Jamie complained, wiggling under the thick layers.

"I don't like it, either," retorted Meredith, "but sometimes you do things you don't want to do."

Jamie glared at her.

"Come on." Meredith scooted her to the door.

Her daughter's mood instantly changed when she saw the blanket of white spread out before her. She ran out into the yard and kicked at the snow, laughing as it scooted away from her feet. She tromped through it, stamping her feet down hard to make a trail. Meredith let her run, but when the cold seeped through her own light coat, she chased after Jamie, wiggling her toes to keep them from going numb.

"Make a Laf," Jamie ordered, ready to get down to business.

Meredith showed her how to roll the snow in her

hands, compacting the handfuls tightly so it held together.

"It's cold." Jamie nodded her head approvingly as reality lived up to the movie fantasy.

As they scooped the snow and packed it into something not remotely resembling a snowman, Meredith kept up a prayer Brian would find the movie soon. *Before I'm frozen.*

****

It started as a distant buzz, and by the time the snowmobiles appeared across the landscape, the sound had worked its way up to a low roar. Two men wearing brown and cream camouflage, with guns strapped on the back of their vehicles, raced toward them. Meredith and Jamie stood by their makeshift snowman and watched the men approach. By the time they pulled up, Brian had stepped out of the house.

"Afternoon," one man called out.

Brian edged forward to stand next to Meredith and Jamie. The men stayed seated on the snowmobiles, idling the engines, and Brian didn't move closer to them. Meredith eyed their guns, ran her eyes over their camouflaged jackets and took in their shaggy beards. One man spat out a wad of black goo onto the snow. *Meredith, you're not in California anymore*, she thought.

"Moving in, are you?" the same man asked.

"Just yesterday." Brian's voice was tight, the tension rolling off him.

The man shifted on his seat and glanced at his friend, who remained silent.

"I heard there might be new people here," the first man said.

Brian moved forward, closing the distance in long strides, and stuck out his hand.

"That's us." Brian put on a smile that didn't reach his eyes. "I'm Brian Lowe. This is my wife, Meredith, and little girl, Jamie."

Brian gestured back toward Meredith and Jamie but his eyes didn't leave the men.

"Colton Shaker." The man grasped Brian's hand.

The second man, sporting an untrimmed auburn beard, spoke for the first time, his voice low and sulky.

"Yeah, there's been talk about you."

His eyes flickered toward Meredith and then sidled away. She nervously looked at their guns again and then over at Brian.

"Merry, you'd better get Jamie out of the cold now." Brian twisted toward her as he spoke. "She's been out here long enough."

Grateful for a reason to go in the house, Meredith grabbed Jamie's hand.

"Nice meeting you," she said, turning away. There was silence behind her and she could feel the three pairs of eyes on her until she climbed the steps into the house. Brian's deep voice carried across the yard as he spoke in a low tone to the men.

"…worked it out," was all she could catch before shutting the front door.

From the house she watched through the window as Brian and Colton talked. Colton laughed at something, but the second man stayed still and silent on his vehicle. From time to time, he glanced over at the house. Again, she studied the guns on the back of the snowmobiles, long, black, and foreign to her. Meredith realized she was trembling and she crossed her arms tightly against her chest.

Her mother had dealt with each change in their life as though it were an adventure, a challenge to overcome. For Meredith, though, each change had brought further misfortune; hunger, loss of stability, or a new school. Where her mother carried off their nomadic life with bravado and confidence, Meredith only became more withdrawn and fearful. The only constant in her life had been her mother until Brian came along. And he had promised a different life for her.

Now he had broken his promise.

It's like I'm visiting a different country. Different people, different rules, different culture. A city that's not a city. A house that's barely a house. The men who carried guns around so casually and their gruff exteriors unnerved her. Her clothes weren't warm enough for the snowy winter weather; it was as though she needed a new, heavier skin to live here. *Not another country. I've moved to another planet.*

The vehicles revved and she watched as the men roared off. Brian came stomping up the steps and into the house. He paused inside the doorway when he saw her at the window.

"They live out there." Brian waved generally toward the window.

Meredith nodded.

"They weren't very friendly."

"No," he agreed, staring after the disappearing snowmobiles. "But I don't think they'll be back."

Chapter 3

"I looked up your grandmother online the other day," Brian said casually as Meredith poured herself a second cup of coffee.

"Brian," Meredith warned, sitting down across from him at their secondhand dining table.

They'd unpacked the trailer together, struggling to bring inside the heavier pieces of furniture. Fortunately, over their five years together, they hadn't acquired much. Their mattress on the first night had been the worst; sagging, heavy, and wobbling as Meredith tried to find a grip on it and carry it over the slushy snow in the dark. Of course, she'd dropped her side, causing Brian to lose his grip too, and the mattress had flopped heavily down between them. Laughter bubbled up in Meredith's throat at the awful sight of their bed lying in the wet mess, but she pushed it down.

"Damn it, Merr," Brian had growled. "Look what you did."

Her laughter died before it began and they wrestled the mattress back up and shuffled it into the house.

It had been secondhand too, left behind by a former roommate of Brian's. *Hardly used*, Brian told her with a knowing snort. Anyway, they had agreed it wasn't worth getting nice things until the kids were a bit older. The dining table wasn't too bad. Small nicks in the legs, a couple of burn marks in the light blonde finish on top.

Nothing a tablecloth couldn't hide. It was nice not having to worry about the furniture. She had her hands full with the kids and now the move. In any case, when had she ever had furniture at all?

Brian shrugged off Meredith's warning.

"What? She's your only living relative. I don't know why you're not more interested in her."

"Because, she's never been interested in *me*. She certainly didn't show up when my mom died."

"You don't have to be interested in her. Think about the money. She doesn't have anyone else to leave it to. All that money would go a long way. College for the kids. No more used cars. You want a house in California? We could have two."

Meredith set down her coffee cup and looked at Brian steadily.

"The money could have been used to pay rent and food for my mom and me while we lived in our car. It could have been used to pay my mom's medical bills. Instead, she didn't go to the doctor until it was too late. That was her daughter. You think she even cares she has a granddaughter?"

Brian sighed loudly.

"Merry. Your mom was a drunk. I know you want to protect her memory, but it's the truth. Anyway, your grandmother's pretty old, right? How much longer can she go?"

"Don't know. Don't care."

Brian's mouth tightened.

"I sent her a card and signed it for you," he said shortly.

"You what?" Meredith sputtered, staring at him in disbelief. She couldn't think of any words to say. Brian knew, he *knew*, how she'd suffered. How abandoned she'd been. How resentful she was of her grandmother never reaching out to her. How wrong it was that they, Meredith and her mother, struggled so much and her grandmother never, not once, lent a hand.

Brian looked at her calmly and sipped at his coffee, not saying anything else. Meredith's arm ached to throw her coffee cup across the kitchen. She wanted to hear it smash and watch the shards scatter. Her breath came fast and she fought to slow it down. *Easy, easy*, she cautioned herself. Every time they talked about her grandmother, and the money, she would yell and cry, and Brian would accuse her of being irrational. She would end up feeling like a stubborn child who was in the wrong. He needed to understand there was no way she would ever accept anything from that woman. Not even after death. It wasn't likely she would inherit anything, anyway.

"You shouldn't have written to her." She struggled to make her voice sound calm.

"Old ladies get sentimental," Brian argued. "She has great-grandchildren. It's not right you keep them from her. Maybe she'd want to do something for them."

Meredith stood up and walked to the sink. Through the window, a light snow was falling, supplementing the icy tundra before her. *God, doesn't it ever stop snowing here*? She stood with her back to Brian, worried about what he wrote in the card. Lies, of course. What she'd once perceived as ambition, Brian's thirst for bettering their life, was nothing more than greed.

She turned around. "If, by some far stretch of a chance, that mean-spirited, stingy, old woman decided to leave me any money at all, I would give it all to a homeless shelter. Maybe it would end up helping some other homeless families even though it never helped me."

Brian's eyes narrowed. "You forget you're married. You don't get to make those decisions by yourself. You don't get to be selfish anymore."

His words stung. When had she ever had the opportunity to be selfish? She never had anything to be selfish about. Brian knew the subject of her grandmother was painful, but he kept pursuing this. He had a job, a wife, two beautiful children, and now a house. But he still wasn't satisfied.

"I'm not the selfish one." Meredith surprised herself. She normally wouldn't defend herself this way, not with a return attack. Meredith cringed inside, waiting for his fury. It was awful when he was angry, when he yelled. Brian had never hit her, but a cold violence lurked under her husband's cool exterior. More and more lately, his hand would squeeze a little too tight on her arm, tight enough to leave a bruise; he would step too close behind her, "accidentally" bumping her hard enough to throw her off balance; or the jostling of her coffee cup, spilling hot coffee over her hand.

It was one reason she shied away from contradicting or challenging him on anything important. She made the little decisions; he made the big ones. After five years, she was still trying to find a balance.

Brian threw back his head and laughed.

"You're funny." His lips curled into a sneer. "Tell me who works in this family? Who pays the bills? You think I always like going to work, spending hours with my butt in a car driving all over the place? You think I'm staying in fancy hotels, eating lobster, and drinking fine wine all day? It's sagging mattresses and fast food out there."

Meredith shrank back at the reproach.

"Want to switch places?" he continued, his voice sarcastic. "Anytime, babe. Just say the word."

He sat back, crossed his arms, and waited.

There was the urge to crumble, as usual, to give in, to agree with him. Was it worth it? To make him this angry? But no, this was something she couldn't back down on. She steeled herself but her legs started to tremble. Meredith sat down at the dining table again and faced her husband.

"I. Will. Never. Take. Her. Money. If you ever contact her again, I…I…I will leave you," she stuttered, amazed and afraid she had suggested such a momentous thing. Would she really leave him over this? She had no job, no skills, and two kids. She would be dooming them to repeat her own childhood, moving from place to place, teetering toward homelessness.

They stared at each other for a moment and then Brian got up slowly. Meredith sat still as he came around behind her and put his hands on her shoulders. He rubbed them softly and then moved his hands to her neck, his fingers circling it easily. He bent down, his breath rasped in her ear. Anger stemmed from his fingers and in his breath. Tears sprang to her eyes and she realized she was afraid.

"Merry, Merry, quite contrary," he whispered.

She swallowed hard, the pulse in her throat throbbing against his fingers. *Are the kids awake,* she wondered suddenly. *Are they listening to this?* She didn't move.

"Christ," he growled in disgust. "You didn't used to be this way."

In an instant, his fingers were gone from her neck and there was a rush of air as he moved away from her and out of the room. Meredith sat there in shock, chilled and confused. Was it her or the slim possibility of an inheritance Brian wanted?

Her mind swirled around and around. Brian's hunger for money. The pressure of his hands on her neck. His constant anger. His disregard for her. Were there shades of these tribulations in all marriages? One of the things she had loved so much in her husband was his passion for things. When he wanted something, it consumed him. Wasn't this just the other side of the same coin? In her mind, a coin flipped end over end in the air. *How is it I can't tell the difference between love and hate?*

She sat at the table motionless as her coffee grew cold, remembering.

****

"Let's go visit your grandmother." Brian had suggested this one day, three years into their marriage.

Meredith looked at him in surprise.

"I don't think so."

They were at a park, watching Jamie play in the sand with two other children. Meredith took Jamie there on Saturday mornings, getting her out of the apartment early so Brian could catch up on sleep. But he had risen with her and announced he wanted to go, too. She'd smiled happily, glad they would have a family morning together.

He breathed heavily for a moment.

"You're the one who told me about her in the first place." He spoke evenly. He was the rational one in their relationship, after all. "Why would you tell me you had a grandmother unless you wanted to get to know her? To meet her. You'll regret it someday if you don't, you know."

Meredith considered her next words for a moment. He must have misunderstood, although she had told him part of this story before.

"I told you about her because she had the power to help us. My mother and me. She *should* have helped us. My mother asked for help. It wouldn't have meant anything to my grandmother. My mother always told me how rich she is. Horse-and-stables rich. Somebody-else-cleans-her-house rich. My mother went skiing in France as a kid. She had been to Switzerland. My grandmother never wrote back. My mother died without her help."

Brian listened in silence, his brow furrowing deeply. He nodded his understanding and licked his lips.

"So your mother wrote to her, huh?" he asked, and then his face brightened. "Your grandmother probably never got that letter. She never knew your mother needed help. She probably doesn't even know you exist."

He stood up, excited now. "Why didn't your mother call her? You should call. Right now, before it's too late."

Meredith looked at Brian as though he had gone crazy. Understanding flitted through her mind. *He likes the idea of a rich relative.*

"Why do you care so much about this?" she asked,

not moving.

He shoved his hands in his pockets nonchalantly and looked over at Jamie.

"I don't care, not for *me*," he said. "I care for you. And Jamie. I don't want you to regret anything later."

Meredith considered for a moment before answering.

"I called her a few times when my mother was dying. The first time, she answered the phone. When I told her who I was, she told me she didn't have a daughter anymore and so she couldn't have a granddaughter, either. Then she hung up on me. I called back but she didn't answer, so I left a message telling her my mother was sick."

Meredith swallowed hard before continuing. She remembered the anxiety, the desperation setting in when she realized no one was there to help her.

"I called the next week and left another message saying we were getting kicked out of our motel room because my mother couldn't work anymore. I called a month later from a shelter and left a message saying we couldn't stay at the shelter anymore. The last time I called, someone, I don't even know who, picked up the phone and told me my grandmother was on a cruise. So I left the message her daughter had died that morning."

Brian stood uncertainly before her now, his shoulders slumped a bit as though in defeat.

"So I doubt I'll have any regrets about my grandmother," Meredith said.

****

Neither one of them had spoken to each other since the argument in the kitchen and the idea of Brian touching her that night made her skin crawl. He was insistent even as she edged away and then pushed at his bulk. But he was an immovable force, moving forward slowly and surely until he was on top of her, inside her. Meredith's unease with the morning's events lingered, and she tried only so hard to make him stop.

In the early days of their relationship, she loved his body and all its little imperfections. She'd tease him in bed about the cluster of hairy moles on his left shoulder, the slight paunch he could never lose, or the way his ears stuck out. He would just smile tenderly at her as he stroked her breasts, ran his hands over her hips and then slipped a finger inside, making her gasp and wordless. It was in those moments she felt the most loved.

Any tenderness faded after Jamie was born and Brian's affections waned. Where Meredith's love expanded twice-fold and more, encompassing their daughter and her husband, Brian apparently only had so much love to give. They still had sex, but he grunted impatiently when she teased him and occasionally she had to tell him to slow down, that she wasn't ready.

She wasn't ready on this night either, but she just wanted to get it over with. Meredith rocked her hips into his, acquiescing completely until he grabbed her behind and changed the rhythm of her movement, changing it from *her* pace to his own. He thrust harder and harder until she started to pull back.

"Brian, stop it." She was breathless from his weight pushing her down. Meredith tried to twist out from under him, but he wouldn't let her move.

"You aren't going anywhere," he grunted into her, and then gripped her shoulders tightly, pushing her down harder beneath him.

The mattress creaked in protest and she gasped little breaths in between thrusts.

Hurry up, she pleaded in her mind, and it'll be done with soon enough. She let her body go limp, making him relax his grip on her. And then he was moaning loudly.

He rolled off her and onto his side, with his back to her. He was snoring within a minute. The pain piercing her shoulders kept her awake, sore and angry.

It's hate. He hates me.

****

Meredith twisted the ignition key again, listening to the engine chug, coughing wearily in the slushy driveway. They had taken a test drive to make sure it ran and all had been fine, if you ignored some random screeching and whirs coming from the engine. A scene flashed in her mind of her trying to start the car, the kids in the backseat, their belongings packed up in the trunk. Brian would be standing in the doorway of the house sadly watching his family leave him. The car would wheeze and hack futilely and she would be forced to creep back in the house. Defeated, trapped, powerless.

Damn! I'm stuck here, out in the middle of nowhere.

She looked up. Brian was standing in the doorway of the house watching her impassively, Atticus in his arms. He was dressed in his work clothes, bags packed and loaded in his truck for a week on the road; down to Boise, over to Twin Falls, up through Burley, Pocatello, Idaho Falls, Rexburg, and around the loop, back to their little homestead again. His truck was parked in front of hers and he waited as she struggled to get her car started and moved so he could back out of the driveway.

He hadn't touched her since that night two days earlier, and Meredith was grateful. They walked wordlessly around each other during the day as he finished unloading the trailer and she scooted furniture into place. He behaved detached and distracted and she was relieved when he left to Mountain Home to return the trailer to the rental business.

It hadn't been the first time he was forceful in bed, but this was the first time she felt he was using sex as a weapon, deliberately trying to hurt her. Or had she misinterpreted the other times? The harsh words he would whisper in her ear, the hands gripping her just a little too tightly.

She hadn't been inexperienced when she met him, but she knew all men were different in bed. Where the boy before him had been gentler, kinder, slower, he had also been an indecisive teenager, unsure where he was headed in life. In comparison, Brian was passionate, a man who knew what he wanted. She took his forcefulness in bed as an extension of his vitality and enthusiasm, and tried to live up to his expectations.

She twisted the ignition as hard as she could, as though it was from a lack of effort that kept the car from starting. The engine whined shrilly and then there was a click. Then silence.

A rap on the hood startled her.

"Pop it open," Brian called. "Sounds like a dead battery."

She sat there as he pulled a small box out of the back of his truck and then lifted the hood of her car. Meredith glanced over to where Atticus was now crawling on the cold, icy ground, only in his pajamas, and then back to the raised hood of her car. She stilled her instinct to dash over and pick Atticus up. *He did it to get a reaction from me. To pick a fight.* Through the gap in the hood, where it met the windshield, she watched as Brian's fingers attached cables to her battery. An idea fluttered through her mind: *What if he gets the wires wrong? Would he get electrocuted?*

"Try it now," he called.

She didn't hesitate. The car chugged once, then twice, and roared alive. Relief flooded through her. The car was fixed. Brian wasn't electrocuted. But, good grief, where had *that* notion come from?

Brian was at her window, staring in at her.

"Keep it on for a while so the battery charges up. It'll be fine."

She backed up the car and re-parked it, leaving the engine running. As she hurried across the drive to grab Atticus, Brian's truck backed away. It'd be another cold war between them. Of course, there would be no apologies for their argument or how he treated her in bed.

"Att-cus is *cold*." Jamie was standing at the door, dark curly hair in a tangle, looking accusingly at her. "Bring him inside."

Meredith forced a smile at her little girl. Not for the first time, she wondered how they had created this bossy spitfire. She looked over her shoulder where Brian's truck was disappearing down the road. Her smile faded.

Asshole. Tears popped into her eyes.

****

The idea crept in, first lurking at the edge of her

consciousness and then hitting her brazenly. *Maybe Brian won't come back.*

She knew in her heart while she could find a way to leave him, Brian would never allow her to take Jamie and Atticus away. But what if *he* left, involuntarily. What if he had an accident and never came home? It was icy and Brian wasn't used to driving in these wintry conditions.

The idea didn't shock her. But then there would come the unpaid bills, the creditors, people no longer sorry for her, the eviction, needing another place to live, and single motherhood. Her kids. She would be dragging them through the same miserable childhood she'd lived. Her kids deserved better. She had an opportunity to make their lives better than hers. She needed to make her marriage work. She would make peace with Brian.

But her shoulders still ached from where Brian had pinned her against their mattress. Blue and green bruises bloomed in the shape of his large fingers and now were turning black. She knew there were similar marks on her bottom, although she couldn't bring herself to look.

In the mornings, as she stepped out of the shower and the bruises on her shoulders reflected back at her in the mirror, anger and helplessness swelled up inside her. She again imagined Brian's truck flipping end over end down a high mountainside.

What if it wasn't an accident?

The prospect startled her at first.

It happens all the time. Husbands murder their wives. Wives murder their husbands. And they get away with it.

Meredith hated herself for these thoughts but, once started, she couldn't push them away. A little fantasy can't hurt, she decided, just to work out my anger. *Call it marital therapy*.

In fact, she chuckled to herself, planning my husband's murder might save my marriage.

Just a fantasy, she reasoned.

Chapter 4

"I want Choco Huffs," demanded Jamie, reaching from her seat in the grocery cart toward the sludge-colored cereal.

"Puffs." Meredith spoke automatically, scanning the long row of cereals. "Puh for P."

"I want them," her daughter repeated. "I want the Puffs."

"Not today. Not ever. That stuff is made out of doggie tails and lizard gizzards." Meredith grabbed three off-brand raisin flakes and two store-brand oat ohs.

"They are not," Jamie protested, but she giggled.

Meredith pushed the cart on, trying to get away from the sugary cereals, but to no avail. Cartoon lions, movie characters, and leprechauns smiled widely at them, all strategically placed at cart height to bewitch young children and drive mothers crazy.

"Mommy, I want a star."

"What?" *What now?*

Jamie pointed down the aisle. "I want a star like him."

Meredith turned, then stood and gaped. At the end of the aisle, carrying a full shopping basket, was a rugged looking man dressed like a sheriff straight out of an old western. His jeans fit snugly around his muscled thighs and his boots were scuffed and well-worn. On top of his blue plaid shirt, he wore a soft chamois vest. Right above his heart was pinned a silver star.

"You've got to be kidding," she murmured to herself, but she couldn't tear her eyes away. The guy was movie-star beautiful.

"Hey Barney," a hearty voice behind her called.

The face above the star looked straight at her and Meredith froze as he smiled widely, showcasing perfect white teeth. *Look away*, she ordered herself. *Look away now*. But she couldn't stop staring. Meredith's face warmed with embarrassment and she smiled back.

"Hi, Mrs. Stohler," Barney called to the woman behind Meredith. "How're the pigs doing?"

"Fat and sassy, just like me," the voice boomed, coming closer to Meredith. A wide-bodied woman moved past her, barreling toward the sheriff.

"Nothing wrong with that," Barney responded, his eyes flickering to Meredith, back to the woman, back to Meredith with a puzzled look, and settling on the woman again.

Barney. Well, nobody's perfect. She wheeled her cart around, blindly grabbed a box of Choco Puffs and quickly left the aisle. She dropped the box in her cart next to the carrier where Atticus slept.

"You got Huffs." Jamie smiled in delight, reaching around and grabbing the box.

"Puffs," corrected Meredith. "Just this once, okay?"

"Okay," agreed Jamie, hugging the box to her chest.

Meredith moved down the aisles, plucking boxes and cans, the image of the handsome, young sheriff fading from her mind. Jamie kept up a chatter, but

Meredith gave practiced one-word responses as her ruminations drifted back to murder. *If a woman wanted to murder her husband, how would she do it?*

"Mac-roni," demanded Jamie.

Meredith considered the boxes picturing day-glo orange-colored pasta and wrinkled her nose. She picked up one box and read the multi-syllabled ingredients, a small-printed listing running down the side of the box of chemicals and quasi-food stuff. *Poison,* she wondered. Where would she get it and would she just put it in his morning coffee? Wouldn't he taste it? How would she even know what to use? What if it just made him sick enough to go to the hospital and the poison was detected? *Prison.*

She dropped the box of instant cheesy macaroni into the cart, pondering whether she could simply poison him slowly over the years with artificial food additives and artery-clogging instant mac-and-cheese. Meredith moved on to the small deli counter, looking at pre-sliced meats and cheeses.

A knife? Could she push a knife into her husband, slicing through skin and sinew, going deep enough to kill him? She rolled the grisly idea over in her mind as she considered between provolone, swiss, and peppered jack cheeses.

"Help you?" a bored voice asked.

She looked up and a pimply faced teen stood behind the counter, tall and thin, wearing a dirty white apron smeared with something dully red.

Kill my husband, Meredith answered in her mind. "Half pound of sugared ham and half of the turkey," she ordered.

"Half pound of turkey or half that amount," the

teen intoned back to her.

"What?"

"You asked for half pound of ham and half of turkey." The teen made his annoyance clear. "Do you mean half as much turkey or half a pound of it?"

Meredith studied him briefly. "You decide."

He glared at her, the pimples on his neck angry and red. "Whatever."

Meredith went back to her reverie. A knife wouldn't work, because he would overpower her easily. What other ways were there? A gun? She was a city girl and had never even held a gun. Brian had one locked in a cabinet in their bedroom closet but she didn't know where the key was. She certainly couldn't ask him. Besides, she didn't know how to load it or shoot it either. *Geez, am I really this incompetent...even in my fantasies?*

"That it?" The teen plopped the two packages of sliced meats, one twice as big as the other, on the counter.

Meredith considered him sadly. Poor kid. What chance did he have growing up in a place like this? He would probably marry the pig lady's daughter and have a litter of kids looking just like him.

"Yes, thank you," she said politely, thinking more kindly toward the doomed teen.

Broccoli, tomatoes, apples, onions; she rolled through the produce aisle, entombed the items in plastic bags and plopped them in the cart next to the sleeping Atticus. Sometimes it practically took a bomb to wake him up; other times, only a whisper.

Maybe an accident would work best. A broken ladder? Leaky brakes on the car? Oh, for heaven's sake.

She might as well lay banana peels around the house and hope he tripped. She couldn't rely on an accident to finish him off.

There had to be some way to commit murder and get away with it. After all, if she wanted to do this fantasy right, she absolutely couldn't get caught because then what would happen to her children? Her breathing came faster. *Fantasy*, she reminded herself. *This is just a fantasy.* She would think this through carefully. No, she thought, she could commit this fantasy murder and she wouldn't get caught.

That decided, Meredith pushed her cart toward the checkout line, and solidly into the firm denim-clad behind of Barney the sheriff. Her cart jolted to a stop; Barney didn't budge.

"Sorry, oh, I'm so sorry." She cringed in embarrassment.

Barney turned around and his eyes brightened. A flutter awoke somewhere inside Meredith; she tried not to stare at him too openly.

"No, it's okay." Hazel eyes looked down at her. "I don't mind."

"Uh, you don't mind?" asked Meredith with a smile. She watched as Barney's ears turned pink and then bright red. Afraid she embarrassed him, she gestured toward his star. "So, are you an actor or something?"

"He's the sheriff." Jamie was firm about this.

"Sheriff." He confirmed it briefly with a nod. Meredith watched in horror as the red spread from his ears to his neck. She judged he was in his early twenties, about her own age, and like her, still unsure about his place in the world.

"Well, sorry again, Sheriff." Meredith was doubtful, reasoning someone barely her own age was unlikely to be a real sheriff. Then again, maybe they did things differently in Idaho. "I really didn't mean to have a run-in with the law."

They both chuckled at the lame joke. He hesitated as though he wanted to say something and so Meredith paused, but nothing came but a discomfiting silence. She recognized the attraction in his eyes too, and fought back a twinge of regret.

Married. I'm married, with kids and Choco Puffs in my grocery cart.

She smiled a goodbye and pushed her cart around him and continued toward the checkout line. She felt his eyes following her and she knew her cheeks were pink. Besides, if she was going to go through with a fantasy plan to become criminally unmarried, the last thing she needed was to goggle at the sheriff.

****

The wind cut through her cloth coat, sliced past her woven cotton sweater, wrapped itself around her bones, and squeezed. She gasped and pushed the cart full of groceries to her car. *This can't be March.*

Quickly she bundled Jamie, still clutching the "Huffs," into one car seat and Atticus, now awake and crying, into another. When she turned to get the groceries, her cart was sailing across the parking lot.

"Oh shit!" She had never been so cold in her life. Her eyes watered against the frigid air as she stumbled after her cart.

"Whoa there. I've got it." The 'fat and sassy' pig lady appeared between two cars and stopped the fleeing cart. She was larger than ever now, bundled into a huge puffy coat that hung to her knees. On her head was a hunter's cap with furry earflaps.

"Thank you." Meredith sighed heavily as she grabbed onto her cart again. "I really appreciate it."

"I'm Honey Stohler." The pig lady thrust out a heavily gloved hand.

"Meredith," she answered briefly, reaching out and watching her own ungloved hand disappear into Honey's bear paw.

"You need some warmer clothes." Honey tsked. "It's hard on you Californians moving out here, no idea what a real winter's like."

Meredith was taken aback. "How did you know I was from California?"

Honey gave her a knowing look. "Word gets around."

Meredith shivered violently. She was too cold to talk and her face was going numb.

"You moved into the place out Road 41, right?" Honey didn't wait for an answer. "I knew who you were the moment I caught sight of you. Too small of a place to go unnoticed."

Meredith realized while she was entering the first phases of frostbite, Honey was unfazed by the cold. How was she going to end this conversation if she couldn't even talk?

"I have some good slow cooker recipes if you'd like some," Honey was saying now. "Do you have one? Best things in the world. Throw it all in, turn it on and presto, dinner is ready eight hours later."

"Kids." Meredith's legs were shaking from the cold.

"Sure, I have five of them," Honey said, smiling

broadly and showing all her teeth. "Judy is thirty-nine and lives over…"

"*My* kids…in the car," Meredith broke in, taking a step backward.

"You'd better get yourself over there," Honey cried. "Those kids are going to freeze in there. It'll be like a refrigerator in your car."

Meredith turned away quickly.

"Come by anytime," Honey shouted, as Meredith shuttled her cart back across the parking lot. "I'm out Ham n' Eggs Road. Ask anyone."

****

Atticus was fed and roaming the house in his bouncer, ricocheting off walls, doorways, and furniture. Jamie was happily watching *Ice Land* for the twenty-fifth time and singing along in her off-tune, childish voice. Meredith took advantage of the lull to attack a pile of unpacked boxes crowding one side of their bedroom.

Their move had occurred so fast that she hadn't marked all the boxes or packed in a logical fashion. Inside a box marked "*kitchen*," she found jars of spices jumbled up with crib sheets and a dustpan. From another unmarked box, she unpacked bras, laundry soap and, gratefully, mousetraps.

"Daddy!" Jamie squealed just as the front door slammed heavily.

She sighed. Brian wasn't due home until the next day and she had just planned cereal for dinner. It drove Brian crazy how Meredith could eat cereal for breakfast, lunch, and dinner.

"How about maybe a vegetable or meat or something normal?" he would ask.

With two young kids, dinner was sometimes too hard to deal with. *Maybe a slow cooker wasn't a bad idea, after all.*

"Hey." Brian appeared in the doorway of the bedroom, Jamie in his arms.

"Hey." Meredith looked up from the box she was unpacking. "You're back early."

"Don't sound so pleased about it." His voice was flat, his face a warning to her.

"Daddy, I saw a sheriff with a star," Jamie gushed. "I got Huffs. Mommy said I can have them for dinner."

"Huffs?" He raised his eyebrows at Meredith.

"Choco Puffs." Meredith wrinkled her nose. "I don't know what came over me."

Brian nodded. "Cereal. I should have known." But he smiled affectionately at his daughter. "Can I have some too?"

Jamie looked at him seriously and nodded. "I'll share with you. Not Atticus though. He's a baby."

"Right." Brian nodded. "Huffs are just for us big kids."

Jamie hugged him and laid her head on his shoulder.

Meredith watched this and a twinge of guilt went through her about her murder fantasy. What would losing their father do to her children? How much would Jamie remember of her father? Her nerve crumbled. Her fantasy about getting rid of Brian hadn't included the hurt she would be inflicting on her children. Of course, Atticus would have no memories of his father but he would have to deal with growing up without knowing him.

"What's this about a sheriff?" Brian asked. "Did he

come to arrest you?"

Startled out of her fantasy, Meredith blurted, "No."

Jamie giggled. "Mommy's going to jail," she sang out.

"We sort of ran into him at the store." Meredith recovered herself quickly. "Complete with cowboy boots and silver star. He looked younger than me. Some sheriff."

"There's no crime out here, so he probably doesn't have much to do." Brian set Jamie down. "It's a good place for you and the kids."

Meredith got up from the floor and rubbed her back. Jamie ran into the living room singing a song from *Ice Land.* Although she knew the melody, Jamie often substituted her own words.

"How was the trip?" she asked.

Brian shrugged and leaned against the doorway. "The usual. I have to go out again tomorrow. Another week."

"A week?"

"There's a sales meeting in Boise." He avoided her eyes. "There's a couple of calls I need to make over there, too."

Meredith mulled this over. It would be nice to go to a bigger town. Anything had to be better than Hay City.

"What if the kids and I went too? We could all use some warmer clothes and there's nowhere to shop out here."

Brian shifted uncomfortably. "This isn't really the right trip for shopping. I'm going to be pretty busy, and besides"—he nodded toward the boxes—"there's a lot to do here still. How about next time?"

Meredith looked at him steadily and nodded. She

was stuck out in the middle of nowhere with two kids and a car likely to blow up at any moment.

"Whatever."

"Ok, then." He mimicked her annoyed tone. "I need a shower. Something to eat would be nice, too. Aside from Choco Puffs."

He turned away toward the bathroom and then turned back.

"Don't unpack my stuff. I have some things I'm just going to store for awhile."

"I know, you've told me, like, twenty times." Meredith rolled her eyes. "I already have enough to do anyway, with my stuff, the kids, and the house."

Brian had already walked away, and Meredith knew he had tuned her out. She stared at the empty doorway where he had stood. *Maybe I hate you, too.*

****

She'd felt like the luckiest girl in the world at first. Early in their marriage, as her pregnancy with Jamie had grown, Brian became more and more concerned about her. Did she want an extra blanket on the bed? A glass of water? He would jump up and fetch it for her. He would wrap his arms around her and tell her he loved his "pumpkin girl," a joke referring to the large round bump growing in front of her. Meredith loved it. She loved him. And, for the first time ever, she loved her life.

They married quietly, registering at the courthouse, agreeing how saving money on a wedding would go toward the baby. Meredith had no one to stand up for her anyway except a few acquaintances from the shelter. She wanted to leave that past behind. Brian had quizzed her about distant family; hadn't she mentioned a grandmother, a rich old lady?

"She's a stranger to me," Meredith had explained.

"People are only strangers until you get to know them," he replied, but didn't press it further then. Brian was estranged from his own family so he understood.

Jamie was a difficult baby from the start, keeping them awake at night and requiring constant attention during the day. Getting her to nap was a struggle, feedings were a battle of wills, and she cried half the day for no reason Meredith could fathom.

Brian quit classes too and took a job requiring travel three days a week. It was a hands-on opportunity to learn about the business world, one more step toward owning his own business, he claimed. *Their* own business. She was proud of him, even as she floundered being a new mother. After all, she had no role model to speak of.

He returned from his trips often tired and sullen, complaining about the driving and idiocy of clients. '*You* wouldn't understand', he'd snap when she asked about the details of his job. They had been married a year and a half when they went bowling with friends of his from work. Meredith was excited at the date, the first time since they married that they went out with others. They were halfway through the first game before she realized Brian was making comments about her as she bowled.

"Here comes another gutter ball from my guttersnipe." The words startled her as she pulled her arm back to toss the ball.

The snickers hurt almost as much as the comment and she dropped the ball early, launching it straight into the gutter. She stood there, humiliated as it rocked wildly from side to side in the gutter all the way to the end, where it dropped finally out of sight.

"You were making fun of me," she said later as they drove home.

"Don't be so sensitive," Brian grumbled. "We were all just having fun."

"You called me a guttersnipe. That was mean."

"Oh, come on," he protested with a laugh. "Gutter *ball*, gutter*snipe*. It was funny."

"Do they know I lived in a shelter?"

"Jesus, Merr," his voice rising in anger. "You take everything too seriously. No one was even thinking about that."

There were good days, lots of them. Nights where Brian would pull her tightly against him, his eyes looking so wild in his passion that she felt powerful in her femininity. He needed her. Jamie needed her. A yearning deep inside her was satisfied. She had a home, a husband, a child. Everything she had ever wished for. She let the occasional cruel barb go by without remark. When he went out with friends, though, she stayed home with Jamie.

****

Three years later, it wasn't just her psyche that was bruised. Brian had become physically rougher with her as well, leaving dark marks on her skin for weeks at a time. Memories of past moments in bed with Brian kept coming back to her now her perspective had changed. *Did he treat me that way because he didn't like me*, she wondered now.

Having sex with Brian had gotten worse and worse for her, especially in the past year. He had become more forceful, more aggressive, turning her one way and then another, twisting her into positions causing throbbing aches afterward.

"Am I hurting you?" he would ask and she wouldn't answer, not wanting to admit she couldn't do what he wanted.

Once, just when Meredith started to cry out in pain, he came with a loud groan and then rolled off of her. She had inhaled deeply, tears welling up in both relief and frustration.

"Jesus, you're good," he had moaned, seemingly oblivious to her pain and tears. How could something so good for him be so wrong for her? She hid her pain and dismay, afraid he would find her lacking.

Now, she wondered, maybe he knew he was hurting her. Maybe he liked it. *What if*, she thought in horror, *what if he had fantasies of killing her, too?* Meredith imagined his large hands on her body, moving up to her throat, pushing down firmly. 'Am I hurting you?' he would ask. 'Can you breathe?'

Is this why he moved her out to this isolated place? She had no one to run to, nowhere to go, no money of her own, two kids to tend, and a car barely able to reach the next town. She couldn't leave him, she couldn't stay.

She lay back, sleepless, wondering what she was going to do. This couldn't really be her life, living way out here on a frozen tundra, sharing slow cooker recipes with the pig lady, and living with a callous, insensitive husband. Five years ago she had been a college student; independent, with the world in front of her. There was so much possibility in her future. She didn't wish her children away. She could never do that, but Brian… Why, if he disliked her, if he hated her, why wouldn't he just leave her? Was he afraid of losing his children?

Even in the dark, the emptiness of the Idaho plain made its presence known. The silence here was so loud it hurt her ears and kept her awake at night. She strained for any sounds at all. The faint ticking of the kitchen clock down the hall grew louder and then the chirping of a lone cricket, wintering somewhere inside her house, began and stopped again. A gust of wind rattled a loose roof shingle and whistled through a gap under the front door. The sounds set her teeth on edge. There was nothing to do out here but think about her life and how things had gone so wrong.

She missed the familiar noises of the city and how they'd connected her to life. Trucks rumbling by, laughter from passersby drifting up to her window, aromas from a bakery and Indian deli blocks away drifting to her bed on a breeze, and distant sirens. Anything she wanted was just a quick walk away and, even on an early-March night, she wouldn't freeze getting there. She wouldn't be so trapped, afraid of the man in her bed. In the city at least, there were distractions keeping her from thinking about her marriage. There, she could pretend her life was normal, satisfying.

I don't want the fantasy. I want it to be real. I want a good life for me and my children. I want to figure out a different life. So, okay, whatever it takes, I want Brian out of my life.

Oh Jesus, am I really going to kill my husband?

Chapter 5

Diaper changes, breakfast, laundry, make the beds. Slice apples and bananas for Jamie, laid out pretty on her purple plate. Clean the floor under Atticus's high chair. Set up crayons and a coloring book for Jamie. Fix a bottle for Atticus.

Meredith plowed through the chores while trying to entertain the kids. The unpacked boxes seemed to have grown in number and she looked at them with resentment. She didn't even want to move here so why did she have to be the one to unpack them.

Mid-morning she gave up and snapped on the TV. They couldn't afford satellite and the TV antenna only broadcasted fuzz, so she popped in a DVD.

"I want *Ice Land*," Jamie complained.

"You've watched it twenty times this week." Meredith knew her head would explode if she listened to the songs from the movie one more time. "How about something different?"

"No! I want *Ice Land*."

Meredith saw with horror that her daughter, eyes furious, was on the verge of a meltdown. What did it matter what she watched?

"Okay, okay, *Ice Land* it is." She quickly pawed through the discs until she found the right one. "Here it is."

Jamie settled on the couch and pulled Atticus next

to her.

"Watch your brother, right?"

"Att-cus loves *Ice Land.*"

Meredith looked at her two children, Jamie with her arm protectively around Atticus, and for the millionth time wondered how she had gotten so lucky. They were healthy, beautiful and loving; well, except when Jamie's temper flared. She loved being a mother even though it was exhausting and she was conscious she often wasn't up to the task. She was sure other mothers didn't let their kids watch TV in the morning. She needed them occupied so she could focus on unpacking. It had been nearly two weeks and there still were stacks of boxes tucked against walls in every room. How did they ever accumulate this much stuff? Where did it all come from?

Again, she attacked the jumble inside the boxes, pulling out clothes, canned goods, and cleaning supplies, organizing closets as she went along. It was a small house. There were three bedrooms and one bathroom, with the small closets typical of houses built when people were just people, not consumers. She flattened the emptied boxes and wondered what she should do with them. If all went well, *if she could really do it,* a tiny voice whispered, she would be moving again soon so she needed to keep the boxes.

Meredith checked in on her kids. Atticus had fallen asleep on the couch and Jamie was swaying to the music, wide-eyed, mouthing words to a song.

Meredith went back to the bedroom and faced the flattened boxes. There was nowhere left to put them. She wandered back through the small house, opening the kids' full closets and shutting them again. She returned to her own bedroom and looked in the closet. This time, she looked up and noticed the attic access. *Perfect.*

She dragged a chair over and popped the access panel up. It lifted easily and a pull cord for an attic light dangled down. She tugged it and was somewhat surprised the bulb still worked. As her eyes adjusted to the attic light, she looked around and amid the spider webs and mouse droppings sat two boxes. One small and one medium, just within reach.

She grabbed the larger of the two, about the size of a boot box, and set it down on her bed, then went back for the other one. Curiosity trumped a passing misgiving that the contents were private; in any case, they weren't hers. But wasn't there some finders-keeper's law covering cases like this?

She ran a finger under the flap of the larger box and lifted gingerly, half-worried she would uncover nesting mice. Inside she found about a dozen men's socks wound into balls.

She reached inside and pulled out one of the socks and her fingers touched something firm inside. Meredith frowned in consternation. Someone had clearly hidden something inside these socks, put them in a box, and secreted them away in the attic space. The last thing she wanted to do was uncover someone's drug stash. She knew an empty house could easily fall victim to squatters or those looking to hide something illegal. This house looked as though it had been empty for years, but the tops of the boxes were free of dust, clearly placed in the attic recently. What if the people who hid the boxes showed up at the door one day and realized she had disturbed their secret?

In the other room, the movie's climactic song was starting. There was only another ten minutes of privacy before the kids would demand attention from her again. She glanced up at the window nervously and then felt foolish. They were miles from anything in the middle of nowhere. No one was going to suddenly peek in to witness what she was doing. Meredith looked down again and realized her fingers were already unrolling one of the sock balls. She shook it out and gasped when a thick roll of money, fastened with a rubber band, dropped heavily onto her lap.

Oh no. Not drugs, but drug money. Shit.

Still, trepidation over where it came from didn't stop her from unwrapping the roll of money. Twenties, fifties, *oh, sweet Jesus*, there were hundreds. Her mind was too rattled to count it. Quickly, she grabbed another sock and shook out another money ball. And another. And another. More money than she'd ever had in her life lay in front of her. More money than she'd ever had in the bank. Without counting, she knew it was easily thousands of dollars. Enough to fully stock the kitchen with groceries. Enough to buy warm clothes for her growing children. Maybe even enough to fix her car.

She piled it all back in the box, money and socks haphazardly, and shut the lid. She would reroll it all again later when her hands stopped shaking. Her breath came quickly and her head spun as she turned to the second box. The box was much smaller and lighter than the first, and the contents inside shifted around loosely. She gingerly opened it.

Inside were pictures. Of women. Correction. Of one young woman. Pretty, with long auburn hair falling to her waist. In the top photo, she was laughing and gesturing toward the person taking the picture. Standing on an old-fashioned wooden porch, she wore blue leggings under a short dress and cowboy boots.

In the next photo, the girl stood on the shore of a lake, her feet bare and toes reaching out to touch the water. Even though her auburn hair was pulled up and twisted back into a tie it was easy to recognize this was the same person. Beautiful porcelain skin, straight white teeth showing as she grimaced while touching the water. Meredith flipped quickly through the photos. The auburn-haired girl hiking, cooking in front of a stove, in bed wearing nothing but that impressive mane of hair spread out behind her on the pillow. Somehow, when she arrived at the final photo, Meredith was already half-expecting what she would see; the young woman, her face looking dreamy as she gazed at the man next to her. Brian.

"Mommy?" Jamie stood at the door. "Att-cus stinks."

Meredith looked up, dazed, her eyes unfocused.

"Mom!"

Meredith quickly put the pictures back in the box and closed the lid. She couldn't think about it now, with her daughter looking at her and her son needing her attention.

"Let's go take care of Atticus, and then how about a nature walk?" she asked Jamie

****

They headed down the gravel road leading toward the mountains, what Brian told her was the Cascade Range. The peaks were rounded, soft and white under a thick layer of snow. Here and there a sharp spire of gray rock shot up as though it had erupted from the peak and was still growing skybound.

Atticus was in a baby carrier on Meredith's back, a fuzzy cap covering his still-bald head and buried under three layers of clothing topped by his thin cloth coat. Jamie ran in front, her own makeshift hat flapping from her head. Meredith had made a game out of fitting a pair of Jamie's tights on her head in an attempt to keep her warm, with the empty legs dangling down her back like elongated rabbit ears. Gloves, tennis shoes, and layers and layers of clothes. It took a half hour to dig out the clothes and then get her kids warmly attired while they wiggled and squirmed. The activity kept Meredith's hands busy, even though her mind was numb.

She hardly felt the wind sweeping down off the mountain. She knew it was too cold to take her kids out, but there was no way she could stay in the house. With those pictures. All that money. She tried to engage her mind but it kept spinning and spinning and spinning.

"Look Mommy! I'm in *Ice Land*!"

Meredith watched as Jamie sat on a patch of ice and scooted her bottom across it. She'd have to think about getting a sled.

"Push me," Jamie called.

Meredith blindly obeyed, squatting straight down so she wouldn't spill Atticus out of his carrier. Who was she? How long had it been going on? One photo was from the summer, another from fall. Where were the pictures taken?

"Sweetie, you're getting wet now," Meredith cautioned. "We're going to have to go back."

"No. Chase me." Jamie took off, her little legs churning down the path.

A surge of anger rose up inside Meredith when she thought of the money. Some months, they ate little but spaghetti and mashed potatoes until Brian's next check came.

When was the last time she had laid eyes one of his paychecks? They were deposited directly into the bank, or that's what he'd always told her. He gave her cash for groceries, cash for clothing, cash for everything. She realized she didn't even know if the bank account was in her name as well; she never had needed to write a check or use a debit card. They had been on a tight budget.

"This is how we get ahead." Brian had lectured her on this again and again. "We're not going to be like everyone else, going into debt and using plastic for everything, never knowing how much money they have. Smart people use cash."

Brian had set the budget early in their marriage, doling out paper bills in little piles. One was for rent, another for groceries, and another for general household expenses. He paid the utility bills. They didn't pay for TV or Internet. They didn't go to restaurants. They didn't pay for babysitters. Meredith would watch him with pride, knowing her mother could never handle a budget. That had been part of their slide into poverty and homelessness. Living on a budget made her perceive herself as very grown up and she was filled with gratitude that she met Brian one autumn day in the college quad. She had never questioned how much Brian's paycheck was because she assumed he shared everything.

Her daughter was far down the snowy path and Meredith hurried after her.

"Jamie! Come back!" called Meredith. "I can't chase you. I have Atticus."

The wind whirled Meredith's words away in the wrong direction and Jamie didn't turn around. She heaved a frustrated sigh and looked around her as she kept up a rapid pace. Her feet crunched over the hard frozen ground.

It seemed to take forever to get back to the house. Jamie complained most of the way, once stopping and demanding that Meredith carry her. With Atticus on her back, Meredith couldn't carry her daughter, too.

"Keep walking, we'll get there soon," Meredith encouraged.

Jamie sat down on the ground and cried.

"I'm tired and cold," she wailed. "I hate snow."

"The only way to get back is if you walk yourself there." Meredith was starting to worry about Atticus. He was a hostage, strapped onto her back without any say in the matter. She turned her back on her daughter and started walking on toward the house.

"Mommy!" Jamie screamed.

"C'mon," Meredith called over her shoulder.

"Mommy!" But Jamie rose and started trudging after her. "Mommy!"

All the way back to the house, Jamie kept up her scream and Meredith swore her ears would explode. Could Honey Stohler hear the screams on the wind? Could Barney the sheriff hear them too and wonder where they were coming from? Could all twelve people in Hay City hear them? She really didn't care.

****

When they got back to the house, Jamie was sobbing. Meredith started a bubble bath, stripped all three of them down, and climbed into the tiny tub with her children. The warm water loosened her numb feet and she relaxed as Atticus and Jamie splashed and played with bubbles.

Steam from the tub rose and fogged over bathroom's window and the mirror above the sink, giving Meredith the sense that the outside world had disappeared. Everything important to her was in the tub. *I'd do anything for my kids.*

"Mommy! Att-cus is peeing."

Meredith looked down at the yellow stream spreading underneath the disappearing bubbles. She sighed.

"Abandon ship!" she called out, standing up and grabbing hold of her son.

Jamie quickly clambered out of the tub.

"That's gross, Att-cus." Jamie wrinkled her nose.

"Yeah, pretty gross," Meredith agreed, though her tone was tender as she wrapped towels around herself and her children.

A sharp rap on the front door made Jamie squeal. "Daddy's back!"

Meredith caught her breath, before realizing Brian wouldn't knock. She gave a small sigh of relief before she noticed her naked daughter was answering the door.

"Jamie, get back here!" Meredith wrapped the towel more tightly around herself and hurried down the hall, leaving Atticus crawling naked on the floor of the bathroom.

"Hey-ya, little chick-a-dee."

Honey Stohler's solid figure was inside the front door, shucking off her huge coat. *All this time alone, and this is the time someone visits?*

"We usually have clothes on," she apologized in greeting Honey.

Honey laughed loudly.

"I'd hate to think what I look like half the time when I'm at home." Her brow furrowed slightly as she looked at Meredith.

Atticus crawled into the room and grabbed onto Meredith's leg.

"We had a bubble bath," Jamie chirped out. "I took a nature walk."

"Then it must be time for sweet pickles and pie." Honey picked up a basket she had set at her feet and headed for the kitchen. "Take your time getting your kids dressed. I'll get the coffee on."

Meredith stood there for a moment, feeling as though a whirlwind had swept into her house.

"Let's go," she said to Jamie, picking up Atticus and heading back down the hall to get dressed.

****

"Never felt the need to go anywhere else," Honey explained over huckleberry pie, pickles, and coffee.

Meredith wondered if the strange combination was an Idaho thing. She sipped her coffee gratefully and spooned the last bite of pie into Atticus's mouth. She wiped his blue-stained lips and fingers and set him back on the floor to join his sister in the living room.

Honey had kept up a nonstop monologue ranging from the weather to chickens to the iffy nature of cell phone service in Hay City's deep valley location.

"What brought you out here?" she now asked. "Most Californians go to Boise where there's at least a restaurant."

Meredith smiled. Restaurants were out of their

budget, regardless of where they lived.

"Brian's job transferred him out here. He sells farm equipment insurance and they gave him the Idaho-Utah territory."

Honey looked down into her coffee. "A salesman. On the road a lot then, huh?"

"It's okay. I have the kids. Once I get organized here, there are a lot of projects I want to do around the house. We never owned a house before. It was too expensive in California. And, you know, with the kids, there's never a dull moment."

Meredith realized she was babbling and she stopped.

"It can be hard for outsiders here." Honey looked pointedly at her. "They don't always fit in. I want you to know you're welcome. In any case, this house has been empty for awhile and it's good to have someone make it a home again."

Meredith wanted to ask why outsiders didn't fit in, but she held her tongue.

Honey scooted her chair back and heaved her substantial body up with a groan.

"I gotta get back but it was good visiting with you. You need anything, I likely have it."

"Thank you," Meredith said. "I'm sure the kids would like to see the chickens."

"Anytime. Just so you know, my bath time is about seven at night. Don't think you want to see all of *me*."

They laughed together and Meredith walked with Honey to the front door. She liked this woman who was so comfortable in her own skin. As Honey shrugged herself back into her coat, she turned to Meredith.

"I couldn't help noticing those mean bruises on

your shoulders." She cast an eye toward where Jamie and Atticus were playing in the living room. "I have some cream that'll help."

Meredith shrank back, horrified she had been so exposed, and then opened the front door.

"Thanks again, Honey." Her voice was stony. "We're fine here."

****

The day had been too much for Meredith and she was exhausted. Fortunately, the kids' energy had waned and they played quietly after Honey left. They all ate cereal for dinner. Puffs were for Jamie, O's for Atticus and Meredith, along with a side of applesauce, and they both went to bed early. Meredith returned to the boxes she had tucked away under her bed and brought them out to the kitchen table. Methodically she counted the cash and then rolled it back up inside the socks.

Twelve socks. Fifteen hundred dollars in each roll. Eighteen thousand dollars. A fortune.

She went through the photos again, slowly, staring into the smiling face of the auburn-haired girl. She stopped at the photo of her husband and the girl together. Brian's face was relaxed, his arm possessively around the girl's shoulder. She was young, Meredith assessed, probably barely twenty. Questions raced through her mind: Who was she and how did he meet her? Where had the money come from and why was he hiding it? What was it for? Did Brian have plans to leave their marriage? If so, why would he buy this house and move all of them here? Had he, did he, love this girl?

She sat back, closed her eyes and let the emotions come. Anger. Fear. Relief. No jealousy though. She recalled the picture of the girl in bed with her hair spread out behind her. Her face was relaxed, her mouth slightly open in a half smile, her eyes slightly unfocused as she looked up at the camera. This time she added her husband in the scene, holding a camera and taking the picture. Meredith realized disappointment, not jealousy, was her fundamental emotion. Their marriage had already self-destructed. It was the money unsettling her the most.

They were always broke, at least that's what Brian would tell her. No money to stay in California, no money to buy warmer clothes for this cold climate, barely enough money for groceries. She had only been grateful they always had "enough," and they could get by. She'd loved the security of being taken care of, and so she never asked questions. She just took the money he gave her and challenged herself to provide good meals for her family.

If the money was for them, she couldn't understand why Brian hadn't told her about it. He would know she wouldn't fight his decision to save it for a car or the house or something important. No. It must be for something, *someone*, else.

It occurred to her Brian may have brought them out to Idaho to keep them out of the way. The memory of Honey asking about her bruises came unbidden to her mind. Meredith had been so distracted by her daughter answering the door that she had run to the door with nothing but a towel around her, with shoulders bare and the bruises clear. The dark blue marks around her clavicle and shoulders were unmistakably pressure marks from large fingers.

She was humiliated that another woman had

witnessed something so private and so painful. How could she explain to her, or anyone, how she tolerated this? It came to Meredith in a rush; she had ignored parts of her life in order to hang onto the stability it offered. *I let Brian hurt me, and I didn't do anything about it. I told myself this was normal.*

Her face flooded with heat and a tremendous shame filled her. Meredith remembered an older woman she met once, in a shelter where she lived one summer after her mother died. The woman came and went throughout the summer, dispensing advice to Meredith each time she arrived. Best soup kitchen, best shelter, best library to spend the days in. Her favorite subject was the stupidity of women staying with their abusers.

"I never put up with any nonsense," the woman affirmed to her more than once. "A man lays a hand on you, get out."

Meredith's early experiences of being homeless, though, had taught her the opposite lesson. She was a witness to shelters full of women who had run from abusive men. That's where you ended up when you ran away. If they took their kids, they were homeless too, just like she had been.

Whoa. Meredith was taken aback at memories leading her to such a conclusion. *I'm not abused.*

She turned the idea over in her mind, doubtful. There were isolated incidents, sure, but Brian had never hit her. She pushed the notion away and thumbed through the pictures in the box again, studying them closely for clues to her situation. It could be true that Brian was planning to leave her so he could go to a girlfriend. There was Jamie and Atticus to think about, though. She didn't believe Brian would leave his children behind. She looked down into the box of pictures, staring into the auburn-haired girl's face. Did she know about Brian's children? The idea struck Meredith suddenly that Brian might fantasize about killing her, just as she fantasized about killing him. It would be so easy if they each disappeared from each other's life.

Poof. Just like that.

Meredith put the boxes back in the attic where she found them, trying to place each exactly where it had been. The contents were too much to think about. She crawled into bed and hugged her pillow. Meredith faced the closet and thought about the gun Brian kept there, locked away in a safe. After awhile, she rolled over, facing the window. Sleep didn't come until hours later, darkness filling the room, her mind and finally, her dreams.

Chapter 6

"Who loves his little pumpkin-girl?"

"Daddy!" shrieked Jamie.

Brian hugged her to him and Jamie wrapped her arms tight around his neck. Meredith watched the welcome-home greeting with a calm impassivity.

Jamie danced around Atticus in the living room joyfully, singing "Daddy's home. Daddy's home."

"Forgive me, Merr." Brian came up to her wearing a serious face, his voice soft. "I don't know what got into me. The move. The new job. Everything, I guess."

Meredith nodded, not trusting herself to speak. Brian bent over her, and when she didn't look up, he kissed her on the cheek instead. He brushed by her and her heart contracted.

"Hey little guy," Brian said, picking up Atticus.

Atticus laughed and squealed as Brian lifted him high and blew a loud raspberry on his belly.

"Presents, I have presents," Brian called out. "One for each of you. Come sit on the couch, Merr."

Meredith obediently sat where he pointed and watched as Brian set a bag on the table.

"Sorry, I didn't have time to wrap things." He glanced at her before pulling out a box and handing it to Jamie. "The potato man," he announced jovially. "Can you believe they still make these things?"

Jamie tore open the box and started pawing

through the pieces.

"Help me, Daddy."

"Wait a minute, it's time for your brother." He pulled out a soft toy. "They call this the spuddy guy. We're in potato-land now, you know."

Brian handed the bag to Meredith and she took it gingerly.

"This is for you," he said, adding gently. "Let's start over, okay?"

Meredith felt herself waver inside. Brian was being so nice and trying so hard. Maybe the auburn-haired girl was from another time in his life. He was older than her. Of course he would have known other women before her. The money, well, the money could be for the business he always talked about starting.

From inside the bag she pulled a small jeweler's box. Formal and expensive-looking. She felt Brian watching her closely as she popped it open. There, laying on a piece of velvet was a pair of plastic potato earrings; brown, lumpy, and terribly ugly.

Despite herself, she laughed. The earrings were so silly, so ridiculous, and so unexpectedly awful. She loved them.

"I knew you'd get it." Brian sounded triumphant. "As soon as I saw them, I thought of you."

Those words made her laugh more. "Yeah, I bet." She cast a look at him.

"Someday, it'll be diamonds," he vowed. "I promise."

****

"Bad timing." She tensed in bed that night as he reached for her.

There was a pause.

"Early, isn't it?"

She swallowed dryly. "It's late. I was worried."

Brian snorted. "Yeah, let's not let that happen. You're not forgetting your pills, are you? Another kid's the last thing we need right now."

Meredith shook her head. "No."

Brian scooted over to her side of the bed and kissed her on the forehead. He hovered there a moment.

"It's not like we haven't done it wet before."

Fear rose up sudden and unexpected in her throat. She hadn't expected fear. Repulsion, rage, maybe. Not fear.

"I've been cramping." She said it in a rush, hoping her face wasn't visible in the dark. "Pretty badly."

He didn't move and Meredith sensed his indecision. *If he touches me, it's all going to come out*, she thought. I'll tell him I found the boxes, that I opened them, that I know about the girl and the money. *Touch me. Don't touch me.* Her mind spun, both wanting and fearful of either option.

Then he moved away and she bounced lightly on the mattress as he flopped on his side with his back to her.

"Why don't we go by the store tomorrow. Get you some medicine or something."

She searched her brain for an answer but nothing came to her. After awhile, she realized he wasn't waiting for an answer. His breath came deeper and fuller. Finally, when she was certain he was asleep, her fists uncurled and the tension in her body started to ease. She knew in her heart the pictures weren't from before their marriage; the money wasn't for a business venture.

Poison. She tried to draw comfort in her newfound fantasy. *An accident.*

Brian began to snore softly and she listened to the rhythm of his ragged breaths.

He's real. Not a fantasy man that can disappear from a fantasy murder. *The fantasy isn't enough. But…could I? Would I?*

****

She couldn't pinpoint the moment when she wasn't happy in her marriage anymore. Brian's sales territory had expanded and he traveled farther and farther afield, staying away for longer periods of time. But it wasn't just the time away causing her unhappiness; it was his more frequent belittlement of her.

The ongoing series of disappointments and hurts led her one day, to think, *Oh well, he takes care of us. He comes home to us. We'll make it work.* She didn't like to think that's all her marriage was.

Then her period was late and she was rocked by a fierce joy she didn't expect. Even before she took the test, Meredith knew she was pregnant a second time.

"You'll have to get it out of there." Brian's voice was icy and distant when she told him. "We can't afford another kid."

She was shocked, partly by the suggestion of killing their baby and partly by the matter-of-fact way he said it.

"I'm not having an abortion," she cried. "I want this child."

He chewed the inside of his cheek and assessed her coldly.

"You'll have to take it out," he insisted. "The timing's bad."

Tears sprung to her eyes and she shook her head. "No."

He stepped forward quickly and hugged her to him. She melted into his body, smelling sweat and aftershave, and her heart swelled with love for him for backing down so readily. *There is nothing wrong with my marriage. He loves me but doesn't know how to show it.*

"I'll go with you if you want," he persisted gently.

She tugged herself free and backed away. She forced herself to look him in the eye. *Don't let him bully you. You can't let him bully you on this.*

"You can't force me."

"You're making a mistake." His voice stayed soft and he became more cajoling, changing tactics. "Think about this. Think about Jamie. We can do more for one child than we can for two."

She shook her head.

"I won't change my mind."

He nodded, staring at her and through her. Then he turned suddenly and punched the wall between them, making her gasp. She started to sob and tremble as he turned back toward her.

"You're right. I can't force you." Then he grabbed his keys and left, not returning until two days later.

****

Brian didn't bring the subject up again. In fact, they never talked about her pregnancy at all, even as she grew large and round. There was an unspoken agreement that she was on her own with this one; no offers of extra blankets or water or a back massage. When Jamie woke up crying in the middle of the night with a nightmare, it was Meredith who heaved herself out of bed to soothe her back to sleep.

Late in her pregnancy, though, with the baby lying low in her womb, Meredith struggled to carry the laundry basket up and down the stairs to the building's machines. A couple of times, she flagged a passing neighbor who was going up or down the stairs and asked for help. People always seemed happy to pitch in, asking when she was due, if she knew the gender, whether they had picked out a name yet.

"Don't you dare try to carry the basket yourself," Beth, the woman next door told her. "You knock on my door anytime if you need help, with laundry or anything."

Meredith's biggest fear was going into labor while Brian was away. She looked up two taxi companies and kept both numbers in her pocket. Beth agreed to watch Jamie if Meredith went into an early labor and Brian was still on his sales rounds. A month before her due date, Brian worked out his schedule so he didn't have to leave town and her anxiety lessened. *I can't do this alone. When I really need him he's there for me.* She was grateful.

****

"How much soap?" he asked at the top of the steps, preparing to haul the full basket down to the laundry room.

Meredith stood on the threshold of their apartment. Jamie, now nearly four, was jumping down the steps with both feet, one at a time, calling out "I'm a fwog! I'm a fwog!" Her small voice echoed in the stairway.

"Just put in half a cup," Meredith said. "It's all it needs."

The door opened next to her and Beth poked her

head out.

"Oh, your husband's here to help," Beth cried out with a big smile toward Brian. "How nice. Your wife needs lots of attention now."

Brian smiled lazily at Beth, giving her his crooked smile, the one he used when he wanted to charm someone.

"Now and always. Big or small."

Beth laughed, her eyes lighting up. *People look at him and like him instantly*, Meredith observed with wonder. *How does he do that?*

"You are so lucky to have a helpful husband like this." Beth glanced over at Meredith and then instantly back to Brian. "Especially one so handsome."

Meredith smiled. Her husband was handsome. He was helpful. He supported them by working long hours. Maybe she wasn't giving him the credit he was due.

"She's my pumpkin-girl," Brian joked, looking over at Meredith affectionately and then explaining to Beth, "I called her that when she was pregnant with Jamie. This time though…" He raised his eyebrows in mock distress. "She's more of a watermelon, don't you think?"

Beth shrieked with laughter and Brian chuckled along with her. Meredith's smile froze on her face. She had gained quite a bit more weight in this pregnancy, especially in this final month when even her face looked puffy and swollen. Her body had never been so ungainly and unattractive, and it hurt when Brian would tease her about it.

Brian looked over at Meredith, registering her reaction before heading down the stairs.

"Guess you're my watermelon-girl now," he

repeated. "I'll have to find a new pumpkin-girl."

Beth disappeared into her own apartment, still laughing softly. Meredith stayed in the doorway for a moment, trying to recapture the earlier mood of the morning. She knew Brian would be annoyed if she told him how it hurt to be called a "watermelon-girl." He would tell her she couldn't take a joke, that she was too serious about things.

Brush it off, she ordered herself. *After all, who's making sure your underwear gets washed downstairs?* Back inside the apartment, she sat down gratefully, heavily, onto the living room sofa. The baby kicked her hard in the ribs, making her gasp, and it shifted inside her as though doing a somersault. "Come out, come out, whoever you are," she sang softly.

Next to her head, by the side of the sofa, the fist-sized hole in the wall remained unpatched.

Chapter 7

"Everyone looks the same here." Meredith glanced around as they walked through a discount department store. "I expected it to be different in a bigger city."

Brian rolled his eyes and snorted. "We're in middle America now."

Meredith found it strange how nearly everyone around her looked the same. After living her entire life in California, she was used to different races, cultures, and languages all around her on a daily basis. Idaho, by comparison, was bland. *Like potato soup*, she thought.

She hiked Atticus up higher on her hip and moved coats around on the sale rack. There were just three left in Jamie's size and one was pink, which technically, left only two. Jamie refused to wear pink. She handed one to her daughter to try on.

"Twirl around, sweetie," Brian coaxed, watching attentively as Jamie spun around in the coat. "You look beautiful in that one."

Jamie beamed at the compliment and hugged the coat to her body. "I want this one, Mommy."

"I guess that's the one then," Meredith agreed, adding quietly to Brian, "Good job."

"Let's get the gloves and get out of here," he said. "I'm hungry."

"Me too." Jamie's expression lit up. "Can I have fries and a chocolate shake?"

"Ugh." Meredith made a face. "No, we cannot eat greasy potatoes with sugar."

"The food's cheap, Merr," Brian said. "We've spent a fortune on clothes here. Anyway, you're buying her Choco Puffs at home."

She glared at him.

"The kids *need* warmer clothes. I could use a better coat too, you know."

"Next paycheck, okay? We can't do this all at once."

He turned to walk toward the cash registers. Meredith couldn't help herself. "Don't we have some savings?"

"I wish," he snapped, over his shoulder. "Everything we had went into the house and the move."

"Everything?" she prodded

There had been reason after reason not to bring up the subject of the hidden money at home; the kids were nearby, dinner needed to be made, laundry to be folded. Anything really was a good enough of an excuse to avoid a confrontation over the boxes she found. The real reason was she was afraid. She knew once the subject was broached, their lives would change, and their marriage would probably be over. And he would be angry, very angry with her.

He turned back to her, his eyes narrowing. "Yeah, everything. It takes everything I make to keep this family going."

Meredith knew she needed to drop it. Having this type of discussion in the middle of a department store wasn't the place. Not in front of her kids, not in front of strangers. But she couldn't stop herself. That eighteen thousand dollars in the attic prickled at her. *Where had it come from? What was it for?*

"You shouldn't have bought the house then. We're out in the middle of nowhere, Brian." Her voice rose. "For God's sake. Hay City?"

A woman looking at clothes glanced over and then strolled casually away.

"I gave you a house to live in." Brian's voice was cold and Meredith's breath came faster. "I pay for the food you eat, the clothes you wear, the heat so you don't freeze. Those earrings in your ears? Your socks? I bought those. Everything you have is because of me. I don't want you complaining to me about your house, about your clothes, about anything at all, actually."

Jamie sidled close to Meredith, her eyes filled with tears.

"Don't fight with Daddy." She wrapped her arms around Meredith's hips.

"We're not fighting, sweetie." Brian's tone lightened and he reached out for Jamie's hand. "Mom's just being silly. Let's go buy this stuff and then we'll get some fries and shakes. Maybe a cheeseburger, too."

"Brian," Meredith was reeling from his words, his cold tone and his lying. "I don't want to be here."

"Merr, enough. You've made your point. What's gotten into you lately?"

The woman was back, browsing the racks nearby and clearly listening to their family drama. Whatever. Give her something to talk about.

"I don't have to be here. Or the kids." She stared him down.

"Stop your complaining. You aren't going anywhere." His voice had lowered again and sharpened, a warning in its tone. "You have nowhere to go. No job skills. No one who will take you in. No money. Your car won't get you over the hill. Let's face it, you're lucky to be with me."

His face was red with anger. She had pushed him further than she had ever dared before. Her legs trembled and, in that moment, she hated herself for being so weak.

"Mommy?" Jamie tugged at her pant leg. A store employee was moving toward them. *Was there a protocol for family fights?* Meredith wondered. *Did they get training in this?*

Brian headed to the line of registers, pulling a tearful Jamie away from Meredith and along with him.

"Everything okay, Miss?" the employee asked, coming up to her. "Do you need anything?"

Meredith wiped her tears away with the back of a hand. Brian was right. She wasn't going anywhere and he knew it. She didn't want to stay, but she was more afraid of leaving. Nothing was okay.

How about a gun, Meredith thought bitterly.

The store clerk took a step away from her, an alarmed look on her face. *Did I say that out loud?* Meredith wondered. Then she followed after her husband.

****

Brian dropped her and the kids off at the shopping mall, telling her he had a couple of business calls to make.

"I'll be back in a couple of hours and then we'll head on home." He didn't look at her.

Meredith was relieved to get away from him for a while. They hadn't spoken to each other since their argument in the store.

"I want to stay with Daddy," Jamie announced.

"No sweetie, Daddy has to work." Meredith unbuckled her daughter from the seat.

"No, no, no!" Jamie screamed as Meredith pulled her out of the car.

Chocolate sugary shake, chicken nuggets, fried potato strips. *God,* she thought, *my little girl has been filled with cataclysmic rocket fuel.* She struggled to control Jamie as she loaded Atticus into his stroller. Brian drummed his fingers impatiently on the steering wheel, staring straight ahead.

Jamie screamed her way through a department store, attracting sympathetic glances from some and winces from most. The path in front of them cleared as shoppers scattered away.

"Here sweetheart, how about a lollipop?" An older woman bent down and offered the red candy to Jamie, who quieted in mid-scream and reached out a hand.

Meredith gritted her teeth and smiled a thanks. More sugar was all her daughter needed. But if lollipops were required to get them through the next two hours, then she would buy a bagful.

What's happening to me? I'm unraveling. Those pictures. That money. Those words Brian said to me. The way Honey looked at my bruises.

"Can I help you find something?" A smiling girl approached her as she absentmindedly stood in front of a row of lotions. Cherry Pie, Mango Lime, Green Apple. They all sounded luxurious and delicious, but she had thirteen dollars in her wallet and no credit or debit card. Brian didn't believe in them; he said using a plastic card made people overspend.

"No, just looking." Meredith tried to sound

confident.

"Well, your little girl's not 'just looking.'" The girl smiled even wider, showing white, even teeth. "I bet she'd love the toy store. It's down the mall, on the other side of the fountain."

Meredith caught a glimpse of Jamie squirting a long strand of lotion onto her arm and then skipping to another display.

"Sorry," Meredith breathed. "I'm so sorry. I'll just grab her."

"No problem, my little sister would do the same thing," the girl chirped out in her cheery manner, adding, "if my mom let her."

"Can you just watch him? For just a moment." Meredith pushed the stroller toward the girl, who backed away quickly.

"I can't watch your baby." The cheerful tone gone. "Hey lady!"

But Meredith had already dashed across the store to grab Jamie who, seeing her mother, ran around a table to get away. Shoppers scooted off to different aisles, avoiding the chase. *Oh please. Transport me somewhere else.*

Time slowed down as she darted around tables after her sugar-loaded child. They went round and round and Meredith finally stopped, panting. Other shoppers now stopped, peeking their way, curious about what would happen next.

"Jamie, knock it off," she called out. "Get over here."

Jamie picked up a bottle and studied it intently. Meredith rounded the table and scooped her up, smelling about a dozen scents coming off her daughter.

She felt the heat radiating from Jamie as well as sticky, greasy lotions on her arms and legs. Jamie laid her head on Meredith's shoulder.

"Can I get a lotion?"

Meredith strode quickly back to where she had left Atticus.

The girl's smile had vanished and her look was stony.

"You shouldn't leave your baby with a stranger," the girl chastised, shaking her head.

"Thanks for the advice." Meredith grabbed hold of the stroller with one hand and awkwardly maneuvered it out of the store. As she struggled to carry Jamie and push the stroller, she wondered how other mothers survived this stage.

"Sweetie, how about riding in the stroller with your brother?" she asked.

"Carry me, Mommy." Jamie wrapped her legs and arms more firmly around Meredith.

Shoppers around her parted to let her through, smiling down at Atticus and then up at Meredith. People moved a little slower here, she noticed, the pace not as frantic as the malls in California. And there was a display of more plaid than she had ever seen in her life; red, blue, green, yellow. Men and women wore it atop jeans and khakis like it was a uniform. Hiking shoes, cowboy boots, tennis shoes. Nothing complicated. She had to admit, the clothing looked comfortable and the people here appeared relaxed.

"I might have to ticket you for inattentive driving." The male voice was at her shoulder.

Meredith turned, startled, and looked directly into the face of Sheriff Barney. Her eyes lit up. She knew exactly two people in Idaho and one of them was at the mall? She didn't really know Barney so he hardly counted. Still, his friendly face was more than welcome at the moment.

"Where's your star?" she blurted, then knew her face was turning red. What a stupid thing to say. She felt off-balance here in this new place, so far from everything she knew.

"Off duty." His voice was warm and relaxed. The awkwardness she had noticed in him before was gone, and that helped her compose herself.

Jamie wiggled out of Meredith's arms to stand next to her. Meredith's shoulders relaxed their tension from carrying a forty-pound four-year-old and she sighed at the respite.

"I'm going to get a star," Jamie announced. "I'm going to be a sheriff."

Barney looked down at her seriously.

"That's a good idea. You'll have to study hard in school, though."

"I'm going to kindergarten next year." Jamie stood tall. "I'm almost five."

"You must like to get into a city on your days off," Meredith said.

Barney turned his attention back to Meredith and shook his head quickly.

"I come to the mall only under protest." He chuckled. "I need a gift for my sister's three-year-old. Apparently she likes unicorns?"

"I love unicorns," shouted Jamie, making Meredith wince in embarrassment, but Barney just smiled.

"A pink unicorn," Barney clarified. "I've been walking around for an hour, trying to work up the nerve to say those words to a clerk. Maybe I should just write them down and pass over a note."

Meredith laughed.

"By the way, I'm Meredith." There was something about him that made her feel nervous and more confident at the same time. She continued on before he could introduce himself. "I know you're Barney because Honey called your name. At the grocery store, you know."

She watched in surprise as he first looked startled, and then threw his head back and laughed loudly. Other shoppers looked over and smiled. Meredith looked at him quizzically, wondering what she'd said to make him laugh.

"My name's Curtis Barnaby," he explained. "Honey calls me Barney, after Barney on the *Andy Griffith Show*?"

Meredith shook her head. She had no idea what he was talking about.

"It's an old black-and-white TV show. Barney was sort of this dumb deputy who never got anything right."

"Oh, I didn't know." Meredith was now horrified she had called him Barney.

His face started turning red as he tried to explain. "Honey means it in a nice way, as a joke, you know. She's a nice lady. The only thing is, other people have started calling me Barney, too. The name's sort of stuck. Not everyone means it in a nice way. Not everyone likes the sheriff."

"I won't call you that again," Meredith promised, inwardly glad his name wasn't Barney after all. "I like Curtis better, anyway."

He heaved his shoulders with a sigh and she

couldn't help but notice how broad they were.

"I'd better get on with this." He bent down to talk to Jamie. "Can you walk like a big girl? Your mom's got her hands full pushing your little brother around."

Jamie nodded and looked up at him adoringly. *Charisma*, thought Meredith. *I'm not the only one he's charmed.*

"Try the bigger stores," she suggested. "There are unicorn toys, clothes, everything there."

"I want a unicorn, too," Jamie demanded.

Meredith winced. "We're not here to buy things. We just get to look today."

"Then I want to *look* at unicorns," Jamie retorted.

Curtis hesitated a moment and then addressed Meredith.

"Do you want to come with me? Help me find something?"

Meredith looked down the mall. Brian wouldn't be back for a couple of hours and she had time to kill. *What could be the harm? It would be nice to make a friend in Idaho.*

"Ok," she agreed. "As long as you're sure."

He smiled his answer. They headed down the mall in search of unicorns.

****

It was dark by the time they got home and both kids were asleep in the truck's backseat. Meredith had closed her eyes on the way back and leaned into the swaying of the truck as it wove around turns and crested hills.

Brian was late in picking them up at the mall, and hadn't answered her calls when he didn't appear at the agreed upon time. Her pre-paid cell phone was for emergencies only, Brian had told her, but wasn't this an emergency of sorts? Finally, he had called her back and said tersely that he was on his way.

"I want to go home," Jamie whined over and over while they sat on the bench inside the mall waiting, aiming an occasional kick at Meredith's leg for emphasis.

"Daddy will be here soon," she kept saying, too tired to chastise Jamie for kicking her.

When he arrived, she was relieved and angry in equal measures.

"I tried calling," she complained, letting her exasperation out. "You just left us here."

"I went in the office and got busy with contracts that were running late." Brian's tone was brusque and not apologetic at all. "Then Jim came in. I've told you about him. We got to talking and he helped me out some, told me of a new prospect out in Rexburg. I may go there in the next couple of days, try to get in the door."

"Didn't you get my calls?"

Brian's face twisted as he glanced sideways at her.

"Can't you ever be happy for me? Think about me for a change? You're the one who wanted to come to Boise, go to the stores. You got what you wanted, okay? What was the big deal? You had an entire mall to keep you entertained. Why didn't you walk through a couple more stores?"

Meredith slumped in her seat, thinking about her afternoon.

They'd spent an hour with Curtis at the mall before he left for his sister's house. A stuffed pink unicorn was successfully found and purchased, with Jamie selecting the wrapping paper and bow. They chatted easily and the time flew by. When he left, it seemed he did so somewhat reluctantly.

Afterward, Meredith slowly circled the mall twice with her children and the second hour disappeared. By the end of the third hour, her back and feet were sore and Atticus was on his 'emergency' diaper. She swore she never wanted to go to another mall again.

Walking through a couple more stores with tired children would have been a nightmare. It wasn't worth saying those things to Brian. *I'm too tired for another argument. I want to go home.*

It hit her afresh as Brian turned the car east onto the highway that home had changed. Home was Hay City. Home was Idaho. Whether she liked it or not.

Chapter 8

There really was a Ham n' Eggs Road. A real road, paved and with yellow stripes down the middle, as though so it saw so much traffic the lanes needed to be divided and dedicated. Her boxy car rumbled over the pavement, the only car in sight, ticking the odometer closer to two hundred and fifty thousand miles, although she wondered if there wasn't a missing "one" in front of those numbers.

The compact white and green farmhouse, with its numerous outbuildings, were the only structures along the road so it was easy to mark where Honey lived. She drove up the gravel drive, and with the car belching a puff of dark smoke, parked at the side of the house. A small iron table and plastic white chairs sat in a puddle. It had rained all the previous day and night, washing the last of the snow off the roads and out of the valley.

"Mommy! Mommy!" Jamie shrieked. "Chickens!"

Two brown hens bobbed across the muddy yard, their heads turning this way and that.

"Okay, sweetie. I see them." Meredith unbuckled Jamie from her seat and her daughter flung herself at the door handle. "Hey, wait for me."

But the door was open and Jamie was racing across the yard. Meredith sighed. Did Honey know she had invited a tasmanian devil into her home? She turned back and pulled Atticus from his carseat as his face turned up to her with a wide smile, two pearly teeth showing. How could two kids be so different? Her son was so easy compared to Jamie.

"Mommy!" Jamie shrieked again as one, and then both, of the chickens flapped their wings and ran in zigzagged terror.

The farmhouse door banged open and Honey filled the doorway.

"Is the fox after my chickens again?"

"Just my wild child," Meredith called, walking up to the porch.

Honey laughed, and put her hands on her generous hips. She watched as Jamie ran figure eights in the yard with her arms out, trying to catch the birds.

"If she catches one, I'll wring its silly neck for dinner. Neither one of those are good layers. They just idle around wasting space."

Meredith smiled, her body relaxing instinctively around this friendly woman.

"You won't have to wring its neck. Jamie'll keep after them until they have a heart attack. Are you sure it's okay?"

Honey opened the door and gestured Meredith inside.

"Let's get some coffee, what do you think?"

****

"Stanford, huh?"

"Oh, no, no." Meredith looked down at her red jersey imprinted with the university name. "I just wear this. I didn't finish college. I barely started junior college, actually. I quit."

Honey looked at her closely.

"You don't look like a quitter to me." She took a

sip of coffee, eying Meredith over the top of her cup.

"I was going to go back, after Jamie," Meredith started. "Then I got pregnant again."

Honey waved a hand dismissively.

"Life happens. You have lots of time. What are you going to study when you go back?"

Meredith appreciated how Honey used the word *when*, and not *if*.

"I hadn't decided yet. I still don't know if I'm going back. I'm not sure if there's anything I'd be good at."

Honey tsked.

"Everyone's good at something. I'm good at raising pigs and chickens. It didn't take college to teach me that. But if you want to go to school, you should go. What does your husband think?"

Meredith looked out the windows facing the front of the house. Jamie was sitting in the wet grass watching as the two hens clucked and bobbed nearby. Meredith knew she was just catching her breath for round two. The chickens didn't have a chance.

"He wouldn't be for it. It's too much money, even junior college. Anyway, he travels a lot and I need to be home with the kids."

Honey rose from the table and refilled their coffee cups. For a large woman, she moved easily about the small kitchen. Though cozy in size, it felt larger because of the tall windows letting in plenty of light and the outdoor scenery.

"There are always online classes," Honey counseled. "And there's always a few dollars to be found if you want it enough. This is your life, not Brian's. Get a backbone, girl."

"Brian wouldn't like it," Meredith said, her voice coming out louder than she intended. She was aware of Honey watching her closely, and before she could think about it, she was saying, "Honey, I'm so trapped."

Her lips trembled, and to her embarrassment, tears sprung to her eyes. *Oh god,* she realized, *I'm oversharing.* But Honey's face was sympathetic and this spurred her on, despite herself.

"It's not just the kids or the money," Meredith went on, the words tumbling out.

Meredith glanced over to the living room where Atticus crawled around the pillow fort Honey had built for him. She knew he wouldn't understand what she was saying, but worried nevertheless that her words would sink into his psyche and unknowingly wound him.

"You sure you're not just tired?" Honey suggested gently. "Being a mother of two little ones is exhausting."

"I'm not just tired," Meredith exclaimed, and then the words poured out of her. "It's Brian. I need to get away from him, but I can't divorce him. He'd never let me go. Then he brought me out here, to this horrible place out in the middle of nowhere. I need to do *something.*"

She stopped, aghast. She had come over for a friendly visit and then taken advantage of Honey's kindness by sharing frustrations and calling Hay City a horrible place. *I should just go ahead and tell Honey I want to kill my husband. Then she could drive over to my house and tell Brian his wife is dangerously crazy. God only knew what Brian would do with that information. Bury me out in the back field somewhere, most likely.*

There was an awkward pause before Honey rose to grab a tissue box. She passed it over to Meredith.

"You *do* sound like you have a lot on your mind," Honey sympathized as Meredith wiped her eyes and blew her nose. "Maybe I can help?"

"Oh Honey, I'm so sorry. I can't believe I said all that." Meredith wished she could take back the last few minutes. "I really didn't mean it. You're right. I'm just tired."

The front door slammed and Meredith jumped in her seat.

"Mommy! I'm *hungry*!" Jamie burst into the room, trembling with fresh energy. She looked at Honey. "Do you have Huffs?"

"I'm all out of Huffs, but I do have jawbreaker cookies." Honey didn't lose a beat. "You have to ask your mom first if it's okay."

Jamie looked at Honey with suspicion.

"What're those?"

"They're my famous jawbreaker cookies," Honey declared. "So hard, they'll break your jaw. Delicious, though. They're worth it."

Meredith took a deep breath and forced a smile. "Go ahead. Break your jaw. It's fine with me."

Jamie climbed onto a seat at the table.

"Can I have three?"

"How about a please?" Meredith coached. "And let's start with one, okay?"

"Please, can I have *three*?"

Honey laughed.

"Your mom's right. We'll start with one and find out if your jaw can handle a second one."

"My jaw's really strong," Jamie protested, but doubt crept into her expression.

Meredith rose and went to get Atticus. She changed him in the living room while she listened to Jamie chatter away to Honey. For the thousandth time, she wondered what Jamie would be like when she grew up. She loved how Jamie had so much force of character and hoped she'd always be filled with this much vitality. As for Atticus, she hoped he would always find it easy to be happy in any situation.

Honey's house had a personality like its owner. It was warm, comfortable, and inviting. Everything was in perfect order without appearing fussy. A quilt was draped over the arm of a chair as though it had been set aside for the moment and was just waiting to be used again. Books were stacked on a table and a handful of family pictures rested atop a low cabinet across the room. A stone fireplace was clean with fresh wood laid inside ready to be lit.

Meredith realized she hadn't asked Honey many questions about herself. Even from across the room Meredith could recognize a much younger Honey in one of the photos, still large in stature, standing next to a towering man and surrounded by their small children. She didn't even know if Honey was divorced or widowed. It struck her that Honey's husband could actually be away on a trip, although it didn't look as though a man lived in the house.

Atticus changed, Meredith returned to the kitchen table where Jamie and Honey were both dunking the jawbreaker cookies into glasses of milk before biting into them. Honey handed a cookie to Meredith.

"These make good teething rings, too." She

chuckled in her good-natured way, as though nothing had happened.

Meredith forced a laugh, glad the mood had shifted. Honey seemed to know how to defuse an uncomfortable situation. She gave the cookie to Atticus who sucked on it contentedly.

"Cookie?" Honey asked.

"No thanks, I need my teeth," she joked, her equilibrium returning.

"Mommy, Honey has baby chicks. She's says I can have one if you say yes. Can I have one, please?"

Meredith looked at Honey, alarmed. Was this payback for her oversharing? She pictured a round ball of yellow fluff squeezed and squashed under Jamie's pillow.

"It would live here though, right?" Honey leaned over toward Jamie. "You could visit it anytime you wanted, give it a name, feed it. But it would be happier living here with its brothers and sisters."

Jamie frowned, considering this.

"I can have a brother and sister chick, too. So he wouldn't be by himself."

Meredith coughed, but Honey smoothly answered, "So you'd put me out of business would you? I need my little workers here to lay the eggs."

"It's okay to have a chick as long as it stays here." Meredith spoke quickly. "Say thank you to Honey."

Jamie face broke into a huge smile. "Thank you Honey."

****

The chicken coops were inside one of the buildings to the rear of the house. Small chicken-sized doors led from the coops through the side of the building to a series of penned yards so the birds could go outside. Inside, the walls were lined with boxes filled with dozens of clucking birds. Near the door were three large boxes on low tables with heating lamps set above.

"Look in here now." Honey pulled a stool over for Jamie to stand on. "These eggs are hatching."

Inside, a number of eggs lay nestled in hay. Jamie watched wide-eyed as several of the eggs rocked and slowly broke apart as the chick inside fought to get out.

"Can I help them get out?" Jamie asked.

"This is their job to do," explained Honey. "This first fight makes them strong and gets them ready for the world. A little fight is a good thing."

Meredith looked over at this, wondering if Honey was making a point to her.

Honey scooted the stool with Jamie on it over to the next two sets of boxes where round, yellow chicks stood about and cheeped, pecking occasionally at the grit and seed under their feet.

"I'll keep a few of these, but most go to other farmers in the area," she said. "Apparently, it's 'in' now to raise a couple chickens, so a lot of families in neighboring towns want them, too." She leaned down to Jamie. "You can pick one of these."

Jamie watched, mesmerized by the roiling mass of yellow.

"I'm letting the hogs go now." Honey stepped back where Meredith stood holding Atticus. "Too much work since Milt's gone. I always liked the chickens best anyway."

"Your husband…" Meredith started.

"People called us Milk and Honey when we were out together, and that's how we were. We just belonged together. When we first got married, he was this huge guy. I'm a big gal. I was back then too, so he was the one for me."

Honey smiled in remembrance. "Big shoulders, tall, and louder than me, if you can believe it. He had a deep voice that could tickle me down to my toes. He built all these buildings himself, from the ground up. The hogs were his, and the chickens were mine. 'Ham n' Eggs go together like Milk n' Honey,' he would say."

A pang of something she couldn't recognize made Meredith tremble. She didn't quite believe people could really love like this and live in harmony year after year. In her experience, love was too closely linked to other emotions. Resentment, bitterness, indifference, and hate.

"What happened?" she asked.

"Cancer." Honey's tone was clipped, pained. "Ate him alive. Whittled him down to nothing inside of a year. It's been twenty-two months, one week, and three days since I lost him."

Honey broke off.

"Honey! I found Laf!" Jamie cried out, causing a couple of the sitting hens to fly off their nests.

"Sorry, she has one volume. Earsplitting," Meredith apologized, as they moved back over to the baby chicks to see where Jamie was pointing.

"That one! That one's Laf," Jamie said.

"Laugh, huh?" Honey repeated. "What a jolly name."

"She means Lafayette, from *Ice Land*," explained Meredith. "It's a kids' movie. He's a snowman."

"Either way works." Honey grabbed a marker off a

clipboard attached to the wall. Deftly, she reached into the box and daubed a blue mark on the top of Laf's head. "Just so I can keep an eye on him and not lose him in the crowd."

****

Later, as Meredith came back around to get in the car, Honey touched her arm.

"Sounds like you're in a heap of trouble." Honey spoke quietly, looking over toward Jamie.

Meredith shook her head quickly. "No, no, not at all. Hormonal craziness, I think. And I'm tired, like you pointed out."

Honey studied her face seriously.

"You going to be able to get some rest tonight?"

Meredith nodded.

"Brian's supposed to get back, but it'll probably be late," she mumbled. "I'll be fine. I *am* fine."

Honey frowned.

"I don't think that's true at all, dear. I'm a good helper when friends are in trouble. You remember that. There's nothing better than a good friend when you need one."

Meredith nodded, not meeting Honey's eyes, and then got into the car. She knew she had shared too much about her troubled marriage. And she needed much more than a friend's kind words.

****

The shrill ring of the wall phone startled Meredith. It'd been hanging on the wall when they moved in, old-fashioned with push buttons and a long curly cord. Brian said ten dollars a month was a lot cheaper than having her use her pre-paid cell phone. More reliable too, he added, since cell service was spotty in their deep valley.

She'd gotten three calls on the house phone since they moved in. The first was someone trying to sell her a timeshare in Mexico.

"I can't even afford to repair my car," she told the man.

"You wouldn't need a car in Mexico," he pitched at her desperately. "You just walk to the beach."

The second call was from Beth. Meredith had called her once the phone was turned on, lonely and looking for a friendly voice. She'd reached voice mail, but Beth called back almost immediately and they talked for an hour, promising to stay in touch. Meredith knew they wouldn't. She had moved enough to know that friends faded away.

This third call was from the bank. The woman on the phone sounded bored as she informed Meredith their account was in overdraft status, or would be if they qualified for overdraft. As it was, checks were bouncing and the woman from the bank wanted to know if Meredith preferred to transfer money from their savings to stop the wreckage.

"How much is in our savings?" Meredith asked. She had never gotten a call from the bank before.

There was a pause.

"$270.26." There was something accusing in the bank employee's tone. "Normally, a paycheck gets deposited about now. But it's a little late this time. Might want to talk to your husband."

Meredith wanted to laugh. All those years of penny-pinching only added up to $270. Of course, she knew where their savings really was, but she doubted if the bank employee could access the box in their attic.

"I definitely will talk to him," she told the bank employee.

A thought came to her.

"I'm wondering," she started. "Our bills? Our mortgage? I keep forgetting when they get paid. Just so I can keep better track."

"Good idea," the woman encouraged. "You should write this down."

There was a pause, and then she came back on the line.

"Electric, gas, insurance, and phone; all go out on the fifteenth. That's it. There's no mortgage payment. You sure it's through us?"

"No," Meredith said slowly. "I forgot. We pay the mortgage out of a separate account."

It was time to have it out with Brian about the boxes in the attic. About the house and how he paid for it. When he showed up again, she would confront him and make him tell her everything. Maybe she would even tell him she wanted a divorce. She would figure out a way to keep herself and her kids afloat. She would get a backbone.

Meredith had expected him home the night before, but he hadn't arrived and hadn't called. Angry, she hadn't called him either. Instead, once again she'd raided his supply of sleeping pills and fallen into a strange sleep filled with shadows and discord. She'd woken exhausted with a nauseating headache, swearing to herself that from now on she'd leave Brian's medication alone.

"Ma'am?" the bank employee interrupted her musings. "Can I help you with anything else?"

I can do it, Meredith vowed to herself. This is my

life, and I do have a backbone.

"You cleared a lot of things up," she responded. "I can get back on track now."

****

The ever-surly boy at the deli counter eyed Jamie's pajamas and her own baggy sweatpants. Meredith's hair was pulled back in a ponytail and she hadn't bothered putting makeup on for the trip to the grocery store.

Brian hadn't shown up for a second night without so much as a call. Meredith briefly wondered if he had abandoned them. She tossed and turned through the night, worrying about bills not being paid, the boxes in the attic, leaving her marriage, and facing up to Brian's temper.

"It was a rough night." She mentally kicked herself for explaining how they looked to the deli boy.

He sniffed loudly, wiped his nose with the back of his hand, then pulled out a tissue and spat into it. Meredith watched disgustedly as he examined it before balling it up and cramming it into his apron pocket.

"You getting anything?" he asked.

"You washing your hands?" Meredith shot back.

They glared at each other, but then he reluctantly turned and washed his hands in the sink behind him. She stood her ground and waited, feeling petty and victorious. *Don't mess with me today.*

"I guess it's easy to let yourself go," he sneered when he returned. "After having kids, I mean."

Meredith gaped at him.

"What's your problem?" she asked.

"Only problem I have is when Californicators come barging in here, telling people what to do." He stared her down. "You buying something, lady?"

She fumed. There was no way she was going to let this kid talk to her this way.

"Is the manager around? I think he needs to know what a little snot you are."

The boy cocked his head to one side and smirked at her knowingly.

"You're talking to him. Manager and *general manager*. While my parents are out of town, anyway. Doubt they'll want to know anything you got to say."

"Time for my break," he added, and walked away, leaving Meredith seething at the counter.

****

She shouldn't have let deli boy push her buttons. He was just an awful kid, even though he was only a few years younger than her.

Meredith wished there was somewhere other than her broken down house on the prairie she could go for awhile. Somewhere she could pull herself together while the children played, like a city park. Hay City didn't have enough people for a community playground. She briefly considered going to Honey's house to vent, but she was afraid if she started talking, the conversation would veer into dangerous territory. Honey was kind and motherly, and her sympathetic ear invited personal confidences.

With no other way to vent her anger, Meredith pressed her foot down harder on the gas pedal. The old car trembled at the demand. No matter. What's the worst that could happen? It would break today rather than a few weeks from now. Fifty-five, sixty-five, seventy miles an hour. The speedometer topped at seventy-two and wavered there. The engine strained and whined at her in protest.

The scenery floated by, appearing to move slowly past them despite their speed. Blue lilies, purple lupine, and tall lime grasses had filled the landscape almost overnight, so intense in color that she felt choked and smothered by it. The mountains beyond were more soothing, just turning green at the feet, but still buried in snow once they rose from the valley.

Her foot was almost to the floorboard when their turn approached. She slowed as little as she dared and turned sharply, the car leaning dangerously to the right.

Jamie shrieked and then laughed. Meredith glanced in the rearview mirror, reassuring herself Atticus's carseat had held, and then put her foot down hard again on the gas pedal. There was an angry grinding noise and then the car leaped forward. Her house was far down the road, a gray meaningless cube that grew and grew as they hurtled toward it. The house changed from gray to dirty white with black trim. The brown roof emerged and dark windows watched her approach.

"Mommy! The sheriff!"

Startled, Meredith looked up at the rearview mirror and the blue and red lights flashing from the top of the sheriff's truck reflected back at her. *Shit, shit, shit.* She judged the distance to the house and considered whether there would be an extra ticket for continuing down the road another half mile. Better to get home, she concluded, and let the kids out of the car while she dealt with this.

Still, a lump of worry filled her throat and her heart beat faster. They couldn't afford a speeding ticket. She wondered whether she could talk him into letting her off with a warning. She remembered how friendly he had been at the Boise mall, his admiring gaze, and figured she stood a good chance. Once he realized it was her, with her kids in the back seat, saw that she was home, surely he wouldn't give her a ticket.

She pulled into her driveway and up to the house, crunching over the gravel and rolling to a stop. There was an unsettling metal-on-metal clunking noise in the engine as she turned the car off and her heart sank even more. A ticket *and* car troubles. The day couldn't possibly get any worse. She unbuckled her seatbelt and opened the door, planning her approach.

"Stay here with Atticus a moment, okay Jamie?" Meredith climbed out of the car.

"I want to talk to the sheriff," Jamie said.

"Let me talk to him first." Meredith's voice was sharp. The day had already given her too many challenges as it was and she didn't need one more. She stood to face him.

Sheriff Curtis Barnaby had his door open and was just climbing out. He bumped his head on the top of the car as he emerged and Meredith had to smile. *Barney*, she recalled. Her mood lifted a bit. Surely she could talk him out of the ticket. Maybe she'd invite him in for a cup of coffee. It would be nice to talk to a rational adult for a while. Meredith put on a bright smile and walked toward him, her hands raised in surrender.

"I did it," she called out. "I confess."

He lifted his head to look at her and she stopped, lowering her hands. His expression was one of shock and she felt a slight unease. Maybe he thought she was making fun of him.

"I'm sorry," she tried again, and then waited. He stood by his car for a moment and then approached her slowly.

"Mrs. Lowe, are your children in the car?" His voice shook slightly and he looked strangely pale. She wondered if he was sick. Didn't he have a backup sheriff to take over when he couldn't make it in, a Barney of his own?

"It's Meredith, please." It appeared unlikely now he was going to let her off with a warning. Or come in for coffee. The mood was strange. "Yes. Both of them."

He nodded toward her car. "Why don't you have them go in the house so we can talk for a moment."

She studied his serious face and then turned quickly back to her car. *Speeding must be a bigger deal in Idaho than I realized.*

"Jamie, take Atticus inside." She opened the rear door and unbuckled her son.

Jamie frowned at her. "You did a bad thing?"

"No sweetie," Meredith reassured her. "The sheriff just wants to talk to me for a moment. Okay?"

"Mommy did a bad thing," Jamie said, climbing out of the car and awkwardly carrying Atticus to the house.

"Great," Meredith mumbled under her breath as she turned to face the sheriff again. "Look, I'm sorry I went so fast. I've had a bad day and decided to take it out on my car. But do you really have to give me a ticket?"

"Mrs. Lowe, I'm not here to give you a ticket." His shoulders were slumped and now he just looked miserable. "I'm afraid I have some real bad news for you."

He gulped and shifted on his feet. She waited, her mind a blank.

"Your husband. Brian Delano Lowe?"

Meredith breathed in deeply and held it. She nodded.

"I'm afraid he…he was found dead early this morning." His voice was shaky as he spoke and he swallowed hard before continuing. "He was shot…shot twice in the head. It was murder."

She sighed, letting the pent-up air escape slowly from her lungs, the world around her stopping.

"I'm sorry," he gasped, suddenly sinking to his knees. "I—"

Then Meredith watched stunned as the sheriff fell over sideways, fainting dead away in her driveway.

Part 2

If you are married and wind up with a bullet in your brain, ninety-nine percent of the time, your spouse was the culprit. Ask any cop.

It's hard being cast as a one percenter. No one believes you.

Some life hacks for committing a murder:

Cover your tracks way in advance.

Don't ever ask a store clerk for a gun.

Keep your fingerprints off the murder weapon.

Don't ever, ever tell anyone the truth about your marriage.

~*~

I should have been more careful. Because the spouse is always the one.

Chapter 9

She couldn't move him, so Meredith knelt over Curtis for a moment trying to get her brain to function.

She kept thinking nine-one-one, nine-one-one, nine-one-one over and over, but it was hard to remember what it meant.

"Emergency," she whispered to herself.

All in a rush, the world started moving and her brain unlocked. She raced into the house.

"Mommy, are you going to jail?" Jamie called out from her bedroom.

"No." Meredith knew she would have some explaining to do to Jamie later. A worry fluttered through her mind that Brian would be angry at this commotion, but then she remembered why the sheriff was there. Brian *wouldn't* be angry.

Her breath caught for a moment and a dizziness swept through her. She cleared her mind, poured a glass of water, grabbed a pillow off the couch, and dashed back outside to where Sheriff Barnaby was just sitting up.

"Don't get up too fast," she cautioned, handing him the water and settling the cushion behind him. "You'll just faint again."

"I fainted?" he asked, rubbing the back of his head. "I thought you hit me."

She sat on the gravel next to him and watched him

carefully as he sipped the water.

"Are you sick?" she asked.

He shook his head, rising off the ground slowly.

"I got the call at three this morning about the bod…er, your husband, and I guess I haven't eaten or drunk anything since," he said. "A group of kids out partying, they noticed the truck parked off the road. One of them went over to look and, well, got a look at more than he needed to."

Meredith hadn't moved.

"You're sure it's him? Brian?" she asked from her knees, her eyes on the gravel below her.

"Pretty sure. I ran the plates, checked his wallet. It looks like him, mostly. Only saw him once before—" He stopped at those words, swallowed thickly, and then went on, "I hate to ask this but we need someone to identify him. I need *you* to come identify him, to be sure, you know."

Meredith's mind swam and she wondered for a moment if this was one of her weird dreams. She fingered the gravel on the driveway, pressing the sharp rocks into her palms. The day felt real and unreal.

She nodded and then looked toward the house. "My kids." Meredith knew her mind was going numb, but was helpless to stop it.

"They can come. The coroner's wife does daycare so she'll watch them while you're inside."

Those words stuck in Meredith's mind, blocking out everything else. She clung to them and turned them over in her mind. She knew it wasn't important, that she wasn't thinking clearly, but couldn't get them out of her head.

"The coroner's wife does daycare," she repeated

back flatly.

Sheriff Barnaby looked at her strangely, clearly not expecting to have a discussion about daycare at this moment.

"They live on one part of the property, coroner's office is on another. She does the daycare in their home."

Meredith imagined children playing in the yard, watched over by the coroner's wife. Did he come home at night and talk about his grisly end-of-life work? Did she then talk about the songs the children sang, their high spirits and energy? How many people left their children with the wife while they went with the husband to look at their dead?

He held out a hand to help her up, interrupting her thoughts and dragging her back to the present.

"I'm really sorry," he said.

"He was supposed to be home day before yesterday." Meredith ignored his hand and hugged the pillow to her chest. "I was mad at him for not coming home, not calling, or anything."

"So you didn't go out looking for him…or anything?"

"I was kind of glad, I think. We weren't getting along." *An understatement.* Their marriage had become a twisted thing.

"You weren't getting along," he repeated back to her.

Meredith looked up, hearing a different tone in his voice. The sheriff shifted uncomfortably from foot to foot.

There was a long silence.

"Mrs. Lowe." Sheriff Barnaby lowered his chin

and stood straighter. “Maybe we should go inside now to check on your kids?”

Meredith rose to her feet slowly. The news didn’t feel real to her. She didn’t like the sheriff’s tone with her. It was cold and…and was it accusing? A cold shiver went through her at the possibility Brian would be just as dangerous to her dead as alive. An anger welled up in her at this. Honey’s words echoed in her head, “Get a backbone, girl. This is your life.” She gulped some air and looked away from him, thinking.

“I need to get the groceries into the house.” She spoke slowly, wondering how she could utter such mundane words just moments after receiving news about her husband being murdered. “Then maybe you’d better eat something before, before I go look.” *At my dead husband,* echoed in her mind.

With that, she turned away and walked shakily toward her car.

****

It was him.

The coroner had cleaned him up but she stared at a smear of blood on Brian’s chin. A cloth covered part of his head, hiding what the bullet had done. Two bullets, in fact, the coroner told her matter-of-factly. As though it wasn’t her husband lying there dead but some stranger they were examining for no particular reason.

She looked at Brian’s face, which had shifted slightly from the damage but still definitely Brian, and wondered why she wasn’t crying, screaming, and making a scene. Her husband had just been murdered and she was just standing there looking blankly at him. She couldn’t believe now that she’d wanted Brian dead, fantasized about this happening. Her thoughts were a jumble.

It was the coroner who took her into the chilled room. Who asked her to identify her husband. Who then led her out of the room to where a pale Sheriff Barnaby was waiting on a bench outside, avoiding her eyes.

"Is this your first dead body?" she asked when the coroner left them alone.

He looked at her, the corners of his mouth twitching downward.

"First murder. It's mainly car accidents out here. And the highway patrol usually gets out to those first." His throat worked a moment before adding, "They cover them up."

She sat on the bench next to him.

"I've seen a couple." Meredith recalled the first time, when she was nine years old and her mother took her to a homeless camp. "My mom and I lived in some rough places. There was one guy who everyone believed was sleeping by the river. It was a few days before someone checked on him. He'd been dead awhile, just laying there. I guess no one missed him."

She stopped, her voice choking up. She had cried over the homeless man, worried someday that would be her and her mom. No one to help them or miss them. She stayed close to her mother for weeks afterward, frightened over what would happen if her mother disappeared. Meredith recalled even insisting on going to the liquor store with her, waiting outside and watching through the window until her mother emerged with a paper bag. Those were the days when her mother started drinking in front of her, too. The beginning of a slow slide to the end.

The sheriff studied her carefully and they sat there for another moment. Then he nodded down the corridor toward the door where the coroner had exited.

"He'll let everyone know I couldn't go in there with you." He shook his head at himself and his apparent failings.

It was another minute before he turned back to Meredith. "This is going to be rough on your kids."

She nodded. They sat in silence again. She breathed in the scents coming off him—leather jacket, old sweat, and an undercurrent of soap. The combination wasn't unpleasant. *My husband is lying dead down the hall,* she wondered at herself, *and I'm thinking how good the sheriff smells. This isn't happening.* Her vision blurred and the room moved around her.

"You still haven't asked who did it."

Meredith looked at him, startled. The room stopped moving so suddenly she thought she would throw up.

"You caught them?" she asked. "You know who killed him?"

He shook his head. "No. I just expected you would have asked."

"I assumed you would have told me, straight away, if you knew anything." Meredith tensed up, and her nausea increased.

"I guess I would have," he agreed.

Meredith stared at him. The sheriff heaved a sigh and stared at the wall in front of him. She remembered something.

"Back at my house, you accused me of hitting you," she mused out loud.

He bit his lip. "Sorry. I just didn't know what

happened to me. It was a stupid thing to say."

She wanted to ask the obvious question, but couldn't say it. It appeared to her the young sheriff next to her immediately assumed she was to blame. He'd turned on the flashing lights on his truck, thinking she was speeding away from him. He thought she hit him. His once-friendly attitude now was cold and serious. Why her?

The reality of it all rolled up suddenly in Meredith's mind. Brian was dead, lying in the next room with two bullets in his head. Someone had murdered him. She was sitting next to a sheriff while her children were with a coroner's wife. Out in the middle of nowhere, Idaho. How had this come to be? She gasped for breath and rocked forward, hugging herself.

"Oh God," she breathed. "Oh God."

The sob burst from her like a bubble popping. She tried to stifle the sound, but, once started, she couldn't stop. Meredith wept. As she cried, her mind raced and fueled her sobs. How was she going to tell Jamie? Who killed Brian and why? What would happen to her and her kids now? She didn't know if she was sad, frightened or relieved, her emotions in a tumult. *This can't be what I wanted. I can't have wished this into coming true, could I?*

She knew this last question was foolish, but it was too coincidental that she'd fantasized about killing Brian. Her sobs lightened and she hiccupped gradually into silence, wiping her dripping nose on a sleeve. All the while, the sheriff sat next to her quietly, glancing at her from time to time, and twisting his hands nervously on his lap.

"What do I do?" Meredith asked. "What happens now?"

Sheriff Barnaby nodded once. "There's going to have to be an autopsy. You can't make arrangements until after the body's released by the coroner. Do you need to make some calls?"

Meredith stared at the blank wall in front of her for a moment, wiping at her nose again with her sleeve. "He wasn't in contact with any family. I guess I need to call his work. Geez, what do you say? I'm sorry, my husband won't be coming into work anymore because he's dead?" She turned to him. "Can you call for me? Tell them?"

He nodded. "I'll need to talk to them anyway. Ask a few questions."

He cleared his throat. "Is there anyone else you'd like me to call for you? Friends who could come stay with you for a bit?"

Meredith shook her head. There was Beth back in Oakland, but she wasn't the kind of friend who would drop everything and drive to Idaho to be with her. The other assorted friends she'd had over the years were nomadic, not the sort you'd trade addresses with. Later, after she married, she'd have a friend for six months at a time before things got awkward. Brian would either flirt heavily with them or say something awful. Friends didn't stick around.

She chewed on her lower lip until she tasted blood. The sheriff shifted in his seat next to her, making the bench creak. The sound of a door closing made her wonder how the coroner's wife was entertaining Jamie and Atticus. She wanted to get them away from this place, away from where their father lay dead.

"No friends," Meredith whispered hoarsely, the words sounding terrible to her own ears. No one who would support her and be with her. How had she become so isolated in the world? "I want to take my kids home."

They rose together.

"Mrs. Lowe…" he started.

"Please don't call me Mrs. Lowe anymore. I'm Meredith. Please."

His face twisted a bit.

"I should be official about this. You know."

"I'd rather be Meredith," she insisted. She was aware that her face must be puffy and red from crying and equally aware how terrible it was she would be thinking about her appearance at this moment.

"Okay," he agreed after a pause. "I guess you can call me Curtis, too. Not Barney, though. Please."

She gave a small smile.

"Meredith," he started again. "I'm going to need to ask you some questions when you're ready."

"I don't know who did this." Her words came out in a rush. "You never asked me. But I don't know who or why or anything. Brian didn't talk about work much. Or much of anything, really. Not to me, anyway."

Curtis stepped back and gestured down the hall.

"We don't need to go through this now," he said. "Why don't I take you and your kids home? I can come by tomorrow and we can go over things then."

****

"You must be devastated." Honey hugged Meredith tightly as she bustled into the house late that afternoon. The sun tilted heavily in the sky, touching the western mountaintops and drawing long shadows over the valley. "What a shock this is."

Tears pricked again at Meredith's puffy eyes, and she was grateful Honey had come over and grateful for the sympathy.

"How did you find out? Did Curtis call you?"

Honey's eyebrows went up.

"I was just down at the grocery store, sweetie," she said. "It's all over town about the murder. I'm afraid everyone knows."

Meredith turned around making sure Jamie wasn't in hearing distance.

"I haven't told Jamie." She spoke in a low voice, blinking back her tears.

Honey nodded.

"You going to be okay tonight? Want me to take the kids? Make you dinner? You know, why don't you come over to my house and stay for a day or two?"

Meredith was speechless. She wasn't used to such kindness, where people invited you into their homes to eat and sleep.

"I want to stay here," she answered. "Keep things normal for the kids. And me. I can't tell you how much I appreciate the offer though."

Honey frowned at her.

"I don't like the idea of you here all by yourself, when you've just gotten this news. And there's someone bad still out there."

Meredith was startled. The idea hadn't occurred to her about a murderer still at large. She hadn't been thinking about much of anything since Curtis dropped her off, telling her he would return the next morning. Atticus had fallen asleep in the truck and had taken a nap; Jamie played with her puzzles. Meredith stood at the living room window for a while and then had lain on her bed staring at the ceiling, not able to close her eyes even as exhausted as she was.

"I can't believe this is real," she told Honey. "It doesn't feel real. I want to wake up."

Honey led her into the kitchen and sat her down at the table.

"We haven't had a murder out here my entire life," Honey said. "It's shaken the town up, I can tell you that. The closest thing to it was when Shorty Harris beat his wife half to death and then set their house on fire. Fortunately, a neighbor spotted the smoke and dragged her out of the house. The wife wouldn't testify at the trial, but everyone knew Shorty did it. They locked him up in rehab for a while."

Honey broke off suddenly and then rustled around the kitchen. Meredith watched silently as Honey opened cabinets, pulling out bread and coffee before rummaging through the refrigerator.

"What happened to her? The wife?"

Honey shrugged.

"Got smarter, I suppose. People don't like talking about all that anymore. Divorce then was as much a scandal out here as a husband beating a wife. Lots of ugly rumors at the time."

Rumors if you leave, rumors if you don't. I wonder if there's going to be ugly rumors about me.

Mayo, mustard, sliced turkey, and cheese; Honey stacked them on the counter and methodically made three and a half sandwiches.

Meredith didn't say a word over the late lunch, but listened as Jamie chatted non-stop, talking about her growing chick and its activities. *Breathe in, breathe out*, Meredith thought to herself. Honey tsked as she wrapped up Meredith's uneaten sandwich and put it the refrigerator.

"I'll be back tomorrow with my slow cooker chicken and homemade bread," Honey said as she left, giving Meredith a hug. "At least I can make sure you're all fed."

****

Curtis showed up mid morning the next day. His first question set her heart racing.

"Do you keep any guns in the house?

"Brian has, had, a gun." *Please don't ask to see it,* she begged silently. "He kept it locked up."

"Do you suppose, I can see it?" Curtis asked.

"He kept it locked up," she repeated. "I don't have the key."

He waited. Meredith had sent Jamie out to play in the yard when Curtis arrived. She hadn't the heart, the energy, or the words to tell her young daughter that her daddy was dead. Hopefully, she wouldn't learn for years yet that he had been murdered. With the autopsy and investigation planned, she had a few days before she had to ready Jamie for a funeral. And with Brian gone so much, Jamie would just think he was working.

Meredith led Curtis into the bedroom and opened the closet door, pushing aside clothes to expose the cabinet at the back. He bent down and studied it carefully. Curtis ran a finger over a series of scratches around the lock and pulled at the handle, before straightening and stepping back out of the closet.

"Someone tried to get in." He looked at her.

She stepped toward the closet and peered at the lock, keeping her face turned away from him. *If he's wondering whether I'm guilty, it won't help if I tell him it was me.*

The night after she first found the money and pictures, Meredith had woken from a troubled sleep. The moon shone into the room and she found herself looking back at the closet and thinking again about the locked cabinet. What else was Brian hiding from her? Her feet crept across the cold floor to the closet and she bent down to look at the small cabinet. She jiggled the handle, knowing it would be locked. *There has to be a way to open it without the key*, she thought, and before she knew it she had a kitchen knife in her hand and she was jamming it into the lock, twisting and poking furiously. She spent an hour working at the lock; trying a screwdriver, a pen, and a paperclip before it finally popped open.

The dark gray lump of metal was the only thing in the cabinet, along with a single box of ammunition. Meredith had touched the gun gingerly at first and then picked it up, surprised at its weight and how solid it felt.

Now, with Curtis watching her examine the scratches, she wondered if she should just tell him she had caused the scratches on the cabinet. What excuse would she give for breaking in to it? Every reason that flitted through her mind added up to reasons for murder; an affair, distrust, fear. She couldn't tell him she wanted to see the gun and experience its weight in her hand. She couldn't tell him maybe, just maybe, she was thinking of killing Brian with it.

"I never noticed those scratches before," she found herself saying instead. "We bought it used. It might have been scratched when we bought it."

"Could be," he agreed, "but they look pretty recent."

She swallowed and his eyes flickered to her throat, following its movement. *He knows I'm lying. And if he thinks I'm lying about this, what else will he think I'm lying about?*

"I'd like to open it. With your permission."

Meredith nodded, a numbness creeping into her mind again. *Stay focused*, she ordered herself.

"You sure you don't know where the key is?" he asked. "It's a lot of trouble to get a locksmith out here. Otherwise, I'll have to drive it into Mountain Home. Have someone there get it open."

"No," Meredith blurted. The last thing she wanted was for it to be opened without her there to witness what was inside. "I mean, I'd rather you didn't take it out of the house. I'd rather be here when you open it."

Meredith watched as his eyes moved around her bedroom, taking in the unmade bed, the clothes on the floor, the dirty walls, and the ripped carpet. For a moment, she viewed the room through his eyes. It was dismal, shabby, and decaying. She wished she had known he would want to see the cabinet so she could have tidied up the room first.

Laughter rose in her throat and she pushed it down. *This isn't a social visit. He's here about your husband's murder. I'm not thinking straight.*

Curtis was staring at her now.

"I guess I could get it open, but I'd have to break the door. It would ruin the cabinet."

He looked at her questioningly. Meredith chewed her lip, wishing she knew for sure what was inside before he opened it. She felt Curtis searching her face and realized she was hesitating too long, acting as though she was the one with secrets.

"I hate having it ruined." She knew it was silly saying that about the inexpensive cabinet. "But go ahead and break it open. I'd rather you did it here."

She paced the room while Curtis returned to his truck to retrieve some tools. *I could tell you how to open it with a screwdriver and paperclip,* she thought. But she simply smiled weakly at him when he returned.

Two quick raps with a chisel and hammer and the door popped open.

The cabinet was empty. Her mouth dropped open and she bent down to look deeper inside. *Where was the gun?*

"There's no gun." Curtis twisted around to look up at her, making her jump back. "Did Brian carry it with him?"

She shook her head, puzzled.

"No, he wouldn't take it with him," Meredith said, before confessing, "He didn't have a permit for it. It used to be a friend's. Anyway, he wouldn't have taken it in the car."

Curtis sighed heavily.

"Not registered, huh? And it's not here. That's a problem."

Meredith stared down at the empty cabinet. *Where was the gun? Why had Brian taken it out of the safe? What was he going to use it for?*

"I haven't seen it in awhile." She told herself this white lie didn't matter. She took it out of the cabinet one night. She held it tentatively in her lap, thinking about her marriage and her children, before returning it and closing the door. "Maybe he sold it."

Curtis looked seriously at her.

"Is there anything you can tell me about all this?" he asked. "You sure there's nothing you know?"

Meredith's heart beat wildly. That was the problem; she didn't know anything at all. *Why am I acting so guilty when I haven't done anything? He thinks I'm guilty of killing my husband, and I'm acting anything but innocent.* But she was afraid if she told him she held the gun, she wouldn't be able to stop talking. It would all spill out…her fear, her hatred, her fantasies of killing him. He would take her to jail and her kids would be taken away.

She wheeled around and marched out of the bedroom to the front door. She stood there until Curtis walked over, his tools in hand, and then she opened the door.

"Next time, bring a warrant." Her tone was icy. Inside, she was shaking.

Chapter 10

On the fourth day after Brian's murder, Meredith threw up upon waking. Her queasy stomach kept her hovering over the bathroom basin for a few moments and a shadow crossed her mind.

God no. Not now. She counted back to her last period and the last time they'd had sex. *Oh god,* she thought, and threw up again.

There had been bad dreams in the night, even without taking sleeping pills. It seemed to her a normal enough response to having one's husband murdered. Maybe, she hoped, her stomach was simply upset over the dreams, which was a delayed reaction to Brian's murder. She wasn't used to having bad dreams and the aftermath left her shaky and anxious. Meredith turned her mind away from her nightmares, away from an unthinkable pregnancy, *oh please Jesus,* and to the unimaginable likelihood she was suspected of murder.

No, she told herself, I can't deal with any of this. She turned on the shower and tried to find positive things in her life to focus on. *My children. A house to live in. That's enough for now.*

She went through the motions, getting her children dressed and giving them breakfast. Atticus was smashing bananas between his fingers and then happily into the table, making Jamie laugh.

"I want a banana too." Jamie giggled.

Meredith absently rose and handed one to her. Jamie peeled it quickly and wrapped her hand around the fruit, squeezing hard. Both children squealed in delight as the white flesh oozed out of her hand. Atticus wiped his banana puree off the table onto the floor, causing another round of laughter.

Meredith watched, indifferent to the mess, uncaring. She knew she should stop her children from playing with the food, but she couldn't remember why. Her head seemed to be falling further and further into a fog.

The phone rang. It was such a foreign sound in the house that at first, in her haze, she didn't know what it was.

"Mommy!" Jamie shouted, after the third ring. "Answer it."

There was nobody she wanted to talk to, but obediently she walked to the kitchen phone.

"Yes." Her voice was anything but welcoming.

"Mrs. Lowe?" a man said.

"Yes."

"Al Robertson from the coroner's office. We're done with the autopsy. What would you like done with the body?"

Meredith gazed out the kitchen window, considering. In the distance, a line of dust moved toward her house. She watched it, slowly becoming aware it was on her road, growing closer.

"Mrs. Lowe? Are you still there?"

At the head of the dust, a truck emerged. The sheriff's truck.

"I don't know," she said weakly. "I hadn't, I didn't… Maybe we can sprinkle him somewhere, you know, in ashes."

"Cremation then." His voice was crisp, hurting her head with his sharp professional tone. "Would you like us to arrange it? There's a place in Blissful, twenty-five miles up the road. They can handle it at a good price."

"Blissful," she murmured, watching the sheriff's truck pull into her driveway and come to a stop. Out of nowhere, she recalled Brian calling their new home paradise. "Perfect."

A banana peel slapped against her leg and her kids squealed with joy. She watched as Curtis stepped out of the car and turned a grim face toward her house.

It was the start of a very bad day.

****

Curtis didn't waste any time.

"We found the gun," he said after Meredith went outside, coldly greeting him with her arms folded across her chest.

He paused, and she was aware he was watching her closely.

"Brian's gun?" she asked. "You found his gun?"

Curtis half-shrugged.

"Well, at least we found the murder weapon. We'll have ballistics done. I found it about a half mile from where he was killed; it'd be quite a coincidence if someone else's handgun was just lying out there."

Meredith didn't say anything. She thought about Brian's body heading off to be cremated and realized she'd have to tell Jamie that her father was gone.

"Meredith," Curtis said, and she blinked. "It would help to get your fingerprints. To isolate which prints might belong to the person who killed your husband."

She nodded absently.

"It might not be his gun." She didn't believe the words even as she said them.

"Well, you can tell us that, too."

Meredith tried to engage her mind. If it was Brian's gun and her fingerprints were on it, wouldn't it look worse for her? There didn't appear to be any way to decline.

"Okay," she agreed.

Curtis turned back to his truck and gestured for her to follow. Her feet wouldn't move and he stopped.

"Here?" she asked. "You brought the gun that shot him here? To my house?"

He walked over to her. Meredith's head spun lightly and her queasiness returned. Curtis put a hand on her arm and led her quickly back to the front steps of her house, where she sat down with a thump.

"Why don't you come to my office later?" His tone softened. "You can look at it there."

She nodded.

"I wasn't thinking," he said. "I'm sorry."

She nodded again, afraid to speak. He stood over her for a long moment watching. Without another word, he turned and left.

It's Brian's gun. My prints are on it. This backcountry sheriff is going to put me in prison.

She closed her eyes.

****

The sheriff's office consisted of a desk inside the two-room Hay City office building. The room smelled of years of dust, old newspapers, coffee, and an underlying scent of pine cleaner. Curtis, the only person there, stood suddenly when she came in and a sheaf of papers spilled onto the floor.

"Oh, crikes." He grimaced and bent down to pick them up. "Not again."

A smile crept to her lips. Surely a sheriff this bad could never be able to put her in prison. A shock went through her at this line of thinking and her smile faded.

I didn't kill him, she insisted to herself. *He's almost convinced me I did it.*

She went over to the window to look out at her car where Jamie and Atticus were waiting. Jamie sat in the backseat next to her brother and Meredith could see Jamie was reading a book to him.

After Curtis arranged his files back onto the desk, he pulled the plastic sleeved gun out from the evidence locker. As she looked at it, Meredith felt his eyes on her, an unreadable expression on his face.

"Yes." Meredith had considered lying but she'd touched the gun, hadn't she? "It looks like Brian's."

Curtis nodded as though he expected this response. He didn't make eye contact as he took her fingerprints and then handed her a tissue to wipe away the grease.

"What happens now?" she asked.

"I send the gun in for a ballistics test and they'll do prints, too." Curtis returned the gun to the evidence locker. "They'll find your husband's prints on it. And yours, maybe, if you ever touched it. And whoever killed him. I should get results back pretty quick."

"Fat chance." A man's voice behind Meredith made her jump.

Thin with humped shoulders, his hair was white and wiry. The old man's eyes darted to Meredith and settled meanly on Curtis.

"Checking in, boss," he sneered. "Unless you're too busy with the pretty lady."

Curtis looked unhappy at the visit. Meredith glanced questioningly between the two, but just as quick decided she'd had enough for one day.

"Can I go now?" she asked.

Curtis nodded and Meredith took that as her dismissal. She gave the old man another glance as she walked past him, catching a whiff of beer and dirty clothes. The man kept his eyes focused on Curtis.

"Playing at sheriff again?" the man scoffed as she walked out.

She leaned back against the door for a moment, relieved to be away from the gun and Curtis's watchful gaze. It shook her up more than she had expected to see Brian's gun, the weapon that had killed him. The early spring sun warmed her face, a welcome reprieve from the long winter. Puddles from melted snow still sat in every rut and dip, but it was finally and definitively spring. Meredith decided she'd get her kids outdoors for the afternoon.

I'll open up the windows to the house and air it out. Maybe a breeze will blow my bad luck away.

****

The windows to the old house were rusted shut, so Meredith propped the doors, front and back, wide open. Then she loaded Atticus in his backpack and took the kids out for a walk down the lane.

Meredith stomped in a puddle, letting the mud splatter up her pant leg, dribble down, and seep into her sock. They should never have moved here. Stomp! She should never have married Brian. Stomp! Wait, then she wouldn't have her children. Well, then she should have left him and taken the kids. Stomp! Her anger honed and narrowed.

The sheriff immediately assumed she murdered her own husband, and with no proof whatsoever. Had she really ever found him charming? He was the local Barney, the joke of the town, no one to take seriously. Stomp! What was it Honey had told her? There hadn't been a murder in Hay City in more than fifty years. Of course, the local sheriff was going to blame her, the Californicator, for bringing murder to their little town. She shouldn't have let him open the cabinet, discover the scratches she made and discover the gun was missing. She'd let him open it because she wasn't guilty. She had nothing to hide. Being open had clearly backfired.

Jamie, tasked with picking a bouquet of flowers for the house, was busy running from flower to flower, examining them closely to select one at a time. Overnight, it seemed, the snow disappeared and their prairie had burst into color, heralding the launch of spring. Blue, yellow, and orange blooms filled Jamie's arms. A brisk breeze wrapped itself around her and she tried to breathe more slowly to calm her anger. She wasn't guilty so nothing could happen to her. She shouldn't be afraid of Sheriff Barney.

I'm free. The idea made her stop. Meredith stood rooted, stunned at this truth. For the first time since she learned Brian was dead…really, since they moved to Hay City…she felt a twinge of hope. She could move back to Oakland, get her old apartment, and slip back into that other life; maybe even take a night class or two. The possibilities lightened her step. *I can find a job, other single moms make it work, I can too.* Honey's words echoed again in her mind, "This is *your* life."

A tightness in her chest rose until it was a lump in

her throat. Brian's voice rang louder: *"You have no job skills, no education, no one to take you in."* She felt the old fear that she was helpless. Her step slowed and she stopped, heaving a sigh. Honey's words fought back: *"Get a backbone, girl."*

I'm glad he's dead, Meredith thought. *If this makes me a bad person, then I guess I'm bad. You don't go to prison for being bad inside.* Meredith swallowed thickly. She had never conceived of herself as a bad person before.

In the distance, she heard the buzzing of ATVs and she remembered the two hunters who had stopped by the house when they first moved in. They had been standoffish and awkward in that visit. Even Brian noticed it and had sent her into the house with the kids. Meredith peered across the prairie but couldn't spot the vehicles. She continued to scan the horizon for movement but the buffering effect of the mountains made it difficult to tell where the sound was coming from.

Don't you care who killed him, her inner voice whispered. *Shouldn't you be obsessed with this question, demanding that Curtis find the murderer quickly and bring him to justice?* Meredith realized she hadn't posed these things to Curtis, hadn't asked if he had any clues as to what had happened that night.

Maybe those hunters were the murderers? They knew how to use guns, but of course, probably everyone out here knew how to shoot a gun. What could be their reason for murder? Meredith searched her brain for a possible reason but drew a blank. They had met once, for a brief moment.

Curtis had confirmed Brian's wallet was still in the

car, so robbery couldn't be a motive. Not robbery and his own gun possibly used to kill him. Meredith snorted. No wonder the sheriff was looking at her so suspiciously.

He can't arrest me. I only wished him dead. The thought had a soothing effect. She strode out more confidently, a happier spring in her step. *I only killed him in my imagination. I didn't really kill him.*

"'Life is messy,'" she remarked out loud to Atticus. "'It's all in how you handle it.'"

****

On the fifth day after Brian's murder, Atticus decided to get up and walk.

Watching her son walk for the first time made Meredith burst into tears.

"Wait 'til Daddy sees!" Jamie cried.

Meredith knew she couldn't wait any longer. She sat Jamie down and, in a gentle tone, told her that her daddy wasn't coming home. She knew it was past time for it, since they'd soon have to make the drive to Blissful to pick up Brian's ashes.

The plans were similar to her mother's; simple, basic, and cheap. She told the funeral home she wanted him cremated and she would take the ashes in a plain, cardboard box.

Meredith knew she'd need to use the money in the attic, and then she remembered the box of pictures next to it. Her emotions swung violently, from anger to guilt to grief. She burst into tears again. Brian was dead, really gone. She couldn't keep pretending he was away on one of his business trips. He wasn't ever coming home again. He'd been killed in a violent, brutal way. She had loved him once, lived with him and had children with him, even if she never really knew him.

I just need to keep moving forward.

The sheriff—she couldn't bring herself to think of him as Curtis now—didn't return over the next few days, with or without a warrant, and Meredith was grateful. Honey checked in with her daily, and Meredith took Jamie and Atticus to her house to watch Laf scratch at seed in the dirt. They talked about the kids' nap schedules, the local school where Jamie could start kindergarten in the fall, and what was needed to build a chicken coop. They didn't talk about Brian. Honey didn't ask any questions. The rest of the week passed quietly and a stillness settled over the house. Meredith realized how anxious she had been, even before Brian's murder.

****

She woke on the eighth day seething. *How could Brian do this to me? How could he hurt me, lie to me, move me out here, and then get himself murdered?*

Her period still hadn't come and the possibility he could have left her pregnant as well was just icing on the cake. The night before had been filled with terrors. Every creak at the window, every gust of wind knocking at loose roof shingles made her think someone was trying to get in her house. She finally took two sleeping pills and sank into a dreamless stupor, waking with a headache.

In a rage, she tore up the rest of her filthy bedroom carpet and threw it out the back door. The sight of the soiled carpet and padding lumped in the weedy yard only made her angrier at the world.

Meredith made pancakes for breakfast, then busied herself as Jamie drew pictures and Atticus toddled from room to room. She washed a mountain of clothes, swept the floors, and scrubbed out the grimy old oven, filling the house with cleaner fumes.

She yanked at the kitchen window, trying to open it, to no avail. She knocked the heel of her hand against the window rim, and then again and again. It didn't budge.

"Damn it!"

Meredith stepped back and glared at the window. It surely had opened in the past and so it could open again. There was no one to help her so she would just have to figure it out by herself.

"I'm heading out to the shed," she called to Jamie. "Back in a minute."

There was no answer except the sound of Jamie's giggling in her room. Jamie's newest game was dressing up Atticus in various costumes. One day he became a flower, the next a soldier or a pumpkin. Atticus loved the attention and Meredith knew Jamie was always careful and protective with her little brother. *My* Atticus, Jamie called him.

Meredith stepped outside and almost sighed at the sun on her face and arms. Her pores responded to the warmth, tingling in delight. Her mood lifted. Maybe they could get some chicks from Honey and raise them for eggs. She was instantly aghast at the notion. *What am I thinking? I'm not staying here. I'm leaving as soon as I can figure out a plan.*

The shed had been left in a jumble by the previous owners, with a mess of old tools lying on a workbench, on the floor, and under a disintegrating tarp. She picked through the clutter gingerly and grabbed up some random tools. A hammer with a broken handle. A rusted wrench. A stiff wire brush, although she had no idea what good it would do.

The crunching of tires on gravel brought her out of the shed. Meredith walked slowly over as the sheriff stepped out of his patrol truck. She fought back a scowl, trying hard to keep her face blank of her annoyance.

He raised his hands up in surrender with a wary smile.

"Checking in." His voice was neutral. "Doing okay out here?"

Meredith raised her handful of tools. Curtis's eyes widened at the sight of the broken and rusty implements.

"I suppose that answers my question. What do you think you're going to do with those?"

Meredith sighed heavily. "Probably give myself tetanus and break a window in the process."

Curtis looked over at the house and then back at Meredith. He shifted from foot to foot.

"I have some better tools in the truck." He hesitated, then added, "And a little time on my hands."

She paused, considering her options. The house needed fresh air and all its windows were apparently rusted shut. Just in time, here was the sheriff, acting genuine and harmless in his offer to help. The last time she saw him, in his office, he took her fingerprints. She was certain he was considering her a murder suspect. Was she simply going to let him walk back into her house? Curtis shifted impatiently and she made a decision. *What's one more bad decision among many?*

"Okay," she agreed.

He pulled a heavy metal box out of the back of his truck and Meredith led him into the house. Curtis stopped abruptly inside the door.

"What's this?" he asked.

Jamie and Atticus stood in the hallway dressed in oversized t-shirts and wearing socks stretched up over their knees. Atticus had a baseball cap on his head that hung down over his ears and mostly covered his eyes.

"Brian's clothes." Meredith looked sadly at her children.

"My daddy's dead," Jamie told Curtis, her face somber and serious.

"I know," Curtis replied. "I'm sorry."

"His car had an accident," Jamie added. "I'll see him in heaven when I die. I have a chicken named Laf."

Curtis cocked his head as though he had misheard.

"A what?"

"She's going to lay eggs for us," Jamie explained. "She has to stay at Honey's house because her family is there."

Curtis looked at Meredith.

"Just go with it," she said.

Jamie had already turned away and was arranging the t-shirt on Atticus to keep it from dragging on the floor. Meredith motioned to Curtis to follow her to the kitchen window. He tugged, and unable to budge it, opened his toolbox and rummaged inside.

"Jamie and Brian were very close," Meredith said. "I hope she remembers him."

"I'm sure she will. Those early impressions are strong."

"Atticus, though," she mused. "He's too young."

"You seem to be adjusting okay." Curtis scraped at the bottom of the window where rust had formed.

She didn't respond and he looked back at her.

"I didn't mean anything."

"Are you here as the *sheriff* today?" she asked.

"I just wanted to check on you. Out here alone like this."

"Checking to make sure we're still here?"

He stared at her a moment and then turned away without comment.

She made herself breathe evenly, reminding herself that Curtis was doing her a favor with the windows. He gave the window a tug and it slid open. Curtis moved to the next one and began scraping at the bottom.

"I'm used to being alone." She leaned against the counter watching him work. "Brian traveled a lot."

As Curtis tugged the next window open, Meredith wondered why she wanted to be friendly to him. *He's here to make sure I'm not running away.* Still, it was a relief to have someone else take the reins for a bit, an adult to talk to, even if it was the sheriff.

"I've been lucky," Curtis reflected, after a moment. "I still have both parents. Life doesn't change all too much out here. I haven't had to do much adjusting, I guess."

They moved on to the living room windows, stepping over a scatter of Atticus's stuffed animals and pieces of Jamie's potato man toy. They could hear Jamie talking to Atticus in her bedroom.

"Sounds like you had a good childhood," Meredith said wistfully.

He chuckled.

"Mostly," he agreed. "Although my mom didn't think I would survive. I was the kid who picked up snakes and tried to pet a moose. I went bear hunting when I was ten, armed with a stick. Fortunately, there aren't too many bears around here."

Meredith thought about a childhood growing up in the country, with two loving parents and people you knew your whole life. It was a world totally foreign to her. She wished she could give some of that to her kids.

A sea of aromas filled the room as the windows opened up, letting the prairie inside her home. Sweet, earthy, clean.

"Any others?" Curtis was asking.

Meredith decided she didn't want him in the bedrooms, his eyes searching for more clues to her possible guilt, reading too much into her life. She shook her head.

"All done then. What else can I do?"

"Know how to set mousetraps?" she asked hopefully.

He laughed.

"Seriously? That's a required subject in school here," he joked. "They'll carry away your house if you let them."

She showed him the traps and he set them around the house, under the kitchen and bathroom sinks where they would seek water, meanwhile advising her that peanut butter was the best bait. She followed him as he worked and they chatted more easily. *He's nice. Really nice, when he's not trying to be a sheriff.*

He moved to the front steps, tapping down protruding nails, and then they sat there together looking out over the yard, the road and the prairie beyond. Jamie hopped down the steps and ran around the yard, flapping her arms. Atticus toddled about the yard on still-shaky legs. The afternoon warmth on Meredith's shoulders loosened her reticence, melted her anger and she talked about her absent father and losing her mother. Curtis listened and asked an occasional question. Meredith found herself trying to come up with other chores she could give Curtis to do.

I don't want him to leave yet. I don't want to be alone out here.

"How did you meet Brian?" he asked.

The mood shifted and Meredith stiffened.

"School." She shrugged and set her jaw against saying anything more.

He looked over at her and waited, but Meredith stood up. She wanted to tell him about her marriage, how good it was at first and how bad it had gotten. She wanted him to understand her, but someone like him, who had led such a normal life, could never understand.

Curtis rose.

"I'm pretty useful. If you ever need anything done around here."

She nodded appreciatively. "Thank you. You've gone above and beyond the call of duty."

"People watch out for their neighbors here."

Meredith walked him to his truck. They stood there for a moment and she thought he had enjoyed the afternoon, too.

"Your husband's murder made the paper in Boise." Curtis had one hand on the truck door and Meredith suspected he'd been waiting to say this to her. "They ran a picture of him."

A chill ran through her and all her good feelings about Curtis evaporated.

"So," he continued. "I got a call from a woman who says she saw you and your husband in a store there last month."

"That must have been the day I ran into you in the mall," she said cautiously. "It's the only time I've been in Boise. I remember how you cheered me up."

"She reported that a woman was arguing with Brian," he added.

Meredith's lips twisted. She'd wanted to confront Brian about the pictures of the girl and the money he had hidden in the attic. She'd wanted to blow up their marriage once and for all, but so afraid to do it too. All that had come out though was a petty argument over buying a coat and whether they should eat fries and milkshakes for lunch.

"I'm sure we were," she confessed to Curtis. "We…we…weren't getting along very well."

"The woman reported that a clerk came over to settle things down, and when he asked if you needed anything, you said 'a gun.'"

Meredith's mouth went dry. She had a vague memory of snapping at the clerk, but didn't recall saying those idiotic words. How could she know her husband would be murdered, shot by a gun, just a couple of weeks later? She gulped and no words came. She shook her head, "I didn't…I didn't…"

Curtis leaned on the open truck door.

"I'm not saying you *did*," he insisted. "You don't come across like a cold-blooded murderer. But tell me, Meredith, who killed Brian? I think you know more than you're saying and it's going to get you in trouble. You can be charged with obstruction of justice, aiding and abetting, or at the very least, it's going to let a murderer go free."

Meredith suddenly wanted to tell Curtis everything about her marriage; her desperation to have a secure life for her children, Brian's strange descent into more belittling and controlling behavior, his secretive nature, his angry outbursts, the girl in the pictures, and the hidden money. All rolled up into one story, she was ashamed she had stayed with him. It was humiliating to say how she accepted his treatment of her in return for a secure life. She had traded her self-respect for a home. Truth be told, she was glad her mother hadn't lived to discover how weak a woman she had grown to be. *Of course* her marriage was poisoned; she could see it now, in retrospect.

At the time, though, living through it day by day, month by month, she had slowly gotten used to her life and surviving the same way she always had, by adjusting and adapting. But none of that had anything to do with Brian's murder. It wasn't a crime to *wish* your husband were dead. No, she couldn't say any of this.

"You're wrong about me," she finally said. "I mean, you're right, I didn't kill him. Of course not. But you're wrong that I know something. Someone must have come along at the wrong time."

She saw the disappointment register in his eyes and then Curtis climbed into his truck and started the engine with a roar.

"I'll come back out in a couple of days," he called out the window.

She watched his truck back away, feeling relief and disappointment that he was leaving. *Friend or foe*, she wondered, as she lifted a hand to wave goodbye.

It's a good thing I didn't murder Brian because I would have been caught by now. On the other hand, she knew with a cold realization, *I may still go to prison for his murder. Guilty or not.*

Chapter 11

It sounded like a rifle shot. Meredith jumped in the driver's seat and Jamie yelped.

"It's just the car." Meredith spoke quickly to calm Jamie and herself. "Gassy today."

That brought a giggle and a round of farting noises from the backseat as Jamie blew through pursed lips at Atticus.

Meredith looked in the rearview mirror. A smoke cloud was billowing out from behind the car and her heart sank. It had been nearly two weeks since Brian's murder. Surely there were things she needed to take care of, mainly figuring out how she was going to support herself and her kids. She needed to know more about the house and whether there was money owed on it. Brian had never told her. Her aim was to sell it soon so she and the kids could leave and start their new life somewhere, *anywhere* else.

This morning, though, she needed to pay the funeral home the balance for her husband's cremation so she could take his ashes. For this, she had taken five hundred dollars from the box in the attic, along with another hundred for groceries. The twenty and fifty dollar bills, still holding their curled shape from being tightly wound in their sock, were radiating bad vibes from Meredith's purse on the passenger seat next to her. She hadn't liked touching the money, knowing it was linked to the problems in her marriage. *Funeral money. Maybe the best use for it.*

Her car problems were getting critical, though, and she needed money for groceries and gas. Bills needed to be paid. She didn't have the luxury to be particular or superstitious about it. The money in the ceiling was the one thing keeping her and her children from being completely broke.

A fine mist covered the windshield as the car rumbled over the highway, clunking as it automatically shifted from one gear to the next. In the distance, a band of rain streaked down onto the far prairie. A bolt of lightning showed above the mountain range as they pulled into the funeral home's parking lot.

Blissful, Idaho was only slightly larger than Hay City. It had a hair salon, a gas station, two churches, and a bar and grill, along with the mortuary. An elementary school, consisting of two mobile buildings and a field full of weeds, sat behind the gas station. Meredith realized this was where her kids would go to school if they stayed in Hay City.

"It's storming over there," she told Jamie, pointing at the mountains.

"How do you know?" Jamie peered through the window where she pointed.

"See those streaks coming down?" Meredith asked. "Those dark clouds over there? It's a big storm. From way over here, you can see where it's been and where it's going."

Jamie watched wide-eyed.

"It's pretty." Jamie's mouth fell open.

Meredith watched the dark storm move over the mountains, regarding it anew. Slim bands of light shone through the clouds from above and the interplay of iron gray and silvery white thunderheads changed as the system pushed its way forward.

"It kind of is, isn't it?"

"Is it going to rain here?" Jamie asked.

"No, look." Meredith pointed again. "The sun is coming out for us. If you feel for the breeze, you can tell which way the storm will blow."

Jamie opened the window and held out an arm for a moment and then pointed toward the mountains.

"It's going over there," she announced. "Away."

Meredith nodded.

"Okay sweetie, you stay in the car with Atticus. I'll be back in a minute."

Meredith took a deep breath, and slowly let it go. Then she went inside to get her husband.

****

Her car backfired and lurched into the grocery store's parking space. In the trunk, Brian's remains were tucked inside a small box. It struck her as strange to combine the trips of picking up his ashes and grocery shopping, but Meredith worried her car could fail at any moment. She didn't want to think about what would happen then.

"Ma'am." Deli boy was wide-eyed as she approached the deli counter, back in Hay City.

"Turkey, turkey, turkey," Jamie chanted.

"Half pound of turkey, I guess," said Meredith, gearing up for a battle. "Half of ham. Surprise, surprise."

The teen nodded, staring at her just a little too long before turning to the meats in the case.

"Cause it's what I always get," Meredith added,

annoyed the kid never remembered her simple, never-changing order.

He grunted.

"Jamie, sit down in the cart before you fall out of there," Meredith ordered, turning to her daughter.

"I want to watch him do the slicer," Jamie argued.

"Sit down or else, young lady." Meredith glared at her until her daughter plopped down reluctantly.

Jamie kicked at the cans of peas, thumping them against the side of the cart.

"Jamie," Meredith warned.

There was a snicker from the deli boy and Meredith shot him a warning look as well.

"Daddy would let me stand up," Jamie muttered.

Meredith gaped. Where did that come from? When had Brian ever taken Jamie to the grocery store?

"I'm not Daddy," Meredith hissed between her teeth.

"My daddy's dead," Jamie said, looking up at the counter where the teen was now standing.

Deli boy slid the packages toward Meredith.

"The guy's still out there, huh?" he asked, stone-faced, adding in a sly tone, "Or could be a gal, right?"

Meredith took the sliced ham and turkey and set the packages in the cart. *What kind of rumors are circulating about me?* she wondered. The boy stood and watched silently.

"Nothing yet," she answered briefly, turning away quickly.

"I'm sure he, or *she*, will be caught soon," the deli boy added to her back.

Meredith looked around at the comment and instantly regretted doing so when she saw a smirk creep up on the teen's face. *Punk. I'll get you back for that next time.*

Meredith rolled her cart down the aisles, pointing out her choices to Jamie so her daughter could pull the groceries off the shelves. In the pasta and beans aisle, a woman abruptly turned her cart around and moved quickly away from them. *Don't be paranoid*, Meredith cautioned herself. She casually rolled by the pharmacy area, plucking a pregnancy test off the shelf and into her cart. The concept of taking the test and its possible results overwhelmed her. *Maybe a glass of wine tonight. Just this once.*

She rolled over to the small beer and wine section where a gray-haired man, eyes watery and red, tapped his fingers against cans of beer as he passed each one. It took her only a glance to observe the trembling in his hands, the lost dreaminess in his face, and a general slackness in dress. She had witnessed the disease come to full-bloom in her mother and the memory stopped her short. The man looked up at her suddenly, startled, and they stared at each other in mutual recognition. She realized it was the same old man from the sheriff's office the day she was fingerprinted.

He moved toward her as though to say something, but Meredith whirled away, a sense of unease filling her. He reminded her too much of her past life, living with a mother who couldn't stay sober for twenty-four hours at a time. For a moment, it was as though her mother was there, judging her silently. Her desire for the glass of wine vanished. It would be too easy to go down that road, she knew, to drown her difficulties and run from life like her mother did.

She hurriedly rolled the cart down the aisles,

grabbing items, mentally tallying the cost so she wouldn't have to put anything back. By the time she reached the checkout line, Meredith realized she was drawing stares from customers and employees of the store. *Are they staring at me because they think I'm a murderer*, she wondered. *Or in sympathy?*

"$92.36." The clerk hit the final tally after ringing up her cart full of groceries and Meredith blew a sigh of relief. She needed to budget more tightly than ever now, until she could figure out her future.

She unrolled the bills into the clerk's hand, trying unsuccessfully to flatten them out.

"Sorry about this." Meredith registered the look of annoyance on his face.

"Guess it spends just the same," the clerk said. "Need help loading this up in your car?"

Meredith flashed to a scene of the clerk putting the bags of groceries in the trunk next to Brian's ashes. *No thanks, my husband's body is in the trunk.*

"It's okay," she replied. "I've got it."

She loaded the groceries in her car quickly, her hands shaking. As she shut the trunk, Meredith noticed the old man from the beer section standing in front of the store watching her. She just wanted to go home, away from these people who didn't know her and yet passed judgment on her just the same. *Maybe it's just my guilty conscience. Or maybe these people sense I had wished Brian were dead.*

****

The sheriff's truck was in the driveway of her house and Curtis was nowhere in sight. She sighed. There was no getting away from the people of Hay City. Meredith unloaded the groceries, curiously looking out down the walking path and scanning the prairie as she walked back and forth from the car with the bags. Jamie walked Atticus slowly to the house, encouraging his chubby legs forward and then lifting him up the steps and inside.

The day had turned still and slightly electric from the far thunderstorm, and the only movement was an occasional rippling of the thigh-high grasses that parted to show wildflowers below. Meredith walked through the house, peeking into bedrooms, but she couldn't imagine Curtis would come inside uninvited. Nothing had been disturbed and her brow furrowed in puzzlement as she stocked her shelves and refrigerator with the groceries.

The mystery was soon solved when a banging from above startled her. She walked outside scanning the roof, circling around to the backside of the house where a ladder leaned against one wall. *What was he doing?*

"Breaking and entering?" she called out.

Curtis looked down from his perch on the roof and smiled widely in greeting. Her annoyance melted as she looked at his wide genuine smile.

"Fixing your roof and keeping the rain from entering. I'll be down in a bit."

Meredith shook her head in disbelief. Was it normal out here for people to show up unannounced and patch your roof?

"Mommy, can I go on the roof with the sheriff?"

Meredith looked down at Jamie, who had brought Atticus outside with her.

"No." Meredith was horrified at the idea her daughter might actually climb on the roof. "Why don't you watch from here and I'll make everyone a picnic lunch."

Jamie nodded happily.

"Stay off the ladder," Meredith warned before heading toward the front of the house again.

"Don't worry," Curtis called to her. "I'll keep the munchkin in line."

"What's a 'munkin'?" Meredith heard Jamie ask as she went back into the house.

****

Atticus was high in Curtis's arms by the large, crooked pine tree behind the house when Meredith returned. Jamie was chatting a mile a minute as they looked up at the tree together.

"Mommy, the sheriff is going to make me a swing," Jamie cried.

Meredith lifted her eyebrows at Curtis as she walked up to them, carrying a blanket and a bag full of sandwiches and drinks.

"Look at that branch." He pointed at a heavy limb elbowing out and up. "If that's not meant for a swing…"

He looked questioningly at Meredith. She gazed up at the limb, and, pretending to assess its strength and worthiness, delayed answering for a moment. Why was Curtis fixing her roof and offering to build her daughter a swing? Brian's ashes were still in the car's trunk, and she suddenly wondered where she would spread them. Something in the pit of her stomach tightened. Dealing with the ashes would make all the events of the past couple of weeks too real, and too final. *Brian is dead and I'm having a picnic.* She spread the blanket under the tree.

Meredith put her hands out to take Atticus and

Curtis handed him gently into her arms.

"I guess it's okay."

"Every kid needs a tree swing," he said. "It's where I did my best daydreaming about my future."

"To be the town sheriff?" Meredith asked, forcing a smile.

They settled down on the blanket and arranged the sandwiches on napkins. Meredith opened a container of applesauce and began feeding Atticus.

Curtis laughed.

"Oh no. For awhile, I was going to be a pirate, then an explorer, then an astronaut."

He leaned back on one elbow. "Let me think," he continued. "Then I dreamed about being a rancher, a mad scientist, a tiger tamer, a spaceship repairman…"

Meredith couldn't help but laugh.

"A spaceship repairman? I thought you wanted to be an astronaut."

"Well…" Curtis said, through a bite of his sandwich, "that changed after I flew off of my swing one day and scraped my knee. I decided to stay closer to earth after that."

They ate quietly for a bit, listening to the subtle sounds of the afternoon prairie. Tall grasses rustled in the breeze, insects clicked around them, and birdsong filled the air. Curtis pointed out a hawk gliding on the high currents above, and then Jamie jumped up and followed a grasshopper across the yard.

"What about you?" Curtis asked. "What were your childhood dreams?"

Meredith went still. Her childhood was nothing like his.

"I wanted a house," she said, and then stopped. She

had wanted so many things others took for granted: a mother and father together, to go to one school for an entire year, friends she could grow up with, her own room, a house, security. "A family."

Curtis nodded. "The important things. You were a wise child."

She looked up at him. *Yes, those are the important things. I grew up and achieved those dreams for myself and my kids. But I'm unhappier than ever.*

"I didn't have a good marriage." The words came out from her abruptly.

Curtis stayed silent, waiting. She felt so comfortable sitting next to him. *He's investigating your husband's murder and you're complaining about your marriage. Is Barney smarter than I've given him credit for?*

"Are you on duty?" Meredith asked.

"Only if you want me to be."

She shook off her concerns. It was good to talk to someone. *And I'm not guilty.*

"I wanted to leave him and I think he wanted to leave me too." She spoke in a quiet tone so Jamie couldn't hear. "For some reason, he didn't leave and didn't want me to leave. But I think he hated me."

Meredith whispered those last words, only realizing the full truth and impact of them as she spoke them out loud to another person. Brian had behaved as though he hated her. That was the truth. When had he stopped loving her?

Curtis was watching her intently.

"Did he hurt you?"

Meredith didn't answer.

"Think he hurt someone else?" Curtis asked,

causing Meredith look at him in surprise. "You know, made them want to hurt him back?"

She looked over toward Jamie hopping on the grass, and then her gaze wandered out beyond the house. Brian had been just an ordinary guy trying to make his way in the world. Not all good, not all bad. Maybe just bad to her. Other people always liked him easily enough. She never considered the possibility he could have hurt someone other than her.

"Brian was…dissatisfied. With me, with work, with life. He always wanted more, but I can't imagine him getting involved with something dangerous. Something that could have gotten him killed."

She thought about the pictures and money in the closet attic space. Where had the money come from? Doubt edged its way into her mind. Her husband *had* been keeping secrets and it was likely he had more undiscovered secrets. Meredith cringed inside, away from these ideas; she didn't want to know anything more that would make her life a lie. She didn't want to find she had been married to a stranger, and her children's father was someone she never knew, someone terrible.

Tears came to her eyes. She shook her head firmly.

"What about you?" she asked suddenly, desperate to change the subject. "Anyone serious in your life?"

Curtis looked down at his hands briefly and then sighed heavily.

"I guess that's fair enough, since I'm prying into your life. There was someone. She married a guy in Montana a few months back. I went to their wedding, nice guy that I am."

Meredith was surprised he'd been jilted and blurted

out the first thing that came to mind.

"She left *you*?" She blushed as soon as the words were out.

Curtis smiled, a bit of pink creeping into his cheeks as well. "Not everyone thinks a small town sheriff is such a great catch."

"I just meant," Meredith stumbled on her words. What was she going to say? Was she going to tell him he was handsome, kind, maybe smarter than she first gave him credit for? "You're a nice guy. Handy with windows and roofs."

He laughed.

"I guess I should have fixed her roof," he joked.

Jamie ran over, swooped up a cookie and ran off again.

"How do you keep up with her energy?" Curtis asked.

Meredith smiled as she watched her daughter run across the grass.

"Mostly I just let her run herself tired," She looked down at Atticus who had fallen asleep on the blanket. "It's good she doesn't understand all this right now."

They sat in silence for a while. Then Curtis rose and stretched.

"I'm heading to Boise for a couple of days to look into some things on the case," Curtis said. "I'll stop by when I get back."

"What things?" she asked, suddenly ashamed she hadn't asked about the case sooner. Surely, she should be more interested in whether there were any leads. Each time she tried to think about it though…what had happened that night…her mind shut down and the nausea returned. "Did you find something?"

"Not really. It's where your husband's truck was taken and they have better resources over there. I'm just a one-man office, you know."

Meredith didn't want to think about the truck and the blood that must be inside. But surely, there had to be a clue in there somewhere. Brian had stopped on the road for some reason and someone must have approached his truck in the dark. Pulled out a gun, aimed it at his head…

"Thanks for coming over." Meredith halted her thread of thought. "I've been at a loss about how to handle all this. Having you come over, and Honey too. I can't tell you how much you've both helped, just by coming by. It's pretty quiet out here."

"I guess it takes some getting used to," he acknowledged. "Make sure you get out in the evening or early morning though when the wildlife is moving around. You'll see the elk. Sometimes even a moose passes through. You'll understand why people live out here."

Meredith rose and walked Curtis to his truck, leaving Atticus asleep on the blanket and Jamie skipping around the tree singing in a high-pitched voice.

"Be careful on the road," she said as he climbed into his truck.

He smiled down at her and her heart twisted suddenly.

A memory came unbidden to her mind from early in her marriage. Brian had finished his college business course and had taken his first sales job. There was an overnight trip he would have to take, away from her and their newborn baby. She had clung to him the morning he left, smelling his aftershave, his strong warm body holding her, and the steady thumping of his heart next to hers. He had kissed her tenderly on the forehead and told her he would hurry back.

"Be careful on the road," she had said then too. She had loved him desperately.

She stood and watched as Curtis's truck disappeared down the road, standing there until she couldn't see it any more.

Chapter 12

"There's a worm," Jamie wrinkled her nose and backed away.

They were in the front yard of the house digging in the soft earth where Meredith decided to create a vegetable garden, something she had never done before. Wasn't this part of having a home of one's own? She wanted her kids to know where food came from and to have the satisfaction of growing it themselves.

I'm not staying here, she vowed, yet again. *This is just a practice garden.*

Meredith picked up the worm and held the squirming brown creature in the palm of her hand.

"It won't hurt you." She sat back and let the worm move about on her flat palm.

Jamie approached carefully and peered at it.

"I don't like him," she announced.

"Shh, not so loud." Meredith mimicked an expression of alarm. "You don't want to hurt his feelings."

Jamie looked wide-eyed at her mother and then back down at the worm.

"He has feelings?" she asked doubtfully.

"Of course. All creatures do."

Jamie took a deep breath and then let it out decisively. She reached out and touched the worm, pulling her hand back quickly when it squirmed.

"I guess he's okay," she said.

Meredith smiled at her daughter and then set the worm back down in the dirt, where it wiggled its way below the surface.

Curtis had called earlier, asking if he could stop by. He hadn't called her 'Mrs. Lowe' but there was a formal tone in his voice again. She knew he had information about Brian's murder to tell her and she was afraid to hear it, afraid to learn what might have gotten Brian killed, afraid her children would be saddled forever with a tainted legacy.

Long ago, when other children at school asked her where her own father was, Meredith told them he was dead. That's what her mother said. Later, Meredith found the story changed from time to time. He died in a car accident in L.A., then Ohio, then Reno. The stories got wilder as Meredith grew older and her mother was less and less sober. He fell off a fishing boat in Mexico. He drowned while diving for abalone in Mendocino. At the end, when Meredith had just turned seventeen and her mother lay dying, she tried one final time to learn who her father was and whether he was truly dead.

"You don't want to know." Her mother's lips were drawn tight, her tone bitter.

At least her own children would know they had a father and that he had loved them. She knew a connection would be important as they grew up, knowing he was there for them while he was alive. She didn't want this memory spoiled. Her mother had protected her from something terrible; Meredith would do the same for her own children.

Meredith saw Curtis's truck approaching in the distance and she stood up, stretching her back and rubbing her neck. Gardening was much harder than she expected. Didn't old people do this for fun? So far, she wasn't having much fun with it.

"Let's go wash up," she said to Jamie. "The sheriff is coming by."

"Can I watch *Gorilla Town*?"

Meredith looked at her in mock surprise.

"A new one today, huh?"

"I've had *Gorilla Town* forever." Jamie rolled her eyes.

Meredith smiled. Her daughter was getting great practice for her teenage years.

It had been four days since the picnic in the backyard with Curtis and she hadn't heard a word from him about the case. Honey stopped by a couple of times, once with a flat of strawberries and another time with Laf in a small wire cage.

"Don't panic," Honey had called out jovially. "He's just here on a friendly visit. Figured he'd like to experience a bit of the world."

Jamie, of course, was overjoyed. She hauled the fledgling chick around from room to room, giving it a guided tour of their house before settling down with Atticus to watch the chick in its cage while Honey and Meredith talked in the kitchen.

"Any word yet?" Honey asked.

Meredith shook her head.

"Curtis is checking up on some leads. But nothing for sure."

Honey waited, but when Meredith didn't add anything more, she rushed on, "People don't like this, knowing something like this can happen here. They're not sure our Barney's up to the task. I mean, bless his heart, but he's a little green."

Meredith bristled inside and found herself defending him. "I think he's doing everything he can. Whoever did this didn't leave a lot of evidence."

"I understand he found a gun." Honey looked sidelong at Meredith. "Any prints?"

A jolt went through Meredith. Was Honey looking for fodder for more gossip? Would she visit someone else and fill *them* in on "the latest?" Annoyed, she snapped at Honey.

"You tell me. It appears you hear more than I do."

Honey sat back and Meredith felt her face redden in embarrassment.

"I'm sorry," she said quickly. "It—it…"

Honey reached out and laid a hand on Meredith's arm.

"You have nothing to be sorry about. I'm prying while you're dealing with a lot right now."

A peal of laughter came from the living room and a flutter of wings beat around the cage. Meredith hoped the chick would survive its visit.

"There's talk about bringing in the state police," Honey continued matter-of-factly. "Just to help out."

Meredith knew Honey was studying her face and she tried to look unconcerned at this. Inside, however, she was alarmed at this possibility. The state police would likely be more aggressive in pursuing her as the murderer. Would they discover she was using Brian's hidden stash of money? Would they tear her life apart?

"I guess Curtis would appreciate the help," Meredith said slowly.

Honey laughed.

"Oh, I doubt that very much. It'll be like boys

fighting over a toy." She stopped. "Oh dear. I can't believe I'm gabbing like a fool about your husband's murder. You know what I mean, though."

Meredith nodded. She knew Honey didn't mean to hurt her feelings in alluding to her husband's murder case as a toy. She was distracted, though, by another idea.

"So if Curtis isn't calling in the state police, who is?" she asked.

Honey nodded, pursing her lips.

"You need to know this, and so does our young, good-looking sheriff." She raised an eyebrow as she stressed 'good-looking.' "People around town have noticed his car coming out here and staying around. If he's not investigating you as a possible suspect, then maybe he's interested in the pretty young widow."

Meredith's mouth dropped open. Who was watching her house way out here? She was worried at Honey's tone and the direction her comments were taking.

"I thought you were my friend, Honey."

"I'm *being* your friend right now," Honey stressed. "You live in a small town now. This murder is the biggest thing to happen here in years and people are going to talk. They're going to watch you and talk about you. They're going to speculate. Right now, most people think you killed your husband."

Meredith gasped. "They don't even know me."

"That's why it's easier for people to not like you." Honey leaned forward. "Might be good to stay away from our sheriff a bit. It'll stop people from jabbering about state police. Not good to get those outsiders poking their noses into our business."

That conversation had rattled Meredith badly and she was more determined than ever to leave Hay City just as soon as she could sell the house. She had been labeled a murderer and a seductress. They could keep their sad, little town and their too-handsome sheriff. She would tell Curtis to leave her alone. She would take her kids somewhere safe, where they could grow up among people who didn't remember their father being murdered and who didn't think their mother was a murderer. Back to a big city like Oakland, where no one cared what their neighbor was doing.

****

Meredith was drying Jamie's hands when Curtis knocked on the door.

"Can I show him the worm?" Jamie asked.

"Maybe next time," Meredith suggested. "Our hands are clean now, right?"

"I'm going to ask him to watch *Gorilla Town* with me," Jamie shouted, running to the door and throwing it open.

Meredith followed quickly. Nodding briefly at Curtis, she looked down at Jamie.

"The sheriff is here on business," she said firmly. "Not to watch movies."

She looked up at Curtis, who had a stony look on his face. *Definitely not here to watch movies and have picnics.*

After Meredith settled her kids in to watch the movie, she led Curtis out the front door to talk. If someone out there was watching—*where could they possibly be?*—they could see this was all official business and nothing else.

She stood with her arms crossed and waited.

"Were you aware that Brian had life insurance?" he asked abruptly. "You're the beneficiary. Twenty-five thousand dollars."

"He never told me." Meredith sat down hard on the front step. *Twenty-five thousand dollars*! "I just don't believe it, that wasn't like him."

Tears came to her eyes as guilt flooded over her. She had wished him dead and he had made the effort to get life insurance. She shook her head. It was so unlike him to pay for something like this. *Maybe he loved me. Maybe not hate after all.*

"How does this work? Will they just mail me a check? How did you find this out?" Her head was spinning with the news. She and her kids wouldn't be homeless. Along with the money in the socks, the insurance money meant security and safety for a long time. She could leave Hay City now. They wouldn't have to wait until the house was sold. She could get away from this place filled with bad luck.

Curtis stood apart from her, looking out toward the prairie.

"I went by his company's office in Boise to ask a few questions," Curtis continued. "They had a few questions for me, too."

She tilted her head to the side. "What do you mean?"

He glanced at her and then back out to the prairie.

"They wanted to know who I was investigating." He paused. "They wanted to know if you're a suspect."

"But I'm not a suspect, right?" she asked, exasperated. "You said you believed me."

She watched his jaw grow tight and fear crept up in her. Again she wondered, was he truly a friend or had it all been a pretense, just to investigate her?

"It's tough, me having to say this to you, but until I close this case, I can't tell them who's a suspect, and who isn't."

Meredith shook her head at this.

"People here are talking about bringing in the state police." Bitterness filled her voice and she felt satisfaction at Curtis's surprised expression. "Maybe you *do* need help on this case."

Meredith stared at him, her chin lifted in defiance, waiting for an angry response. Instead, he studied her for a moment.

"Check on your kids," he said haltingly, "then let's go for a walk."

****

They headed down the lane Meredith had walked along so many times now. She liked the way it curved gently away from the house so that in moments the house, and all the problems associated with it, seemed to disappear. Huge, black bumblebees droned among wildflowers under the cloudless sky. Tall grasses had started to encroach on the lane, narrowing it so Curtis and Meredith walked almost close enough to touch.

Curtis matched his stride perfectly to hers, and they walked in silence for several minutes. Why had he brought her outside, away from her children? She glanced at him, liking him despite herself. *Except when he doubts me. Except when I doubt his intentions.*

"Meredith." He stopped suddenly.

She turned and faced him, looking up into his eyes. His mouth turned down and small wrinkles showed at the corners of his eyes. As he looked at her gravely, for the first time he looked older than her. *Brian's murder is taking a toll on everyone here, not just me.*

She wondered what it would be like if they were just out for a walk, nothing more. Just two people enjoying each other's company and not talking about murder and guilt.

"I was thinking," Meredith began, "do you have to find the guy who killed Brian? I mean, what would happen if you just let it go."

Curtis's eyes widened in surprise. Something else flickered in his expression.

"You would want that?" he asked flatly. "I would think you'd want the murderer caught."

"I want it over."

He shook his head.

"I can't let it go," he said, sadness in his voice. "I wish I could."

Meredith stepped closer to him and put a hand on his arm.

"Maybe it's better not to know." She was thinking again of her children and the knowledge they would carry with them for the rest of their lives.

"We don't get to make those decisions." His voice was soft, counseling her, and something approaching regret showed in his eyes. "You can't just run away from all this."

Meredith still had her hand on his arm and she felt the tension underneath. He didn't move away and she wondered at her emotions; one moment hating him and the next minute attracted. Strangely, his presence comforted her even as she worried he would arrest her. She gazed up into his face and he looked down at her, a confused expression in his eyes.

"Meredith, I..." He paused and shifted closer to

her, their bodies close now. She closed her eyes and tilted her head back, anticipating the touch of his lips on hers. It had been a long time since she felt cared for and safe. *God help me, don't let me fall in love with him.*

There was a moment and then another and then she realized he wasn't going to kiss her. She opened her eyes, her cheeks burning in embarrassment.

"I'm sorry," he said.

"No, I'm sorry." She spoke quickly and stepped back.

"I can't." His voice was choked.

"Please. Don't explain. It makes it worse."

"You're a suspect," he snapped out, startling her in his bluntness. "You had a strong motive to kill your husband. No alibi. Your fingerprints are on the murder weapon."

Her eyes widened. The gun in the cabinet *had* been the murder weapon. She had broken into the cabinet and held the gun. Her prints were on it.

"I didn't kill him," she protested.

"I can't rule you out as a suspect. And it's not just that. You're my only suspect. I have no other leads."

"I didn't kill him," she repeated, her voice rising. "You said you believed me. You had a picnic here. You told my daughter you'd build her a *tree swing*."

He swallowed hard and didn't respond. A flutter of fear was growing, starting in her stomach and rising up to clutch her heart.

"Did you come out here to arrest me?" Meredith asked, breathing hard now.

Curtis looked away and then back at her as some decision seemed to settle in his mind.

"I did," he confessed. "I want to believe you didn't

kill him. But, by your own admission, you weren't happy in your marriage."

Meredith looked down, regretting telling him anything. How could he pretend to be a friend, get her defenses down, and encourage confessions?

"*Somebody* killed him. If I can't find another explanation…" He trailed off, but Meredith didn't need him to finish the sentence.

"Then obviously I did it," she finished for him.

He looked at the ground and shook his head miserably.

"I've lived here all my life and people trust me to find the person who did this and arrest them," he said. "The only way they'll feel safe in their homes is if they trust me to do what's right. I can't just let this go."

"Even if you arrest the wrong person?" Meredith asked. "And the real killer stays out there?"

Curtis looked up. "Help me believe the real killer is out there somewhere. Do you know something you're not telling me?"

How many times had he asked her this question already? She had been honest in saying she had no idea why someone would kill Brian. But her honesty was going to put her in prison for life and she would lose her children forever. Atticus and Jamie would have worse childhoods than she had, growing up in foster homes with a murdered father and a mother in prison. They would hate her. Fear swept through her. There must be something she could say that would put the suspicion on someone else. The lesser of two evils, she finally decided.

"Maybe I know something." She pictured the boxes in the attic. "Can I show you?"

****

"You don't know where this came from?" Curtis asked, as he unrolled the second sock full of bills.

They sat side-by-side on the bed, the box of rolled socks on Curtis's lap. At the last minute, Meredith couldn't bring herself to show him the box with the pictures. It was too humiliating to show him the pictures of her husband with another woman.

"You never asked him about this." Curtis looked down at the money, his expression sober. It wasn't a question.

She shook her head miserably.

"I was going to. But then…then he was killed."

"You were afraid of him." It was a statement.

Meredith studied her hands, not wanting to look at Curtis. She doubted now her impulse to keep the pictures secret. Maybe Curtis would understand she didn't want people talking about Brian's affair. Maybe he'd understand she was afraid people would judge *her* for this. That they would gossip about it and that her children would someday learn about it. That people would think she was just plain stupid for not knowing Brian had this other life.

"If we can figure out where the money came from, we may find the person who killed your husband," Curtis said. "Why didn't you tell me about this before? What else aren't you telling me?"

A ripple of unease went through her. The pictures of the girl came to her mind again and she closed her eyes. She didn't really want to know what Brian had been up to. Again, she had the impulse to run from her reality. *Get a backbone girl,* she ordered herself.

She opened her eyes and looked at Curtis, prepared

to tell him everything. Instead, she heard herself saying, "We've been living on this money, to pay for groceries and Brian's cremation."

He looked at her doubtfully.

"That's it?" he asked. "You didn't think this might be important?"

"Why would I tell you my husband was keeping secrets from me, lying to me, hiding money in our attic?" she spat out miserably. "Anyway, it's one more reason you'd think I killed him, right?"

He nodded slowly.

"Could be," he agreed.

She gasped softly, thankful she didn't show him the second box. A cheating husband would be just one more reason for murder.

"Could be," he repeated. "But it possibly gives me another suspect, depending on where this money came from."

Curtis reached into the box with the money and unrolled another one of the socks.

"Small bills," he mused. "That tells me he probably had accumulated this bit by bit. Were you missing money from your bank account?"

Meredith shook her head. She didn't want to tell him she never paid attention to their finances.

"I need to take this," he added, gesturing to the box. "It might be evidence."

Her heart sank. She rose and went to her dresser, opened the top drawer, and brought out another rolled sock.

"This was in there, too," she confessed, looking down at the sock in her hand. "I'm broke. This is all I have left."

Curtis silently rolled the money he was holding back into its sock and stood. He hesitated before crossing the room to her.

“You’ll need more than that.” He handed her the rolled sock.

Meredith looked up at him in amazement, tears springing to her eyes at his kind nature. She knew he didn’t need to give her anything, that he could have taken the money she already had. ‘You just don’t seem the type,’ he’d told her. Maybe she could trust him after all. *I should tell him about the pictures.* The words bubbled to her lips but Curtis spoke first.

“Meredith,” he said gently, looking kindly down at her. “I’ll do what I can for you here, but it’s best if you don’t leave town for awhile.”

She swallowed her words, realizing he wasn’t to be trusted at all.

Chapter 13

She sat on the hood of the car. The blackness closed in around her, squeezing her heart until she thought it would burst. It'll be okay, *she soothed herself.* I'll get through this.

Headlights approached and she ducked her head deep into her hoodie until, with a roar, the car went past. Not him, *she determined. Her heart beat faster.*

A familiar car neared, slowed, pulled off the road, and stopped in front of her. She hopped off the hood and walked over.

The driver's side window rolled down.

"How did you end up out here?" he asked. His face was in shadow.

The gun was already in her hand. She was aiming, shooting. So easy.

Driving back to the house, she realized the gun was still in her hand. She opened the window and let the cold wind lick her face. She flung the gun away. Then drove back home to her sleeping children. She showered twice, climbed between her sheets and let the blackness of the night take her away.

****

Meredith woke with a headache and chills. There had been a dream. She had been driving somewhere… Shivers swept through her. *God, no, I can't be sick.* She struggled out of bed, wincing as the headache swelled and sent a series of knives through her temples.

"Son of a *bitch*," she groaned.

"Sonna *bitch*," echoed Jamie from the floor.

Meredith looked down where her daughter had curled up with her pillow and blanket next to the bed.

"What are you doing down there, sweetie?" she asked.

"There was a monster in my room." Jamie's voice was calm and matter-of-fact.

Meredith forgot her headache as she knelt down to hug her daughter.

"Baby, there aren't any monsters," she soothed. "You know that."

Jamie struggled free. "It had big eyes and it wanted to eat me," she whined, her voice starting to rise.

Meredith stood, making her quickly remember her headache. She moaned, putting one hand up to the side of her head.

"Sonna bitch," said Jamie in sympathy.

"Son of a *witch*," Meredith corrected, thinking quickly. "My head hurts, like the son of a witch hit me with her broomstick."

Meredith held out her hand and Jamie scooted free of her blanket.

"Let's go check out your room and you can show me where you dreamed there was a monster."

Jamie's room was an explosion of primary colors; yellow-haired dolls wearing blue dresses, books with red titles, and a white-and-blue dollhouse with miniature blue furniture inside. Meredith had fought for and gotten Brian to buy new furniture for their daughter when she had graduated from the crib. It didn't matter to Meredith that it was inexpensive and somewhat flimsy. She wanted her child to start out with something belonging only to her. The white metal bedposts had ceramic toppers and a small matching dresser stood against the wall. The clean furniture looked incongruous on the stained worn carpet and against the dirty walls.

Jamie hung back in the doorway, unwilling to go back into her room.

"Over there." She pointed at the wall above her dresser.

Meredith let go of Jamie's hand and walked over to the wall.

"There's nothing here," she said. "You just had a bad dream."

Jamie stamped her foot. "It was real," she cried emphatically.

How would an experienced mother handle this? Meredith looked back and noticed two faint spots against the wall, as though it had once held oval pictures and left a shadow of their shapes.

"Here it is." She traced a finger around one large circle and then the other.

Jamie took a careful step into the room, and then another, her whole body poised to flee.

"Look here, and here?" Meredith pointed out the spots. "How about we paint your room and get rid of these spots?"

Jamie's face lit up.

"Purple?" she asked, the monster now apparently dismissed.

Meredith mentally calculated how much money she had in the socks and whether she could afford something as frivolous as paint in a house she didn't plan to keep. She bit her lip, wishing she had considered her solution more before offering to buy paint.

"Can we do it today?" Jamie pressed.

"Purple, red, and green if you want," agreed Meredith, her headache overwhelming anything else. "But I'm not well today. I need to go back to bed. Can you change Atticus and watch him for awhile?"

Jamie gave her a disapproving look.

"*You're* the mommy."

Meredith gave a tired smile. She wished someone else could be the mommy for a while.

"How about I change Atticus and you watch a movie with him?"

Jamie jutted her chin out, sensing room for negotiation.

"We're eating Choco Huffs."

"Deal," said Meredith before her daughter made any more demands.

****

She was back on the hill sitting on the hood of her car. Waiting. What was she waiting for? She struggled to remember. A movement from the road caught her eye and she watched puzzled as it traveled toward her. Not a car. Not a person or animal. More like a shapeless dark cloud. Somehow she knew it was coming for her. Sure enough, it slowed as it crested the hill and then hovered in place before her. Two oval circles opened up in the middle of the vapor—huge eyes that made Meredith's breath catch in her throat. Jamie was right, *she thought.* There are monsters.

****

"Meredith."

She opened her eyes to see Honey standing over her bed.

"I'm taking your kids to my place for the day, no arguing." Honey spoke firmly. "I'll bring back some chicken soup later."

"Honey?" Meredith's tongue was thick in her mouth and perspiration pricked at the back of her neck. Her pajamas were damp with sweat. "What time is it?"

"Lunchtime and your kids are eating jam out of a jar," Honey said brusquely. "Atticus has a full diaper and here you are sick as a dog."

Meredith started to sit up but Honey gently stopped her.

"Didn't mean to sound so harsh." She sighed. "I don't like seeing someone as helpless as you. Makes me squeamish. You need to rest today."

Meredith sank back against her pillow and closed her eyes gratefully. Her head hurt, her eyeballs hurt, her bones hurt. Honey was talking but the words didn't filter all the way into her brain. After awhile, from what seemed far, far away, the front door clicked shut.

****

She woke to Jamie giggling and Honey's voice. She moved her eyes and when that didn't hurt, she slowly sat up. The headache was still there but not nearly as bad anymore. She swung her feet off the bed and slowly stood up. The light filtering in through the closed shades had dimmed. Meredith glanced at the clock and realized she had slept most of the day away.

After she brushed the sour taste out of her mouth and washed her face, she stopped for a moment to stare in the mirror. Looking back were her same brown eyes, flecked with green, big in her thin face. *Same, but different. I don't know myself anymore.* Meredith pulled her hair back in a loose ponytail, brushing out the tangles and long pieces of hair broke loose onto the brush. *I'm coming apart.*

The pregnancy test had been negative, though moments of nausea continued to hit her and her period had yet to return. She figured stress was to blame for her stopped period, the nausea, the bad dreams, and now being sick. *Life goes on around me like normal, but my body knows there's nothing normal at all about my life.*

Meredith stepped carefully down the hall and into the kitchen. Atticus was seated in his highchair and Jamie was kneeling on another chair. The table was covered with marshmallows, chocolate chips, maraschino cherries, and toothpicks.

"We're making mallow mice," Jamie chirped happily, her face smeared with red syrup and pieces of marshmallow.

"And I'm the Pied Piper," added Honey. "What does the Pied Piper do?"

"Toot, toot, toot!" Jamie's high-pitched toots set Atticus to giggling too.

Meredith plopped down on a chair, her head a little less thick and foggy.

"What year is it?" she joked.

"You sure picked up a bad bug," said Honey. "The kids and I had a good day together. We pickled some pole beans and fed the chickens. Oh, and there's homemade chicken soup for you on the stove."

"I don't deserve you, Honey."

Honey shook off the compliment and rose to ladle soup in a bowl.

"We look out for each other out here. Besides, I enjoy having children around again. Your Jamie is an especially smart girl and Atticus is the happiest baby I've ever been around."

Jamie beamed at the praise and stuffed a whole marshmallow in her mouth.

"I understand you're going to paint Jamie's room purple," Honey continued.

Meredith vaguely remembered her promise with a wince.

"I guess so. I'll have to find the paint first."

Honey set a bowl of steaming soup on the table in front of Meredith, making her realize she hadn't eaten since the day before. She dug in gratefully.

"You'll want to hit the hardware store," said Honey.

Meredith mapped Hay City in her mind. There was only the small grocery store with its two-pump gas station and a couple of abandoned buildings next to a silo a half-mile down the main road. Aside from one small neighborhood, a couple of homes on the edge of the cemetery that functioned as the coroner's office/daycare, and the two-room city hall/sheriff's office, there was nothing but prairie and the occasional isolated home for twenty-five miles.

"What hardware store?" she asked.

Honey smirked and waggled her head knowingly.

"Haven't found it yet, have you? It's our local secret, though why it's a secret, I haven't a clue," she said. "You'd think a store would want business, wouldn't you?"

Meredith let Honey talk as she chewed contentedly on a tender shred of chicken.

"You know the old Porter Grain silo by the city sign?" Honey asked. "There's something near it that looks like a big log cabin."

"That's it?" Meredith asked, surprised. "It looks abandoned."

"Don't go in through the front," Honey continued. "There's a door around the side."

Meredith tilted the bowl in front of her and spooned up the last of the soup, before holding the bowl up to Honey.

"More, please," she asked.

Honey took the bowl with a smile and served up another helping.

"You run into any trouble at all down there, you just mention Honey sent you."

****

It was two days before Meredith finally was up to leaving the house. Atticus had started sniffling and Meredith was holding her breath Jamie wouldn't get sick, too. Deciding they just couldn't stay cooped up inside the house anymore, she loaded them into the car for an excursion to find the hardware store.

Two dusty trucks sat outside the log building, marked only with a small faded sign above the door reading:

"*Not the Hardware Store*"

Gun racks hung in the back of both truck cabs and Meredith remembered again the men who came to her house on their snowmobiles. Brian had told her they were unlikely to come by again, and they hadn't. Meredith was grateful. The visit had unsettled her, for the men's unfriendly demeanors, their guns, and the feeling she had that Brian knew them but pretended otherwise.

As Honey advised, Meredith drove by the silo, marked by the faded Porter Grain sign, around to the right side of the building, and noticed another small sign:

"*Not The Bar*"

"Guess that's plain enough," she muttered.

The inside was dim and cool, filled with the mixed scents of tools, oils, wood, and mustiness. As Jamie ran from aisle to aisle, Meredith wandered down the short narrow walkways stacked to the ceiling with merchandise. One aisle had everything from screwdrivers and boxed whitewater rafts to boots and wind chimes. The rear of the store was crammed with motor oil, several car tires, a bicycle seat, an assortment of beef jerky, and packages of men's underwear, size extra large only.

"Holy cow," Meredith breathed.

She searched the shelves for paint but it appeared to be the only thing the hardware store didn't carry after all. The yellow counter at the front was empty, with no one in sight. She was beginning to wonder if the place was actually closed. Just then, a door behind the counter opened, and, as a tall man walked through, the sound of clinking glasses and voices came from the room beyond. The smell of cigarette smoke trailed the man as the door closed behind him and all was silent again.

"Help you, Miss?" His voice was deep and threatening.

"Um, yes," Meredith wondered what Honey had gotten her into. "I'm looking for paint."

The man scrutinized Atticus in her arms and Jamie

standing nearby, before his gaze landed back on Meredith.

"I don't carry art supplies," he said dismissively. "You'll need to go to Mountain Home."

Jamie stepped forward.

"I'm painting my room purple," she announced.

The man studied Jamie carefully and nodded his head, stroking his bushy gray beard. His expression lightened somewhat.

"Purple, huh? You sure that's okay with your mom?"

Jamie looked at him haughtily. "It's *my* room."

A smile touched the corner of his eyes as he looked at Jamie.

"So, if I have this right, you came all this way, from New York City or some big fancy place, to my famous little store just to get purple paint for your room."

"York City?" Jamie repeated, looking pleased to correct him on this. "No, we live *here*, in *Hay* City."

"My mistake," he said, giving a little bow. "You looked like big city folk. Since you're locals, let's see what I can do."

He came around the counter and led the way down one of the claustrophobic aisles, Jamie marching close behind. Meredith followed from farther back, doubtful the paint, especially purple paint, would be found.

"Boys don't have ponytails," Jamie declared, examining the man's long, gray hair tied behind his back.

The man was pushing aside items on one shelf, rearranging boxes, and looking here and there for the paint.

"Why not?" he asked.

Jamie looked back at Meredith, who shrugged.

"They just don't," Jamie said firmly.

"Hmmm," he responded. "Doesn't seem like a good reason to me."

Suddenly, he whirled around and did a little hop, his eyes lighting up.

"Wrong aisle!" he exclaimed, and then hurried around the corner.

Meredith's mouth twitched in amusement, and then she and Jamie followed after him. They watched as he crouched to the floor and pulled out pots and pans, boxes of nails, a scarlet red toilet seat, and a series of potato-shaped coffee mugs.

"Here we go." His head and shoulders were deep into the shelf. He pulled out can after can of paint onto the floor in the aisle and then emerged with a triumphant look on his face. "This is what makes my place so famous. There's nothing you can't get at my hardware store."

He held aloft a gallon can of paint.

"Is it purple?" Jamie asked tentatively.

"As purple as a September sunrise." He grinned and Meredith wondered how she ever thought he looked threatening. The man was an overgrown puppy dog.

She shook her head in disbelief that purple paint had been hidden amongst the shelves.

"Not possible," she said.

"Possible and true." He rose to his feet and handed the paint can over to Jamie. "Here you go, young lady. You can carry this for your pretty mom."

They walked to the counter, which Meredith for the

first time noticed was painted like a bale of hay.

Acknowledging Meredith's look, he patted the counter proudly. "The only hay you're going to find in Hay City. And the site of Hay City's Post Office. Need any stamps today, ma'am?"

Meredith shook her head in wonder at the strange place. She sat Atticus on the counter and pulled out her wallet.

"If there's no hay then why the name?" she asked.

He made a scoffing noise.

"Don't see a city here either, do you," he quipped. "Whatever were the city forefathers thinking? If you really want to know, one of them is drinking whisky on the other side of the door behind me."

She laughed appreciatively.

"You mean, in the bar named 'Not the Hardware Store?'"

"I guess nothing is ever quite what it seems. For example, my name is Crusty." He leaned forward on the counter. "But I started life as Sean. Which name do you think gets more business?"

Meredith smiled, liking this big friendly man with his mountain man beard and surfer-dude ponytail.

"Crusty's not a name." Jamie broke into the conversation.

Crusty leaned over the counter and looked down on her.

"You have big opinions for such a little person, don't you?"

Jamie looked questioningly at Meredith, who gave a small nod.

"It's been my name ever since I accidentally cut off my little finger while skinning a muledeer." He displayed the four-fingered hand. "It stayed crusty for months. Hurt like a son-of-a—" He broke off and nodded toward Meredith. "Whoops. Little ears."

"Son of a witch," Jamie filled in, nodding her head in understanding.

He roared with laughter.

"Just so, just so. Hey," he said, looking at Meredith, "can I take your little girl next door to introduce her around? They'll love this one. She's like one of the gang."

Meredith looked indignantly at him. "Of course not! She's barely five years old."

The sound of glass breaking came from the other side of the wall. Crusty took a step back and pounded on the wall.

"Probably the mayor." He edged toward the bar's door. "Let's say five dollars for the paint and whatever other paint supplies you need."

Meredith started to protest his generosity as he opened the door, letting in a wave of raucous laughter and cigarette smoke.

"Just tell Honey I want one of her chicken dinners soon." He winked, letting Meredith know he had been expecting their visit, and then the door closed and he was gone.

Chapter 14

"It'll be a long time before I sit down to dinner with Crusty Connery," said Honey, when Meredith told her of the visit to the hardware store.

They were sitting on the floor of Jamie's bedroom, a half empty paint can sitting on an old sheet Meredith had put down to protect the floor. Two walls were now painted a bright purple color, which Meredith had to admit made the room more cheery.

"You're not telling me Crusty's last name is Connery." Meredith gave a small laugh. "As in Sean Connery?"

"007 himself. As he reminds me. Often."

Meredith laughed again and Honey joined in.

"He seems nice," Meredith offered, "and he's a businessman, too."

Honey shook her head firmly.

"Not interested. There was only one man for me. Besides, I have to be careful. At my age, a man is either looking for a nurse or a purse."

A warm breeze came through the open window, moving the thick odor of paint through the room. On the floor of the hallway, within view of Meredith, Atticus sat stacking wooden blocks. The sound of *Ice Land* came from the living room where Jamie once again was watching her favorite movie.

"I didn't have that kind of love." Meredith looked

over at her kids. "Where they were the *one* person."

Honey sighed.

"Pardon me for saying it, but I didn't think so. My mother used to say you might kiss a couple of toads before your prince comes along."

"You were lucky, finding your prince the first time."

Honey opened her mouth as though she was going to say something and then stopped. They sat quietly for a moment. Meredith was about to rise to start cleaning up, when Honey cleared her throat.

"What about our sheriff?" she asked.

Meredith tensed, recalling how she felt when she was sure Curtis was about to kiss her. It had made her realize how lonely she'd been in her marriage. The world had melted away and all she could do was anticipate how it would be with his arms around her and his mouth on hers. She grew warm again at the memory but pushed it away. Curtis believed she killed Brian, and that was that.

"I don't think so."

"I'm just saying, in a town this small, you're a little hard to ignore," Honey persisted.

Meredith looked at her questioningly.

Honey rolled her eyes.

"Beautiful femme fatale? Tragic tale? Mysterious past? Hard for a man to resist."

Meredith snorted.

"Let him see me now, covered in purple paint from head to toe, and he'd run the other way," she said. "And there's nothing mysterious about me. I just attract bad luck."

"I know it hasn't been long, but I've always been

one to speak my mind. You could do worse than Curtis," Honey advised. "I've known his family my whole life and they're good people. But if you're really not interested, don't lead him on. He's been hurt once, pretty hard, and doesn't need to go through that again."

"Believe me, I'm not interested." *I wonder what Honey would say if she knew I'm a suspect,* she thought. "It's the case he's investigating."

"He's sure investigating something," Honey muttered, but Meredith heard it clearly.

Honey got to her knees with a groan and, grabbing onto the bedpost, pulled herself to a stand.

"Well, I need to get on home and check on my chickens." She looked around the room. "This house is starting to look lived in again. It's nice having you here."

Meredith wanted to tell her she didn't plan to stay, that she was leaving as soon as she could figure out where to go. It was true though that the longer she stayed, the more she felt at home in Hay City, something she never believed could have happened. There was beauty in the stark prairie and spiked mountains, and a satisfaction in driving up to her own home. The quiet at night no longer bothered her, and the song of crickets now lulled her to sleep. So, instead of speaking, she rose to her feet also, and walked Honey to her car.

"You're good for this house," said Honey as she settled into the driver's seat. "It needs you here."

Meredith smiled at the idea of a house needing her.

Honey started to back her car out of the driveway and then stopped and rolled down her window to call out to Meredith.

"You mind my words about our sheriff," Honey called out, and then gestured for Meredith to look down the road. She pulled out of the driveway and headed home. Meredith stood there watching as Honey raised her hand in greeting out the window to Curtis when their vehicles passed.

"Oh boy," Meredith said to herself. "What now?"

****

"Just wanted to check on things out here and make sure everything's okay." Curtis stretched as he stepped out of his truck.

"I'm still here." She spoke flatly, still embarrassed and angered by their last meeting.

"Good."

She raised her eyebrows, but he looked past her at the house.

"It doesn't look purple." His mouth twitched at the corners as he looked at her.

Meredith realized her hands and arms were speckled with the purple paint and it had splattered the front of her shirt as well.

"Jamie's room." She picked at the paint on her fingers. "Somewhere along the line, I apparently promised her a purple room. To cover up the monster."

"Monster?"

"Bad dreams." She shrugged. "Watch out. They're going around."

Curtis gave her a long look, frowning. She sighed.

"Jamie dreamed a monster was on her wall so we covered him up with new paint," she said. "I'm having trouble sleeping, too."

He nodded.

"You don't look so good. I was going to say

something."

She lifted her chin at his comment. Her nights had continued to be filled with strange dreams. A terrible idea was growing in her mind, prompted by the nightmares, and she'd fought back by taking an extra sleeping pill each night. She would wake feeling heavy and lethargic, but she judged it to be the lesser of two evils. Then, the night before, she'd woken to find herself outside, keys in hand, standing by her car.

"What do you want?" she asked.

"We need to talk."

"Right."

Meredith looked at him waiting, thinking about what Honey had just said. Curtis was kind and handsome, but he could never understand her past. What if something truly terrible came out about Brian and what he had been up to? Curtis would never believe she had no idea what her husband was involved in. He would despise her for staying with Brian. It would be one more sign she was a terrible person and a terrible mother.

"You okay there?" asked Curtis, looking at her quizzically.

Meredith shook her head, clearing her convoluted thoughts. She ran a hand through her hair, realizing it was a mess. *What am I thinking? My husband was just murdered and, once again, I'm daydreaming about the man who thinks I'm the murderer.*

"Bad headache. Want some iced tea? Or do I go directly to jail?"

He frowned again and held up his hands in surrender.

"Are you always this prickly?" he asked.

She sighed heavily. "Tell me whatever you've come to tell me about the case now," she said. "Don't act all friendly to me and then hit me with some kind of bad news later. Let's get it over with."

Curtis took a step back and gave her an assessing look.

"I haven't been putting on an act." His tone was solemn. "I don't like coming over here asking questions and giving you bad news. I know things are hard for you, out here alone now with your kids. I'd guess things have been tough for awhile."

Meredith bit her lip, wondering if he knew more than he was telling her about Brian's murder.

"Let's start over," she said. "Let's talk."

The front door slammed and Jamie barreled out.

"Come see my bedroom!" Jamie cried. "It's purple."

Curtis looked at Jamie with a smile. "Ah, that's why your mom has purple hair today."

Jamie giggled.

Meredith reached up to her hair, touching stiff bits of paint where it had dried. She followed Curtis and Jamie into the house to her daughter's bedroom.

"It's the perfect color for you," Curtis said, but he glanced at Meredith as he spoke. She flushed, confused, even as she watched her daughter beam in delight and pride.

"It killed the monster," Jamie announced.

"Monsters hate purple," he assured her, glancing again at Meredith.

"I'll make coffee," she said, and he nodded.

****

The coffee did little to lift the fog from her mind.

No more sleeping pills, she promised herself once again. Her supply, Brian's supply, was dwindling quickly and she didn't have the money to go to a doctor or buy medication. *It'll all be gone soon anyway and that'll be that.*

"I got copies of your bank statements," Curtis told her, sipping at his cup. "Did you know Brian had been cashing his paycheck and leaving just enough in to cover bills?"

She shook her head.

"I let him handle the money," she admitted. "Pretty dumb, huh?"

"I think that's where the money in the socks came from. It's your money. Eventually. I need to keep it 'til the case is closed. I'm sorry."

"It never felt like mine anyway."

They sat quietly for a moment. Meredith realized she'd been hoping the money would lead him to another suspect. Instead, it had turned out to be a dead end. She waited to see what he would say next.

"I can loan you some money if you're running short." He didn't look at her as he spoke.

Meredith shook her head, hiding her surprise. She wondered what had changed.

"No, no. Thank you. If anything, I know how to live cheap. We'll be fine for awhile."

They sipped their coffee. As she looked over at Curtis, he leaned forward toward her and she automatically leaned toward him too.

"He might have been thinking about leaving." His voice was low.

She leaned back again.

"He must have been planning this for a good while,

to get that much money together." He shifted in his seat. "Another thing." He stopped and stood up abruptly. "Let's go outside for this."

Curtis set his cup down on the table and walked out the door before she had a chance to respond. Meredith fought back a wave of nausea, but obediently rose and followed.

Curtis stood still in the middle of her yard, looking up at the mountain ridges to the west. *He's as solid inside as those mountains,* she thought distractedly.

"I never get tired of looking at them," he said as she walked up to him. "They always look different."

"Tell me."

He chewed the inside of his cheek.

"You didn't know about Brian's life insurance policy." It came out as a statement, but Meredith shook her head anyway.

"He never told me."

"Did you know he had one out on you, too?" Curtis searched her face.

She shook her head again. That made sense. His and hers.

"Sounds like Brian. If there was money somewhere, he wouldn't leave himself out."

"For a hundred and fifty thousand dollars."

"But why..." she started, her breath coming faster.

His policy was for twenty-five thousand dollars; hers was six times larger. Suddenly, she turned and walked away from him, away from the house, trying not to think what the difference meant.

"Meredith."

His steps moved quickly behind her and she started running. She didn't want to learn anything more about the stranger she married and his secret hateful plans. Tears blinded her and she wiped them away, stumbling, and then falling. She stayed on her hands and knees, sobbing.

He was next to her, bending down and touching her arm. She wrenched away.

"I wanted him dead, I fantasized about killing him, I even broke into his safe to get his gun," she blurted out in a rush, and then started laughing through her tears. Hysteria rose inside her. "He wanted to kill me, too. That's what the insurance money means, isn't it? He was planning to kill me."

She looked up at Curtis, who had pulled back from her and was watching her carefully.

"But who was killed first?" she continued with a gulp.

"Meredith," he said again slowly, as if in a daze. "You broke into the safe. To get his gun."

She didn't notice his shocked expression, but went on.

"He lied to me. He hurt me. I had bruises. He put his hands around my throat. I was afraid he was going to kill me. But not really."

Her words slowed to a stop and she sat back, panting.

"Is there something more you want to tell me?" Curtis asked, saying the words slowly, his words sounding choked.

Meredith looked up at him, shocked that all those words had come out of her mouth. Why would she say all this to the *sheriff*?

"If you tell me now, maybe I can help you. If he hurt you. If you were afraid of him. If you tell me now, we can figure something out."

Meredith took a deep breath and got to her feet.

I think I killed him. I think I snapped one night and went out and waited for him. I think I took his gun and...

"Meredith."

She blinked at the sound of her name and realized she'd been standing in a daze.

"Did you? Did you kill Brian?"

The baldness of the question cut straight through her. For a moment she wondered if she had confessed out loud. She looked directly into his face, recognizing his doubt, and she lifted her chin in defiance.

"No," she said, trying to sound confident despite the tremor in her voice. "We had our troubles, but I didn't kill him."

Meredith knew he didn't believe her. She didn't believe her words either. *I killed him. I don't remember, but somehow I did it.* She read something else in his eyes. Disappointment? Wariness? She waited for him to tell her she was going to jail.

Curtis turned and walked away, back toward the house.

"Wait," she called. "I know what you're thinking. Why aren't you arresting me?"

He shook his head and kept walking.

"Get some rest," Curtis called back without turning. "You look like you're about to fall over."

Meredith tilted her face to the unblemished sky. It was a deep blue, a hue almost purple. It was a sky you could fall into and disappear, a sky traveling forever in all directions. She stood there until Curtis's truck roared to life. When she was sure he was gone, she walked slowly back to the house.

****

"I think I killed him."

"That's ridiculous," Honey gasped. "Why would you think such a thing?"

Meredith stood at Honey's door, Jamie behind her on the lawn picking a dandelion bouquet. Atticus toddled toward a tabby cat stretched out in the sun.

"I wanted to," Meredith said. "My prints are on the gun. I *dreamed* I did it."

"You'd better come in so we can talk about this." Honey opened the door, her tone just as comforting as if Meredith had told her she stubbed her toe or asked advice on a recipe. "I just made some lemon tea."

Meredith stepped into the kitchen and sat down heavily. She watched the older woman pour the iced tea, stirring a little sugar into both glasses before setting them on the table.

"Now what's this about dreaming you killed your husband?" Honey sat next to Meredith.

"I don't remember exactly." Meredith frowned. "I've been having these dreams. I think I must have killed Brian and I'm blacking it out. My dreams are telling me I did it."

Honey tsked gently.

"That's just stress talking to you." She patted Meredith's hand. "Don't you worry. We all dream about killing our husbands at one time or another. You'll feel better over time. It takes a while."

Meredith made a frustrated noise.

"Why is it no one believes me?" she asked. "I tell Curtis I didn't do it and he doesn't believe me. I tell you I did it and *you* don't believe me."

Honey frowned at her.

"You told the sheriff all this?" she asked. "Not a good idea."

Meredith slumped in her chair.

"I kind of wish he'd just get it over with and arrest me. I can't stand this waiting, his watching me."

Honey paced the kitchen, straightening items that weren't out of place and wiping areas that weren't dirty. Meredith appreciated how her friend understood and commiserated so severely with her problems. Honey was like the mother she should have had, a woman who would listen to her worst dilemma and not judge her. Honey was someone you could lean on in a crisis.

"He must have a reason why you *couldn't* have done it," Honey finally said. "He must know something he's not telling anyone."

Meredith caught the annoyance in Honey's tone. She knew Honey prided herself on knowing everything first. But if Curtis wasn't sharing everything he knew about Brian's murder and wasn't arresting her…then maybe her dreams were just dreams. She looked hopefully at Honey who was vigorously stirring more sugar in her tea.

"Why doesn't he just tell me?" Meredith asked.

Honey sat down across from Meredith and sipped at her drink.

"Appears our sheriff likes to keep some things close to his vest." Honey's expression was thoughtful and distant. "The question is why."

Chapter 15

"Half of turkey, half of ham."

Meredith didn't make eye contact with the deli boy, but she knew he was staring; knew he was examining her face, her clothes, and the contents of her cart. She knew every bit would be known throughout the community by nightfall. They would tear apart her comments, find underlying meanings, and tsk-tsk over her lifestyle, her parenting, and her hairstyle. Nothing would be too petty to discuss. Regardless of what the deli boy saw, it would again confirm community speculation, that she was the type of person who would murder her husband. *He was planning to kill me,* she wanted to shout.

She looked up. Deli boy hadn't moved.

"Half turkey, half ham," she repeated.

"State police are coming in." He watched her face intently for her reaction.

Meredith blinked twice and fought to control her face.

"Really?" She arched her eyebrows in mock surprise. "What for?"

"To catch the killer. Figured you'd be happy about it. But you don't look it. Happy, I mean."

"I'd be happy to get my ham and turkey," she said, swallowing.

He cocked his head at her. She knew he was

struggling to find something else to lob her way, to find something that would hit its mark. *If only this wasn't the only option for buying groceries*, she thought for the hundredth time. She waited. His apron, surely once white, was dingy yellow with brown stains at the pockets. Underneath, he wore a gray-green t-shirt frayed at the neck. Meredith watched as his confident expression began to fade and he started to turn away to get her order.

"Mommy, what's a killer?"

Jamie's small voice yanked her back to motherhood. Why was it that ninety-nine percent of the time kids paid no attention to adult conversation until an inappropriate topic came up?

"Killer whale." Out of the corner of her eye, Meredith registered deli boy's smirk. "It's a kind of whale."

"There are whales in Idaho?" Jamie asked.

Deli boy leaned forward on the counter as though he, too, was anxious to learn. Above, fluorescent lights hummed and the wheels of a cart clacked noisily down an aisle.

"Um, maybe," said Meredith. "They're checking it out."

Jamie looked from Meredith to deli boy, deciding if they were playing a joke on her. She shrugged. "Okay," she said.

Meredith glared at the boy, who turned nonchalantly to slice her order, a half-smile on his face. Going into the little grocery store and facing the people of Hay City was becoming more awkward than ever, with people even outwardly staring at her these days. She had tried ignoring them, then staring back, and now she was starting to wonder if she should just walk up to them and ask, *Tell me, who do you think murdered my husband?* She knew what they would say. *The sheriff believes in me*, she wanted to shout.

Her deli order slapped loudly on the counter and she reached over to pick it up.

"Mommy, is the sheriff going to be my daddy now?"

Meredith whirled around to face her daughter, the packages forgotten.

"No. Jamie, don't be silly." Meredith's heart twisted as she forced out a laugh. She was acutely aware of the deli boy standing there, listening and surely preparing to broadcast the scene later to everyone who came to his counter.

"I like him," Jamie said.

"How about some cereal?" Meredith asked, rolling the cart away quickly before Jamie added anything else the boy would gossip about.

"Don't forget your order," deli boy called out.

Furious now, Meredith marched over and grabbed the white paper packages from the counter. The teen stood by his deli-case, taking in her fury with unconcealed glee.

"Out of the mouths of babes, huh?" he snickered.

"Why can't you shut up," she snarled, and walked away. *I could really kill that kid,* she thought.

****

Meredith couldn't stand the idea of going directly home. She drove down the pothole-riddled road behind the grocery store where about two dozen small homes slumped together in Hay City's version of suburban blight. A few homes marked off their territory with chain-link fences and some were surrounded by sagging wood picket fences, any paint color long since chipped and weathered away. In a dusty lot next to one house squatted an A-frame building, not quite a house or a shed. A cross was hung on the door along with a sign:

"*First Prairie Church*"

A piece of paper was taped below the cross with writing too small to read from the road.

Meredith rolled to a stop. *Churches were supposed to be open to everyone, even possible murderers.* Maybe it was time to pray. Her mother had taken her to church off and on when she was a child, vacillating from belief to nonbelief. These days, Meredith still wasn't sure what she believed, but she loved the solemnity of churches and decided it couldn't hurt to pray. As she unloaded the kids again, she looked around and wondered who was watching her even at this moment. The neighborhood was eerily quiet, more ghost-town than town.

As she approached the church's door, she read on a piece of paper:

"*Welcome to paradise. Thrift store open daily*"

This was more like it. She and her mother had always loved going to thrift stores together, picking out a back-to-school backpack for Meredith, winter boots, a frying pan, or a vase in the shape of an angel. Clothes were best bought used, her mother explained, so that they were pre-shrunk and soft from repeated washings. Meredith had believed this all the way until she was in junior high and the girls around her had turned mean, cattily making her aware and ashamed of their poverty for the first time. The girls called her "motel rat" and had turned her thrift store treasures into trash in her mind, prompting her to beg her mother for department store clothing. It stayed this way until her mother got sick and Meredith sought to please her by bringing home thrift store "treasures" again. They laughed over the two-dollar radio that only tuned in to one station, the jigsaw puzzles invariably missing several pieces, and the game of Life that had lost all its male characters. "That's my life, all right," her mother joked with a hearty laugh.

Meredith tried the doorknob of the church but it was locked. *Open daily?* She looked around and down the street for some sign of movement but Hay City's only neighborhood was silent and still.

"Nothing here is like it seems," she muttered, hefting Atticus over to her other hip. The kid was gaining weight fast now, rapidly turning into a chubby toddler. She wouldn't be able to carry him much longer at this rate.

"Mommy, can I play on the slide?" Jamie asked and then disappeared around the side of the building before Meredith could answer.

"Jamie!" she called and then quickly followed. She rounded the corner to spot Jamie climbing the ladder to a shiny red slide, its newness startling in the town's dinginess. "Jamie!" she called again, only to have her daughter turn and wave enthusiastically.

A chuckle from behind her made her turn. A weathered face, heavily wrinkled, white hair topped by a baseball cap, shaded eyes.

"Let her play. That's what it's for."

"You startled me," said Meredith.

"Well, it's my house."

"Oh." She cringed, abashed. "I'm sorry. My

daughter got away from me."

He smiled and his eyes disappeared further into deep folds.

"They do that. Better get used to it."

Meredith stood there uncertain whether she should call Jamie back or not. She looked over as Jamie slid down the slide with a squeal and then ran around to climb the ladder again. The man's attention had shifted to Jamie and Meredith sighed, setting Atticus down.

"I have two of my own, though the wind blew them away long ago," the man said. "I think there's a great grandchild on the way too, but I'm a bit forgetful these days. That one might have been a dream. One of those waking dreams. I have those, you know."

He reached down beside his chair and lifted a beer to his lips and Meredith recognized him. She'd seen him in the sheriff's office and then in the grocery store, his trembling fingers touching the cans of beer. She glanced over at Jamie, now trying to climb her way back up the slide.

"Are you the minister here? Of the church?"

"That's right." He took another sip of beer before setting it down again. "Sinners and saints welcome, one and all. Mostly sinners, though, aren't we?"

He looked keenly at her as he spoke and she wondered if he was rudely making a point. *The only safe place to be,* she decided, *was at home.* Maybe that's why most people in Hay City lived in remote areas, so they wouldn't have to put up with their neighbors' prying eyes and comments.

"You're that girl come from California," the man remarked. "The one whose husband was shot and killed."

She nodded, even though it wasn't a question.

"Bad business," he continued. "Bad for you, bad for your children. And especially bad for your husband."

He chuckled and she looked icily at him, aghast a minister would make such a joke.

"God has a plan for all of us," he preached, and as his eyes rolled upward toward the heavens, Meredith noticed for the first time a cloudy film covered his watery eyes. She knew he wasn't as old as he looked. Her mother had looked far older than her years, too; the heavy drinking took its toll. "Your man's time was up, that's all. There's a plan for you. Best get on with it."

She stood straighter.

"I'm not sure I believe in all that. Plans, I mean."

"California girl," he mused. "Crystals and yoga, tofu and nuts, organic stuff, nonfat, lowfat, no carb nonsense. On the search for the perfect plan but the perfect plan is already in place."

Meredith edged away from him, toward the slide. She wasn't in the mood to be preached to, especially by a drunk who implied she was a sinner and said Brian's murder was part of God's perfect plan. *Since when did God plan out murders*? she wondered.

"Time for us to get going," she said. "Thank you, um, for letting my daughter play."

She turned to the slide. "Jamie, we're going now."

Jamie ran up. "Did you watch me? Can I come back? Can we get a slide?"

The man chuckled softly behind her. "You're welcome anytime. Just like the sign says, we're open daily."

Jamie stopped as they passed the man. "What's

wrong with your eyes?" she asked.

"Jamie!" Meredith exclaimed.

"I looked upon the face of God and his brilliance blinded me to the world," he sermonized, rocking slightly in his seat.

Jamie's mouth dropped open in wonder. "What did he look like?" she asked, awe in her voice.

Meredith paused, curious how he would answer.

"You ever been told the story of Adam and Eve in the garden of Eden, little girl?" the man asked instead.

"There's a snake," Jamie answered immediately, wrinkling her nose.

The man nodded. "Good, good. Know what the story means?"

Jamie bit her lip, thinking.

"Be careful what you ask for," he concluded, answering his own question. "You might get it."

Jamie frowned. "It's about a bad snake and an apple," she protested.

Meredith reached out to grab Jamie's hand.

"C'mon sweetie, time to go now." She tugged to get Jamie to walk with her toward the car.

"It's about greed," the old man called after them. "It's always about greed in the end."

"Thank you again," Meredith called back to him as she hurried Jamie around to the front of the house.

Jamie climbed into the backseat of the car as Meredith buckled Atticus into his carseat.

"I don't want to go back there, Mommy," she said quietly. "I don't like that man."

Meredith nodded. The old man was probably harmless enough but slightly off. She would look into buying a used slide of their own for Jamie and Atticus.

Maybe she would put it out by the tree swing so the kids would have their own place to play. She could dig a flowerbed behind the house and garden while keeping an eye on them. *If* she stayed.

As they drove back toward the house, Meredith looked out over the prairie and sighed at the sight of the green jagged ridges looming over the valley. *Wickedly beautiful.* She spotted her home in the far distance. It no longer looked lonely and old to her. It looked like a safe haven.

****

She planted pole beans, tomatoes, cucumbers, peppers, and strawberries too although Crusty told her they probably wouldn't survive the winter.

"There's always someone who wants to give it a try so I carry the starter plants," he told her with a loud laugh. "If they want to buy it, I want to sell it."

Jamie poked the seeds into the earth, tasting a couple along the way.

"It doesn't taste like a cucumber," she said, disappointed.

Meredith waited for Curtis to return, looking toward the road dozens of times a day. She didn't understand why he didn't come back, worried about it and was grateful for it, too. *He's out there somewhere, gathering evidence for or against me. But if not me, who? Who else wanted him dead? Who else had held the gun? Who else knew he was coming home that night?*

The more questions Meredith asked herself, the more she was certain she *had* killed him. *Somehow, I did it. Sooner or later, he's going to come to the same conclusion.*

He came back a week later, late in the afternoon, driving his truck slowly up to her house. Meredith watched warily from the kitchen window as he sat in his truck for several minutes before emerging. *Is this it?* She looked around at her kids, Atticus in a corner of the kitchen examining two pots he had pulled out of the cupboard and Jamie reading a book in the living room. Her stomach did a flip-flop and she looked back out the window. Instead of coming to the door, she watched in surprise as Curtis lifted a hefty looking box out of the back of his truck and carried it toward the back of the house.

Meredith ran to the back door and peered out its window.

"What in the world?" she asked out loud.

Jamie burst out the door past her, racing to the giant tree where Curtis had set the box. Meredith stayed back, watching as Curtis leaned the ladder against its massive trunk and carried a heavy coil of rope up into the branches.

Jamie danced around the tree as he knotted the rope into a wide plank of wood, and lowered it slowly down.

Meredith went back to the kitchen, pacing back and forth, unsure what to do. Was he looking for something? It wasn't right that he just came onto her property and nosed around. She headed back to the door, intending to order him off her land. Then she stopped and walked back into the kitchen.

"Let's go outside." She hefted Atticus up off the floor. "See how our garden is doing."

The afternoon sun blinded her for a moment, and she blinked hard, squeezing her eyes against the foreign brightness. Winter had been long and spring was an alien being here, so disorderly compared to the temperate California season she'd always known. Nights still brought a chill to the valley and she'd kept heavy blankets on the beds. The days, though, warmed the earth and promised the coming summer.

Meredith set Atticus down and let him toddle around the side yard as she dragged the water hose over to the emerging plants. Each day, Meredith dribbled water carefully over each green sprig, letting the ground around it soak thoroughly. It was amazing how quickly the seeds had sprouted and sent their shoots up through the dirt, seeking the sun. Within days, tomatoes, beans, and cucumbers had emerged and there were tiny bumps in the earth where the pepper plants had taken root.

She glanced back to the tree where Curtis was watching Jamie swing higher and higher. He looked her way, picked up his box and then said something to Jamie. She looked firmly down at her plants again.

I could just drive away, take my kids and disappear somewhere. Start over somewhere new. The idea depressed her. She didn't want to leave. The decaying house Brian bought for them in this bleak countryside was changed to her now. It wasn't all so bleak. All it needed was a bit of paint, a garden, a swing, and a few repairs. *Maybe more than a few*, she mused. The landscape was different now, no longer a wide open frozen wasteland. The snow had been replaced by lush fields and deep-green mountains. Even she had to admit the place was astoundingly beautiful.

I don't want to move. Besides, moving from place to place is what her mother had done with her, each situation getting worse than the last. *If I stay here, though, I'm going to get arrested for murder. I'm making it easy for him, sitting here and waiting for all the evidence to line up.*

She looked up. Curtis stood at the edge of the garden.

"Meredith," he said.

She searched his face for a sign of what he was thinking.

"Thank you, for the swing. That was a nice thing to do for my kids."

He nodded.

She swallowed. "Anything new?" she asked. "Have you found anything?"

"I don't think it was random," he asserted. "I think someone planned this out."

Me, she thought.

"Who? Why?"

He looked as though he was going to say something, but then shook his head.

"Don't go away," Jamie broke in, running up. "Come push me on the swing."

Meredith bit her lip. She wanted him to stay, wanted to talk to him about what he suspected, wanted his comforting presence. *Not a good idea*, she warned herself.

"I need to get back," he said. "Your mom can push you now."

Curtis looked at her somberly for a moment and then turned and headed for his truck. Jamie skipped alongside, telling him about the garden they had planted. Meredith stayed where she was, watching him the entire way, wishing he wasn't the sheriff, liking him and hating him at the same time.

****

That night she went to bed early, dropping in exhaustion as soon as the kids were asleep. Curtis's visit had haunted her for the rest of the day and through the evening. He clearly wouldn't tell her what he knew and what evidence he was discovering. She was afraid and relieved Brian's case was moving forward. Whoever killed him would soon be caught, whether it was her or someone else. But who else could it possibly be?

She listened to the crickets chirp and a pod of toads croak outside her window. Their music lulled her into a welcome drowsiness and she realized it was the first time since Brian's murder that she hadn't taken a sleeping pill.

Whatever happens, I'm not running away, she decided right before she fell into a heavy sleep.

****

There was a scraping at the front door and a jingling of keys. The metal-on-metal sound of a key going into the lock shocked Meredith, and she sat up, her heart jumping into her throat. For a disoriented moment, she was sure it was Brian returning home, a ghost. The doorknob shook and then Meredith heard a key go in the lock again. Not a ghost, but a real person trying to get into her house. Someone with a key.

She scrambled out of bed and looked around for some type of weapon. Nothing. She darted into the hallway and into the bathroom, in her confusion thinking she'd find something useful there. The door rattled insistently. She grabbed her hair dryer and, wielding it, went to the front door. Meredith leaned against the door for a moment and looked down at the doorknob, watching it move futilely back and forth. Her thoughts went to her children, sound asleep in their rooms down the hall, and her breath came quick.

"Damn!" A woman's voice on the other side of the door.

Meredith relaxed slightly. Obviously someone had come to the wrong house late at night and was putting the wrong key into her door. She looked over at the kitchen clock and saw it was only ten thirty p.m. Okay, this was a reasonable explanation.

Meredith took a deep breath and opened the door.

The girl was more beautiful than she remembered from the pictures, her long auburn hair, more strawberry blonde in person, draped over one shoulder. A light smattering of pale freckles dotted her nose, something Meredith hadn't noticed either. Those green eyes, those long legs, and that bronze skin. No wonder Brian had been in love with her.

The full mouth though was twisted, ugly in disappointment. The girl was studying Meredith too, as though she was reconciling the real person with pictures she had seen as well.

It's true, Meredith thought, *time does freeze.* How long had they stood there looking at each other? The girl made an impatient move and Meredith noticed for the first time the firm roundness pushing out from under the girl's t-shirt. *Four months, maybe five. Five would mean it could be Brian's.*

Meredith's throat closed and her heart flopped in grief. Why was the girl here? What could she possibly want from Meredith now Brian was dead?

The girl stood straighter, pulled her t-shirt taut over that round bump, and looked Meredith in the eye.

"I want the money," she sniffed.

Part 3

Murders are crimes of passion. But isn't passion what makes us human? Some days, it's just too hard to not murder someone.

Chapter 16

"What?"

"He promised it to me," the girl said. "Your husband."

Meredith wanted to shut the door on her and go back to bed. She wished all of this were a bad dream she would wake up from in the morning, barely able to remember and left only with an aftertaste of uneasiness and nausea.

"I don't know what you're talking about," Meredith said. "My husband is dead. You have the wrong house."

The girl reached out and put her palm against the door. Meredith gripped the doorknob tightly.

"I'm not leaving here without the money," the girl asserted. "All of it."

"I don't know you," Meredith repeated. "You have the wrong house."

"You don't know, do you?" The girl laughed scornfully, her face turning into something less than beautiful.

"This is *my* house. Now let me in before I get the sheriff over here to evict you."

Meredith's knees went weak and her hand loosened on the doorknob. The girl shoved the door open and pushed her way past Meredith, walking confidently through the living room and down the hall to her bedroom. Breathing hard, Meredith trailed after her. The words echoed in her mind: *my house, my house, my house*.

In the bedroom, the girl had already dragged a chair to the closet. Meredith stood powerless as she watched her climb on the chair and reach up into the crawlspace. *How does she know? Why aren't I stopping her?* The girl turned around on the chair, reaching farther as she rose on her tiptoes and stretched. She stepped down off the chair and faced Meredith, assessing her more closely this time.

"Where is it?"

Meredith swallowed dryly.

"This is your house?" she asked.

The girl shrugged. "My family's house. No one's lived out here in years. And Brian needed a place. Close, but not too close, you know."

Meredith winced when the girl spoke her husband's name. It made their relationship real. *Close, but not too close. Close to the girl, but not so close that I would run into her. He put his family in his girlfriend's house.*

Meredith's head was spinning, her mind trying to grasp these new facts.

"You really don't know any of this, do you?" the girl continued. "Geez, Brian was right about you. Dumb as a stump."

The girl stepped forward and made a gesture toward the bedroom door.

"Let's go in the kitchen and have a chat. I'll fill you in, and then you can hand over the money. Sound like a good trade?"

In a daze, Meredith walked down the hall to the

kitchen. *The money's gone,* she worried. *What will the girl do when she finds out? Who is she? Where did she come from?* And under all these questions, pulsed one, *Whose baby, whose baby, whose baby?*

"Would you like to sit down?" the girl offered, pulling out a chair at the table.

Meredith sat, feeling like a guest in her own home. The girl—because she couldn't be more than twenty, could she?—started opening cabinets as Meredith watched stunned into silence, her mind frozen.

"Don't you have anything to drink here?" the girl asked, opening the refrigerator and peering inside.

"Fruit punch?" Meredith suggested, getting a you've-got-to-be-kidding look in return. "No alcohol, if that's what you're looking for. I don't drink."

The girl heaved a sigh and closed the refrigerator door. She turned, leaned against the door, and crossed her arms.

"I'm Gemma."

"Meredith." She had to be in a bad dream, making introductions with her dead husband's pregnant girlfriend. "You shouldn't be drinking anyway, should you?"

Gemma rolled her eyes. "It was for you… You're going to need it."

Meredith closed her eyes. The thought that she should call Curtis flickered through her mind. The girl could be here to murder her and her children. Meredith opened her eyes. Gemma hadn't moved.

"You and Brian." Meredith's voice was low and choked. "How long?"

"Long enough." Gemma looked down and smoothed her shirt over her round belly. "About a year and a half. Right when he started with the insurance company. I was there as a clerk and he started making a move on me his first day there. He was something else."

"I would have been pregnant with Atticus then," Meredith murmured. "Before we moved here."

Gemma made an impatient sound and stepped to the kitchen table. She pulled out a chair but remained standing behind it. Her eyes roved around the kitchen and into the living room, looking over the sparse furniture, the kids' toys, and the green eyelet curtains Meredith had joyfully found on clearance at the hardware store.

"I didn't chase *him*," Gemma said. "And, for the record, he didn't act like a married man, either. Does all that matter anymore, anyway?"

Meredith didn't respond. Of course it mattered. It mattered to her and it mattered to their two children. If Brian never met this woman, none of them would be there right now. If they hadn't moved to Hay City, Brian would still be alive. Maybe this affair would have ended and the girl wouldn't be pregnant. And Curtis? She was annoyed he entered her reflection.

"Brian had big plans," Gemma continued. "He was going places. He told me about you and how small your plans were. How he regretted marrying you. How you held him back."

None of this was news to Meredith. She had felt those regrets in Brian's attitude toward her, his anger, his barely restrained violence.

"He should have left," Meredith said softly.

Gemma snorted.

"He was going to leave you, when we saved

enough." Her tone was brittle, that of a resentful teenager. "He talked about it all the time. He was going to start his own business."

Meredith had a strong sense of déjà vu in those words, the same things Brian used to tell her. Why then had he moved his family to this solitary place, if he was planning to leave her? The memory of his hands around her throat came back to her along with his words, *Haven't I waited long enough?* Her stomach flip-flopped, her queasiness increasing.

Being away from Brian's influence for the past weeks helped her gain some perspective on him and their marriage. She hadn't realized before how empty his words were. He had her convinced that everything he did was for her and the kids. She had been so young and malleable.

"He promised me lots of things, too," said Meredith.

Gemma tossed her hair back. "Brian had it all worked out."

"Apparently not." Meredith recalled Brian laying in the morgue, the cloth covering where the bullets had entered.

Gemma's eyes widened and she moved away, to lean against the kitchen counter. She glanced over at the boxes of cereal lined up by the refrigerator, the purple plate sitting on the stove, and the high chair in the corner.

"We were going to get married," Gemma prattled on, "move to Texas or Florida. Somewhere warm. Brian was going to leave you some money. We wouldn't have bothered you."

Meredith wondered again about the life insurance

money. Was killing her the backup plan or the plan?

"I was nineteen when I met him," Meredith said. "How old are you?"

Gemma didn't answer, but moved around the kitchen touching the toaster, the coffee pot, and the knobs on the stove.

"My mother lived here. A long time ago. You like it here?"

A sense of unreality swept over Meredith. Had Brian really brought her to live in his girlfriend's former house? It occurred to her the girl had no reason to tell her the truth about anything.

"You killed him," Meredith said. It came out as a statement.

"Fat chance. You're not pinning this on me."

"Then who?"

Gemma stared at Meredith for a moment.

"Look, I just want what's owed to me and then I'm gone," she said. "Whatever else you've got going on, well…that's on you."

"You have to come to the sheriff with me. You have to tell him what you know."

The girl gave a short laugh.

"I don't think you want me to do that." Gemma's tone was sly, accusing. "Brian told me you were snooping around, scratching up his safe, trying to get inside."

Meredith went still. Brian never confronted her about the scratches, but he'd known she was suspicious of him. Maybe that's why he removed the gun. Maybe he'd moved up his plans to remove her…

"Hey, I can keep a secret, okay?" the girl continued. "The only reason I'm here is because we're trading, right? Information for the money. I don't care about the rest of it. Honest. And now it's time for you to pay up."

Meredith swallowed.

"The money's gone." She didn't want to admit she had some of it still rolled in Brian's sock in her dresser drawer. "The sheriff took it as evidence."

The girl's mouth dropped open and disbelief filled her face.

"All of it? You gave him all the money?"

The girl paced around the kitchen, her eyes darting around, clearly furious. She whirled on Meredith.

"Did Brian tell you about it?" she demanded. "Did he tell you our deal?"

Meredith shook her head. She worried again about her sleeping children down the hall. She didn't want this angry girl in her house, but didn't know how to get rid of her. For a moment, she wondered if she was dreaming all of this.

Gemma pulled up a chair across from Meredith with a screech and sat down heavily into it. She stared at Meredith fiercely.

"Damn." She shook her head. "Maybe you're smarter than you look."

Meredith stood up. She didn't want to sit across from this girl. She didn't want Brian's pregnant girlfriend in her house at all.

"I want you to go. There's nothing for you here."

Gemma didn't move. Her jaw was tight and her chest moved quickly as her breath came faster.

"You killed him, right? Damn. I need that money. I have expenses coming."

Meredith watched all this in amazement. What was

this girl saying?

"I have no idea what you're talking about." Guilt overwhelmed her anyway. "I didn't kill him. *You* probably did."

Gemma stared narrowly at her and then spoke slowly as if to a three-year-old. "You better get the money back."

Meredith swallowed. The girl was young, but it was possible she was dangerous.

"If it makes you feel any better, I'm broke, too." She remembered something the girl mentioned earlier. "You said you and Brian had a deal, about the money in the attic. What deal?"

The girl's mouth turned down and she looked like she was going to cry.

"It was for the house." Her voice rose to a whine. "He promised he'd pay me when he got all the money together. But I already signed it over to him."

"That was true then? This was your house?"

Gemma nodded.

"He didn't pay you," Meredith murmured as if to herself. "He left both of us broke."

"*You* have the house," Gemma pointed out, looking straight at her.

Meredith thought for a moment. This was why Brian wouldn't talk to her about the house or how he paid for it. This was why the bank didn't know of a mortgage. He told this young, impressionable girl some of his smooth lies and possibly talked her out of a house.

"It was only eighteen thousand dollars," Meredith clarified. "The money in the attic. You couldn't have sold your house for eighteen thousand dollars."

"Brian told me it didn't matter." Gemma's mouth sagged in a pout. "We were getting married. He just needed a deed just in case you ever wanted proof he bought a house. He said there was going to be a lot more money soon anyway."

"You believed him?" Meredith shook her head.

Gemma got up suddenly.

"Maybe he had it coming." Gemma's tone had sharpened. "Boy, he sure had you pegged wrong."

Meredith went to the door, trembling at all the revelations.

"There's no money," she said. "Brian lied to both of us."

Gemma walked to the door and opened it. Meredith was struck again by how young the girl looked. Anger toward Brian welled up in her. What had he told this girl in wooing her? What false promises had he made?

"We were going to get *married.*" Gemma's voice rose back into a whine. "He promised. And this *was* my house. Good luck in it; it's a bad luck house."

She leaned against the doorframe for a moment and then glared at Meredith.

"Everyone around here knows you killed your husband," she spat out, taking a parting shot. "And everyone knows about you and the sheriff. Smart move, I'd say."

Then she was gone.

****

Meredith stood in place, staring at the door for what seemed like an hour. Was the girl telling the truth? Had this really been her house? Had Brian tricked Gemma into signing the house over to him? She had a sick feeling it was all true.

With the door locked, she walked down the hall and looked in on her children. Both were sleeping soundly, undisturbed by the visitor and their conversation. Atticus slept on his back, arms and legs flailed out, his lips moving slightly in his dreams. She reached out and softly touched his head, rolling his silky brown hair between her fingers. Gemma was pregnant and they hadn't talked about that and whose baby it was. *I must be 'dumb as a stump' to think it could be someone else's other than Brian's.*

Meredith went next into Jamie's room and her lips twisted into a smile when she looked down at her daughter. Jamie's legs were tangled in the blankets and her pillow was on the floor. At some point, she had gotten out of bed and changed into one of Brian's t-shirts. Jamie worshipped her father. Meredith's heart tightened. It would kill Jamie to ever find out any of this. *Damn Brian. Damn the girl. Damn it all.* Meredith gently untangled the blankets from Jamie's legs and put the pillow under her head.

Were she and her children in any danger? Would Gemma come back and create trouble for them? And still unanswered was the main question: Who killed Brian? Gemma surely wouldn't have killed him, if she was telling the truth.

Still, Meredith went around the house and shut the curtains, making sure all the windows were closed and locked. She leaned back against the front door. *Everything comes back to me. I just need to accept it already.*

She closed her eyes and wished she could run away from all these troubles. This bad luck house. Her bad luck life. She wanted to take her children some place where they'd be safe, where *she'd* be safe. But where was this safe place? How long would the money in the sock last? How long would her car keep going? The questions kept coming and her heart thudded in her chest.

For the first time, she really wanted to know the truth: Who killed Brian? At first, she wanted nothing more than to run away from it all. *I was just glad he was gone. I was afraid of the sheriff. Then I was afraid it was me. Now I want to know for sure. I can't stand this not knowing.*

Still, an idea came to her. If she told Curtis about Gemma, then suspicion might fall on the girl. Wouldn't a thwarted girlfriend have reason to kill him? Maybe there was a way out of this, after all.

****

One a.m., two a.m., three. She knew sleep wouldn't come. At some point, Jamie came in her room and crawled into bed with her.

"Mommy, I can't sleep." Jamie rubbed her eyes sleepily before promptly falling asleep next to her.

Meredith rose quietly and went to the bathroom, picking up the last and nearly empty bottle of sleeping pills. Brian had kept the supply coming and she'd hoarded the bottles, doling out the pills on her worst nights. *Lately every night has been a 'worst night.'*

She shook the remaining five pills into her palm and clenched them into a fist. Then she dropped them into the toilet, flushed and returned to bed. She settled into her pillow and stared at the ceiling, tracing her life backwards and forwards and then started over again. This couldn't be her life.

Meredith pushed her mind back to her seventeen-year-old self, the one who fell in love with Brian. He had loved her back, too. She was sure of that. When had he stopped loving her, and then, why did he stay?

Brian met Gemma when she was pregnant with Atticus. The girl was only a symptom, though. Meredith knew their marriage had already unraveled, his work trips lasting longer and longer. When she refused to have an abortion, it was the first time she had dared to be openly defiant toward him. That was when his hostility grew and settled into a quiet rage.

She realized now their marriage had disintegrated into rubble, but she had been too tired to notice it then. Fatigue wore down her defenses. All she knew was she needed to keep going. *Life is messy. It's all in how you handle it.* She'd always believed she would handle life better than her mother.

As she looked back now, she knew that hadn't happened.

Chapter 17

Laf ran for his life, his neck full out, stick legs churning, full-grown wings none-the-less flapping uselessly. Behind him was an equally determined four-year-old. Together, they weaved and dodged around the yard as Honey and Meredith sat on Honey's back porch sipping iced tea.

"Gemma?" Honey repeated back to Meredith. "I don't think so. Do you have a last name?"

Meredith shook her head. She had lied, telling Honey she'd found a letter stuck in the floorboards signed 'Gemma.'

"Just curious, that's all." Meredith looked down at her tea and took a sip. "Who lived in the house before us?"

Honey gave her a long look, hesitated, and then sighed.

"I was waiting for you to ask. Remember the old guy I mentioned, Shorty Harris? Who beat his wife up and then set the house on fire?"

Meredith's jaw dropped.

Honey nodded.

"You told me the house burned down," Meredith protested, thinking back.

"Did I?" Honey frowned. "It's the way we all remember it now. But I guess it didn't burn down because there it is. It was pretty terrible at the time, just awful. But Shorty didn't go back to the house again. It's been empty ever since. I sort of remember it as being gone. That was all so long ago; now it's just a story people tell. And you know how stories grow over time."

Meredith shook her head. It didn't surprise her that Gemma lied about the house being hers. The girl was full of lies; about Brian, about the house, about being owed money. None of it was any worse than living in a house where an attempted murder had taken place, where a husband beat his wife and then tried to kill her. She recalled the burn marks on her bedroom's wood floor and the faint smell of smoke she had noticed when they first moved in. *I sleep in that room.*

A panic of wings beat the air as Laf ran straight across the grass in front of them with Jamie close behind.

"No one wanted to say anything to you, either," Honey continued in a soothing tone. "They thought maybe outsiders, people who didn't know the story, were the only people who would live there afterward. You've been good to the place. Making it a home again."

Meredith was outraged.

"*Two murders*!" she exclaimed. "To people living in the same house."

"Shorty never actually killed his wife," Honey corrected her, then added sympathetically, "It makes you almost believe in curses, doesn't it?"

Meredith's mind was working. If Gemma had lied about the house being hers, she probably also lied about everything else. It seemed so obvious now that Gemma had killed Brian; she killed him because he'd lied to her, because she found out she was pregnant and realized he wasn't going to follow through on his promises.

The afternoon air was still and the damp scent of sugar beets growing on neighboring farms hung in the air.

"Honey," she started, ready to tell her friend about her visitor the night before.

Honey continued to talk in a soothing voice. "That stupid old man served some time and now he's working on drinking himself to death. People want to put all those bad memories behind them. They're all talked out about those times," she said, her tone speaking a warning. "I'd leave that story alone if I were you. No Gemma out here either, sweetie."

"But Honey…"

A squawk from Laf and squeal from Jamie made them both look up. Jamie had pinned the chicken to the ground with her entire body, her arms wrapped around the bird. Laf's one free wing flapped against Jamie's face.

"I swear, that chicken's gonna be dinner before its time." Raising her voice, she called out to Jamie, "Don't squeeze the eggs out of her, Jamie, or they'll come out scrambled!"

"Mommy, look at me! Look at me!" Jamie called, trying to struggle to her feet. "I caught him."

Meredith looked up. The bird was half Jamie's size and putting up a valiant fight.

"I'd better rescue Laf from that amazon you're raising." Honey rose and stepped down off the porch onto the lawn below.

"Honey," Meredith tried again. "I need to tell you

something."

Honey looked back at her with a frown.

"Not another word out of you," she said sharply. "Leave it be."

Meredith watched as Honey knelt down next to Jamie and spoke to her. Whatever she said worked its magic and Jamie opened her arms to release the terrorized bird. It ran quickly away and flew over the fence toward the barn and its nest. Honey and Jamie stayed in place talking for a moment and then they rose together and walked toward Meredith.

"We're going to go out front and see if we can find some magic four-leaf clovers," Honey called. "You just relax for a bit. You're off duty, Momma."

This is the moment. No more just thinking about whether I run or stay. This is when I make the decision.

She took a deep breath.

I'm getting out of this awful place right now. I'm going back where people don't care enough to lie to me. I'm going back to neighborhood cafes and cable TV and car horns at night. I'm going back to places where people don't know every move I make. I'm going back to where I don't have a history, where my children won't have a history, where the past doesn't matter.

She didn't move. Months ago, she found the silence of Hay City oppressive. Now, she was attuned to the low buzzing of insects, the distant clucking of hens and the faint rustling of trees. She listened closely to the country melody, an ache in her chest.

If I run, I run forever. What kind of life is that for my kids?

She rose and went around to the front of the house where Honey was helping Jamie search for magic in the grass.

****

Curtis lived in a tidy one-bedroom house he built with his father on the family's twenty-five-acre property. It sat about a hundred yards from the sprawling well-kept main house surrounded by a line of soaring tamarack pines. The two homes shared a drive, and as Meredith passed the main house, she hoped no one was witnessing her visit, but she was doubtful. In Hay City, someone was always watching.

Honey initially tried to talk her out of going.

"You're having a tough day. Why don't I make us all a nice lunch? You can take it easy here."

"I need to talk to Curtis." Meredith was determined to tell him about Gemma and the affair her husband had conducted with a girl barely out of high school. "I can take the kids with me if you can't watch them."

She watched irritation flicker across the older woman's face. Meredith knew not many people would disagree with Honey. She had a force of will that pulled you along regardless of what you really wanted.

Honey's face settled into a scowl and Meredith knew she was risking their friendship. But she also knew if she didn't talk to Curtis right away, she'd change her mind again.

"I *have* to talk to him," Meredith repeated.

"Go on then, if it's what you have to do," Honey said. "I'll keep your kids. But you're making a mistake if you dredge up these old stories with him. They're nothing to do with anything. Just gossip."

Meredith knew this was probably true, but she needed to tell Curtis about Gemma. As she drove to his house, a deep-rooted instinct told her trusting Curtis was the wrong thing to do. Trusting Brian had led her into a world of trouble. Here she was, trusting another man, this time the sheriff. Yet, if she wasn't going to run, she needed to find out who really killed Brian. It was the only way she would be able to stay and make a home for her children.

What was it that had happened between Brian and this girl? Meredith wondered. Was she truly the link to his murder or had it merely been a random act along the highway? But why did Brian have his handgun with him? There were so many questions still unanswered and Gemma could be the key.

There was the risk Curtis would eventually arrest her, no matter what she told him. *I bet he doesn't trust me, either. So we're even.*

No one was in the office, just a sign saying the sheriff would be in late. She didn't let herself hesitate before driving north into the empty country landscape. His truck sat in front of the tiny square of a house. Meredith took a deep breath as she opened her car door and stepped out onto the gravel drive. The heavy scent of pine was thick in the air and she stood for a moment breathing in the heady aroma. *How wonderful*, she thought, *to walk out your door every day and breathe in this clean purifying scent.*

A small porch, large enough to hold one chair, fronted the house. Meredith stepped up to the door, swallowed, and knocked firmly. She wiped her palms on her jeans, waited, and then knocked again even louder.

This is a mistake. I shouldn't be here. I should take what money is left and go as far away as I can.

The door swung open and Curtis stood there,

wearing nothing but pajama bottoms. He looked at her in surprise. Despite her worries, she took in his taut stomach and broad chest. She swallowed again.

"Is everything okay?" he asked quickly.

"I didn't know I'd wake you up. I need to talk to you."

He yawned and stretched.

"Long night." He rubbed his eyes. "There was a fight down at Crusty's bar after closing. What time is it?"

Meredith checked her watch. "Almost noon. Sorry."

Curtis shook his head.

"I slept too late anyway," he said. "Everything okay?"

Meredith glanced over toward the main house, feeling conspicuous. She shifted on her feet and wished Curtis would invite her inside. The sensation of being watched was oppressive.

"Something's happened. I need to tell you some things."

He nodded briefly.

"Give me a minute and I'll be right out." He shut the door.

Meredith backed away. She turned around toward the main house and this time noticed the tire swing hanging from a tree. She felt a twang of longing for the life the swing symbolized. Movement caught her eye and she watched as an older woman came out the back door of the main house and walked across the lawn into a gated garden, disappearing into the foliage. The woman didn't look her way, but Meredith was certain she knew Curtis had a visitor.

The door opened behind her and Curtis walked out, looking as though he had hurriedly dressed with whatever he grabbed first. The faded red t-shirt had a rip under one arm and looked as though he pulled it directly out of the laundry basket. Blue jeans, flip-flops, and a baseball cap completed the outfit.

"There's a bench out back." He gestured for her to follow.

She glanced back toward the garden behind the bigger house. Curtis's family would be appalled she was there, a likely murderess at their son's doorstep.

"Okay." Curtis sat down and slapped his hands on his thighs for emphasis. Then he waited for Meredith to speak.

"Brian was having an affair," she said. "I think she killed him."

"I know about the affair," he shot back. "I'm looking for her."

"You *knew*?" Meredith asked, her voice filled with surprise. "You *knew* he was having an affair and didn't tell me?"

"I'm trying to find the person who murdered a man in *my* county, close to where *my family* lives." Anger laced his tone. "I keep wondering why you aren't nearly as interested. It occurs to me you've known all this from the start."

She swallowed hard.

"I don't know," she said. "I mean I do know but…"

Tears of frustration came to her eyes. She couldn't explain the range of emotions seizing hold of her every day, from depression to anger to fear. Even joy, if she was being honest with herself.

He waited for her to finish.

"She's pregnant," Meredith spat out.

Curtis looked confused. "Who?"

"The girl…the girl Brian was having an affair with."

"Wait," he said, standing up. "You know her?"

"No. Yes. I mean, she came to my house last night. I hadn't met her before, but she came to the house and wanted some money Brian had promised her. Brian lied to her, too."

Curtis held up a hand to stop her. "Who is she? I've been looking for her. What's her name?"

"Gemma. She didn't say a last name. She told me it was her house though, that she and Brian had some kind of deal—"

"Gemma," Curtis sputtered, breaking in. "Gemma!"

Meredith stopped.

"You know her? You know a Gemma?"

He looked at her, a puzzled look on his face, cocking his head slightly.

"I know a Gemma." He spoke slowly. "I know a Gemma connected to your house."

"That's the one then!" she cried. "That's her. The girl Brian was having an affair with."

Curtis didn't say anything for a moment and Meredith began to worry. What did he know about Gemma?

"And Honey. She knows? You talked about this with her?"

"Honey?" Meredith asked, confused about where this was going. "I asked if she knew a Gemma, but she said 'no.'"

Curtis chewed his lip, nodding slightly to himself. Meredith wanted to shake him.

"What does any of this have to do with Honey?" she demanded.

His face took on a grim look. "Hopefully nothing. Are your kids with Honey right now?"

Meredith felt a chill. "Yes. But, tell me, what does that have to do with Gemma?"

"Honey owned your house before. I assumed you knew about what happened. And Gemma, she's Honey's granddaughter."

Meredith's vision blurred and her head spun. She shook her head.

"No," she said weakly. "Honey told me she didn't know a Gemma. Why would she say that?"

"Your kids. Where are they?"

Meredith gasped.

"Honey has them." She turned and ran for her car.

"Meredith! Wait!"

She pulled open the door, fumbling with the keys. *Honey*, she thought. She must have known about Brian and Gemma. She must have known everything. She must have stayed close to me to know what Curtis knew. And under all that pulsed the fear: *my kids, my kids, my kids.*

Curtis grabbed her arm, pulling her back sharply. She pulled away, slapping at him in a panic.

"I have to go. *Now*! Honey has Jamie and Atticus. She knows I'm telling you about Gemma and the house."

Curtis shook her slightly.

"Listen to me," he said. "I don't know what all happened, but Honey's been using you. You can't just go charging in there, not like this."

Tears ran down her face.

"My kids," she pleaded.

His face tightened and he looked down the long driveway.

"We'll go together. But you'll let me talk. We'll take it slow."

She nodded quickly. *Anything. Anything so I can go, now.*

"Now," she begged. "Can we go now? Please."

He nodded and put his hand out for the keys. She reluctantly dropped them in his open palm, her hand shaking.

"Give me a minute. Let me get my gun."

****

The five-minute drive to Honey's house took forever. They drove in silence as Meredith berated herself for not suspecting any trace of the truth before. It was Honey who showed up at her house the day after Brian's murder, offering consolation and an ear. Honey had been the one she turned to for comfort, the person she sought out when she wanted to escape the weight of the investigation. Instead, Honey must have been using her to keep tabs on the investigation, protecting Gemma.

It was clear when they rolled up to the house that Honey was gone, her large SUV no longer parked in the drive. They got out of Curtis's truck anyway.

"Jamie!" Meredith called, hysteria rising in her voice. "Atticus! Time to go home!"

She pounded on the door to the house and then ran around to the back, her eyes darting around the yard. Curtis went in the chicken barn, quickly coming back out and shaking his head.

"Where did she go? Where did she take them?" Meredith's voice rose higher and higher. She turned on Curtis. "Why didn't you tell me I lived in her old house?"

Curtis stood helplessly, his shoulders sagging.

"I assumed you knew, that it was why you became friends so quickly." Then, she saw the dawning of an idea strike him.

"Her house. I bet she went to her old house. Your house."

They sped back to the truck, the trip to Meredith's house taking just a few minutes. They were a half-mile away when Meredith spotted the red SUV in her own driveway.

"She's here," she cried out in relief. "She brought my kids home."

Curtis stopped the truck and she whirled on him immediately.

"What are you doing?"

"Listen to me. You didn't know this was Honey's old house? You didn't know what happened here?"

Meredith's mind raced, wanting to answer his question, anything to get him to move his truck forward.

"Shorty Harris?" she asked. "That story?"

He nodded.

"Honey's first husband, Shorty, our local drunk and self-declared minister. He tried to kill her here. She was pregnant."

Her eyes widened. She realized she'd run into Shorty several times, even visiting his house near the supermarket.

"The old man? The drunk?"

She tried to comprehend Honey and Shorty together all those years ago, and couldn't.

"Shorty went to rehab, but Honey never lived in the house again," Curtis explained. "Their daughter later had Gemma."

Curtis looked down the road to Meredith's house. Meredith followed his eyes, searching for movement across the distance.

"I don't understand," she said.

"I'm worried she never told you any of this," he said. "I'm worried that her granddaughter was having an affair with your husband. Your *abusive* husband."

She looked quickly over at him as he made that last point, understanding dawning on her.

"You don't think it was Gemma." She spoke slowly. "You think Honey killed him to protect Gemma. You think Honey killed him because she was afraid for Gemma."

Curtis looked grimly down the road.

"I'm not saying anything." But there was doubt in his voice and a sob escaped her throat. "I want to know why she's been lying to you all this time."

He turned to Meredith. Tears flowed freely down her face. She had trusted Honey and been grateful for her friendship.

"She wouldn't hurt your kids," he said.

Meredith wiped her tears away and looked out toward her house.

"I won't let her," she vowed.

Chapter 18

Curtis opened the front door to Meredith's house carefully. Meredith stood just behind him, heart jumping in her chest. It seemed he moved too slowly, when all she wanted to do was rush inside to find Jamie and Atticus.

"The sheriff is here!"

Meredith heard Jamie's gleeful shout and tears of relief filled her eyes. *Safe, safe, safe*. Meredith pushed past Curtis now, rushing inside and then stopping suddenly. The living room was a tunnel of blankets and sheets, stretched from couch to chair to table. Jamie's head popped out of one end of the tunnel and Atticus's laughter bubbled up from inside the crawl space. The tunnel bulged in the middle and it lifted, making one of the blankets fall. Honey pulled the blanket off her head and looked up at them. Atticus crawled out the other end of the tunnel and, with a giggle, turned around and crawled back in.

"I had my old key," Honey said. "I hope you don't mind."

Meredith stared at her stone-faced.

"Your old key," Curtis pointed out. "To your old house."

Honey looked over at Meredith and shrugged, a sheepish look on her face.

"I guessed all my secrets would be out now," she

said. "So no reason I couldn't just bring your kids home for you, make it easier."

Meredith still couldn't trust herself to speak. She wanted Curtis to put handcuffs on Honey and haul her away. Instead, he just stood there, hands far from his gun, not making any move at all.

"Help me up now, would you?" Honey asked, putting up a hand.

Meredith didn't move. Curtis stepped forward and gave a heave and then another before Honey rose to her feet with a grunt and a laugh.

"Crawling around is the easy part, getting up is a challenge." She brushed at her knees.

"Why don't the three of us go outside while Jamie and Atticus play?" Curtis suggested.

Honey sighed heavily. She glanced over at Meredith and then back at Curtis. Meredith took one more relieved look toward the waving tunnel of blankets, hearing her kids laughing inside. Then the three adults walked out to the driveway.

"You....you lied to me!" Meredith spat out as soon as they were out of earshot of the children. "You lied about everything. My house, Gemma, Shorty!"

She couldn't bring herself to say the worst of it, that Honey killed Brian. Looking at the older woman, the person who talked about slow cookers and raised baby chicks, she couldn't picture her holding a gun and shooting someone in cold blood.

"I started to, a couple of times." Honey's tone sounded sincere and artless, but Meredith watched her with skepticism. "I told you about Shorty weeks ago, but I just couldn't say it all. I almost told you today, when you brought it up again, but those memories are bad ones. They're best left in the past."

Meredith snorted in disbelief.

"I'm not the only one who doesn't want to talk about being hit, being hurt by a husband," Honey added pointedly.

Meredith stepped forward and Curtis grabbed her arm.

"Hold on, there," he said.

"Why aren't you arresting her?" Meredith asked, turning on him.

"Arrest me?" Honey asked, eyes widening, her tone innocent. "For what? Lying?"

Curtis was frowning, looking steadily at Honey.

"We need to talk about Gemma," he said. "I need to know where she is."

Honey sighed heavily and shrugged. "She comes and goes. Her mother has never been able to control that girl." Honey glanced at Meredith. "She got a good job and then got mixed up with the wrong guy…"

"My husband," Meredith burst in.

"…and quit. Gemma told her mother this guy was the one, he wanted to marry her, but she never told us he was so much older, already married, with kids. Then Gemma shows up one day with bruises on her arms, crying…" Honey broke off and shook her head.

"You killed Brian," Meredith accused.

"What foolishness…" Honey sputtered.

"Okay, okay," Curtis broke in, his voice cool. "Let's not do any accusing here. Honey, I need you to think where Gemma might have gone. I just need to talk to her. I'm going to need a statement from you, too, about where you were on the night of the murder."

Honey's lips tightened. She looked at Meredith.

"You're being ridiculous. I'm your friend." Honey insisted, but Meredith looked away. "You don't believe me, I know. But I haven't done anything wrong. And I never killed anybody."

Meredith shook her head.

"I'll get your car keys." Meredith turned away as she spoke. "I don't want you near my kids anymore."

"Meredith." Curtis stopped her. "I'll be back later, so we can go back to my house and get your car."

****

The sun had dipped below the mountaintops and the valley was in shadow by the time Curtis returned. He told her briefly about Honey's statement, which didn't offer much more than she already heard. Honey claimed she had seen Gemma only once since Brian's murder, the girl showing up to ask for money.

"Honey gave the house to Gemma's mother years ago, hoping the two of them would move closer," Curtis explained. "It turned out Gemma's mother didn't want it either, so she passed it along to Gemma. That part of the story checks out."

"Great," Meredith mumbled.

Jamie whooped with joy when she learned they would get to ride in the sheriff's truck and visit his house. Meredith was glad to use her kids as a buffer so she wouldn't have to talk to Curtis during the drive to retrieve her car. All the anxiety and pain of the past weeks had rolled up in her and focused on Gemma and Honey. It was so obvious to her that Honey was involved in Brian's murder and it infuriated her Curtis wasn't doing anything about it. Her anger far outweighed her relief at having the investigation focused on someone else.

"Can you hang on a moment?" he asked when they arrived at his house.

Jamie ran straight off to the tire swing at the main house and Atticus slowly toddled after her. Meredith leaned against his truck, the warmth of the day radiating out from it.

"There were three sets of prints on the gun," Curtis said, not hesitating. "Brian's, your's and…" he trailed off.

"Whose?" she demanded.

He shook his head.

"They were partials. But…I think…I think they belong to the person who killed your husband."

Meredith gaped at him, stunned. Then fury set in.

"You let me think… Why didn't you… I can't believe…" she sputtered.

"It didn't necessarily mean anything at first," he explained. "But the longer you stayed here, the more I've thought about those other prints. If you killed him, you wouldn't have stayed. You knew the evidence was stacking up against you and you didn't run. "

"Why didn't you arrest her?" Meredith asked. "Honey admitted she lied about everything. She's been lying all along."

Curtis shook his head.

"Lying's one thing, murder's another," he said. "I don't think I have the whole truth out of her yet. And no evidence to say she held the gun either."

Meredith's heart sank. Why couldn't Curtis do his job and find the murderer? Immediately, guilt overwhelmed her. Curtis *was* trying to help. And Honey was loud, manipulative, and bossy, but could she commit murder?

"Gemma, then," she decided. "Make Honey tell you where she is."

"She claims she doesn't know where the girl is, but she's got to be somewhere close. I'll find her."

He paused. "Brian wasn't very popular around here. It appears a few people had reason to dislike him."

"More than just me, you mean." Her tone was bitter.

Across the yard, Meredith watched as the same woman she saw earlier in the day come out the back door of the main house and talk to Jamie. The woman turned to Curtis and gave a wave before pushing Jamie on the swing. Tears came to Meredith's eyes. She knew her daughter still didn't understand her father was gone forever, that death was forever. *It doesn't seem real to me, either. It's like a bad dream that goes on and on.*

The last glow of the long twilight had dimmed away and a huge moon hung over the mountain in the east. Curtis leaned his back against the truck door, both of them watching the kids play in the moonlight. Meredith thought about the difference between her house where so much turmoil had happened and this peaceful home.

"Have you ever considered living somewhere else?" Meredith asked quietly.

"Sure," he answered, "but it didn't last long. This is where I want to be."

"It must be nice knowing that, knowing where you belong, I mean."

He folded his arms and his expression was serious. "I'm lucky."

Meredith knew she should take her kids home, give them baths, and put their pajamas on. A riot of crickets and grass frogs belted out the asynchronous melody she'd come to love.

"I never could have killed him," she said, gazing at her children.

"Wishing isn't doing." Curtis's voice was gentle. "Otherwise, there'd be a lot more dead people around this county. Other places, too."

Meredith sighed. That's exactly how it was. *I wished it, because wishing is safe. Doing is another thing.*

"My third grade teacher," Curtis added seriously. "She kept me in from recess because I was talking in class. I'm sure I wished some terrible things on her."

Her temper flared for a moment at the comparison before she realized he was trying to create a light moment for her.

"My dad," she stated. "For never showing up."

"My sister, a couple of times while we were growing up. Not dead, but I'm sure I wished her a disfiguring disease or something."

Meredith gave a weak smile. "Is she okay?"

"Never better."

They watched the stars appear one by one.

"Wishing isn't doing, but I still feel so guilty." Tears pricked at her eyes.

"I know," he said softly.

"Please find who did this," Meredith burst out, surprising even herself with the emotion in her voice.

Curtis nodded firmly. "I'll find them."

They stood there another moment and then she went to get her children. Meredith felt him watching her all the way across the grass.

****

After the long day was over and she was in bed, it finally struck her with certainty that she hadn't killed Brian. Her strange dreams didn't mean she had driven out late at night, waited for him, and then shot him when he pulled over. They were just dreams prompted by stress, anxiety and fear.

I'll never take sleeping pills again, she swore to herself. *They made me doubt myself and doubt reality. I almost believed I committed murder.*

****

She decided to go looking for Gemma the next day. The girl had to be somewhere close, Meredith reasoned, if Brian wanted to be here. She considered her rundown car and then counted out the money she had left.

Gemma better be really close, she thought, realizing she couldn't afford car repairs. *I need a job*, but she pushed those worries away for later. *After this is over.*

With no one to watch her children, Meredith loaded them in her car. She packed coloring books, storybooks on tape, a stroller, diaper bag, toys, and snacks, hoping Jamie and Atticus would have the patience for the trip. In her pocket, she put the picture of Gemma and Brian and then headed to Blissful.

The small frontier town had a series of early twentieth century bungalows perfectly fitting the age and look of the house in the photo. A shiver of apprehension went through Meredith as they drove slowly by. None matched the picture and she drove on to Malady, a larger town twenty miles farther down the highway.

Malady was appropriately named, with a closed gas station next to a bullet-ridden sign proclaiming

*"Welcome to Malady!
Home of good, plain folk."*

Farther on was a short main street that had boarded-up buildings with an ice cream shop, a bookstore, and a grocery store in between. Meredith circled around, passing a couple small neighborhoods, before returning to the main street.

"Let's get some ice cream," she announced, deciding to give her kids a break from the driving. She'd told Jamie that morning they were going exploring for the day, but knew her children could only be cooped up in the car only so long before they rebelled.

"We haven't had lunch yet," Jamie said, eyeing her with suspicion.

Meredith shrugged.

"It's our lucky day." She parked near the shop.

"Woody's," a boy behind the counter called out cheerfully as they entered. The sweet smell of rich cream struck Meredith immediately and her taste buds awoke.

"Always a good day for ice cream," the boy chirped.

Jamie ran to the counter and pushed her nose against the glass looking at flavors.

"I want the green one and the red one," she ordered firmly, looking at the boy.

"One Christmas special coming right up," he sang out. "Cone or cup?"

Jamie looked over at Meredith.

"Do you want it in a cone, sweetie, or do you want to eat it with a spoon?" Meredith prompted.

"Cone, cone, cone!" Jamie chanted.

"Roger that." The boy grabbed a cone with a nod and a smile. "Anything for the little guy?"

Meredith mentally calculated the money in her wallet. "Scoop of vanilla for him in a cup. Just water for me."

He pointed over at a carafe and cups. "Help yourself."

Once Meredith got Jamie and Atticus settled with their ice creams, she poured herself water and gratefully drank it down. She fingered the picture in her pocket and wondered whether she should show it to the helpful boy behind the counter. Meredith glanced over at her kids focused on their ice cream and then hesitantly back at the boy. What if he knew Gemma and told the girl someone was looking for her?

"Can I help you with something else?" the boy asked, noticing how she lingered near one edge of the counter.

Meredith made a decision. She walked back to him and pulled out the photo and handed it over.

"I'm looking for this girl. Or the house. Either one," she stammered, wishing she sounded more confident. She watched him study the picture.

He handed it back and shook his head.

"She's pretty. Your sister?"

Meredith cringed and shook her head quickly.

"No, no. Just a friend I'm trying to find. I think she came to Idaho."

"The house looks like it could be around here somewhere," he added. "There're a lot of houses like that, though."

She nodded and turned back to her kids, seeing their faces fully engaged in the ice cream. Meredith hurried over with a handful of napkins. She wiped at their faces while Jamie squirmed away.

"Can I look at the picture?" Jamie asked to Meredith's horror.

There was no way she could let Jamie see the picture of Brian with his arm around Gemma. She should have known her sharp-eyed daughter didn't miss much.

"It's a picture for grownups," Meredith said. "Let's go."

"Why is it just for grownups?"

"It just is," Meredith blustered.

"Good luck finding your friend," the overly cheerful boy called out as they left the shop.

Outside, Meredith looked left and right, trying to decide if it was worth asking around about Gemma. A woman walked down the block toward them and Meredith bit her lip, wondering what she should do.

"Do you want to look at the picture my mom has in her pocket? It's just for grownups so I'm not allowed to see it."

Meredith looked down, horrified at the question Jamie was asking the woman. She grabbed Jamie's hand and tugged them quickly away.

The woman gave them a strange look. Meredith smiled weakly at her and quickly walked on, half dragging Jamie along.

"Don't you want to show the picture to the lady, too?" Jamie asked.

"No, I don't. Let me ask people about this."

Jamie's mouth turned down and Meredith worried that a tantrum was pending. The day was warming quickly and Jamie needed more to do than drive around with occasional stops.

"Tell you what. Next time I want someone to look at the picture, I'll let you ask, okay?"

Jamie's face brightened and she nodded, content. Meredith shifted Atticus higher in her arms.

"How about you ask them like this: Can my mom show you a picture?" Meredith coached. "Just like that, okay? Nothing else."

Jamie nodded again. They walked down the block, passing an antique store Meredith had no intention of taking her high-energy daughter into, and then entered a bookstore. It was in an old, yellow Victorian style house and the cool interior was another welcome relief from the heat. The rough wood floor creaked as they stepped past the front counter heaped with piles of books. Meredith led Jamie to the children's section and had her sit on the floor with Atticus and a couple of beginning reader books.

Jamie turned her face up to Meredith.

"Don't ask about the picture," she demanded. "You told me I could ask."

Meredith nodded distractedly and looked around what appeared like an empty store.

"Stay here a couple of minutes. I'm going to find a book."

Jamie nodded and Meredith looked at her firmly.

"Don't go anywhere," she ordered. "I'll be right back."

Jamie's face was already turned to the books on her lap, Atticus sitting contentedly next to her. Meredith stood there a moment and then headed back to the counter to look for the clerk, or anyone at all to ask quietly about the house, or the girl, in the picture. A creak of floorboards above her made her realize there was someone upstairs. A small sign at the bottom of the narrow steep stairway announced:

"*More to read up here*"

She glanced quickly in her children's direction before heading up.

At the top was a small room, where a group of six women sat in a circle knitting quietly, their eyes focused on the work in their laps. Meredith quickly scanned the group, trying to assess who was in charge or at least who might be the friendliest. Hay City had taught her to be careful between friends and foes. The ladies appeared to range from their late fifties to one well into her eighties, and had well-worn looks. None of them glanced up, even though Meredith was sure they knew she was there.

She took a tentative step forward, hesitant about interrupting, hoping one of the ladies would speak to her first. One of the women, painfully thin and wearing heavy makeup, sighed heavily and glanced over at another woman who sported a tall beehive hairdo. The sigh couldn't have been more clear in its meaning. It meant, "Do something."

I don't care if I'm intruding. I need answers.

She cleared her throat softly and beehive looked around her circle before peering up at Meredith and putting on a welcoming smile.

"I'm looking for someone." Meredith slid the picture out of her pocket. "Could you please take a look?"

"Who's lost, honey?" beehive asked in a friendly voice, reaching out her hand and taking the photo.

The other women looked up at Meredith now,

clearly intrigued by a mystery involving a missing person.

"A…um…friend of mine," stuttered Meredith, stumbling over the word "friend." "The woman there in the picture. Or if you recognize the house, that would help, too."

Beehive passed the photo to the woman next to her while the rest of the group shook their heads and tsked in unison over the lost friend.

"What a nice couple." The second woman stared down at the image before passing the photo on. "He must be sad to lose her."

Meredith gulped and nodded silently.

The next two women shook their heads silently.

"Looks familiar," the second-to-last woman said, the oldest of the group, her deeply wrinkled face bent close to the photo.

"Oh, you don't know anything," the last woman in the circle complained, trying to snatch the photo from her.

"I do so," the older woman protested, holding tight to the picture and pulling it out of reach. "I've seen *him* somewhere. He's a good-looking young man and I'm sure I've seen him."

"She's not looking for *him*," beehive corrected. "She's looking for the woman."

"Where did you see him?" Meredith broke in, her voice cracking.

All six women turned to look at her, took in Meredith's stricken face, and then they exchanged knowing glances at one another.

"It could have been at the grocery store on the corner," the wrinkled woman mused. She sat up in her seat, happy to be the center of attention. "Memory tells me he was buying apples. I'm pretty sure it was apples. Could have been the co-op but I don't go there much anymore."

"Olive, you're wasting this young woman's time and getting her hopes up," beehive chided.

Olive's chin jutted out.

"I saw him," she insisted, her voice indignant. "I just don't know where."

"Here in Malady then?" Meredith prompted. "Was he with anyone?"

"Would have been Malady since I don't go too far anymore," Olive said. "My eyesight isn't what it used to be, so I don't go out much."

"If you can't see, then how do you know it was him?" the woman next to her challenged. "I'm telling you, you don't know anything."

Olive shot her a mean look.

Meredith's hopes wilted. She held out her hand to take back the picture.

"Thank you anyway."

"Sorry." Beehive's face looked truly apologetic that her group couldn't help.

"I guess it could have been onions, not apples," Olive continued, holding out the photo, "but for some reason I'm recalling they were apples."

"Well, I haven't looked at it yet," the last woman in the circle complained. "I can at least look at it."

Olive reluctantly handed it over and the last woman studied it, her expression serious.

"Hmmm," she murmured, scratching inside her ear as she looked at the photo. "Sure it's not Blissful? Looks a lot like Blissful homes."

Meredith shook her head and took the picture back, returning it to her pocket.

"I'll try over there," she promised. "Thank you all for your help. Sorry for interrupting."

"No problem," beehive said. "Hope you find what you're looking for."

"It might have been last year," Olive offered helpfully. "I hope it wasn't at the co-op, though. Their prices are terrible."

Meredith backed away toward the stairs, nodding. *This is ridiculous, thinking I could find Gemma like this. That girl must be long gone.*

"I hope it doesn't have anything to do with the murder over in Hay City," she overheard one of the women say as she walked down the stairs. "That girl could have been *murdered*."

"Oh hush up, Olive," another voice chided. "She'll hear you."

"Don't you hush me," Olive complained. "You never let me talk."

Meredith paused on the bottom step, leaning against the railing. She felt useless, waiting for Curtis to arrest someone. Wasn't there anything she could do?

****

The drive back home was quiet, with all three of them eating peanut butter and jelly sandwiches. Halfway home, Meredith pulled the car to the side of the road to wipe her children's hands of the sticky jelly and dig out the drinks she had packed. She put the car into drive and then back into park, settling back in her seat. She stared sightlessly at the fields by the side of the road.

Had Gemma really been the one to kill Brian? As

much as she disliked her, Meredith couldn't imagine the young girl as a killer. *Don't be silly. You don't have to look like a monster to be a murderer.* It could just as likely be Honey, no matter what Curtis said.

She reached down and touched the picture in her pocket, with Brian, his arm possessively around Gemma, pulling her close against him. Those weeks and weeks he had been away on his sales trips, this was where he stayed. Had he thought about his wife and children at all? Or didn't they exist in his mind when he drove away from the apartment in Oakland or the house in Hay City?

"Why are we stopping?" Jamie asked.

"Mommy's thinking."

"About what?"

"Daddy," Meredith whispered.

Jamie peered at Meredith, her four-year-old face serious.

"Do you miss Daddy?"

Meredith nodded automatically. *I wished he were dead. He was planning to kill me and he would have done it. I sensed it every time he walked by.* Her heart broke for her daughter. What terrible parents she'd been born to.

"I miss him, too," Jamie said sadly, reaching a hand out to touch Meredith's shoulder. "I wish he didn't die."

Startled, Meredith looked over at her daughter, touched at her caring and grief.

"We're going to get through this," she promised. "We're going to be okay."

Meredith knew she was making a promise she didn't know whether she could keep. She remembered

Brian's first promise to their children, before either one was born.

"Our children won't know what being poor is like," he told her, holding her close one night. Jamie had been still tucked snugly inside her womb and Brian's hand gently stroked her growing belly. "I'll send them to the best schools and their friends will come from rich families. They'll live in a different world than us."

Meredith had listened to that and felt secure in Brian's plans for their future. He was so passionate about his plans, so confident and driven. Here was a man who would never let her slip through the cracks of society again. She clung to him and believed.

That was only five years ago, she realized now.

"Can we go home?" Jamie asked, dragging her out of her memories.

Meredith nodded and pulled back onto the two-lane highway. If it took everything she had, she would give her children a home.

Chapter 19

"Sheriff." She stood in the doorway of the office. It was a two-room building consisting mainly of one large room divided by a long reception counter. Curtis stood with his back to her at one of the cluttered oak desks behind the counter.

Curtis turned at Meredith's voice and his eyes brightened. There was that smile, those shoulders, those large strong hands. Something in her stomach flip-flopped.

In his hands was a hefty stack of mail. He noticed her looking at it.

"City clerk is off today with sick kids," he explained with a shrug. "I'm opening and sorting mail for city employees."

Meredith gave a short laugh. "You're doing mailroom duty?"

"Everybody pitches in here. I really should sweep the floors too before I lock up later."

Meredith looked around the office, taking in the three cluttered desks, apparently belonging to Curtis and the absent city clerk, the lines of mismatched file cabinets against the walls, and the dusty crowded bookcase climbing to the ceiling. She wondered whom the third desk belonged to and where they were.

"City clerk's assistant," Curtis said, following her gaze. "We haven't had one in two years. Budget cuts."

Meredith had dropped Jamie and Atticus off with the coroner's wife, the one who ran a day care in her home. There was no way she would go near Honey now, not after everything that had happened. The coroner's wife was more than happy to help and there were three other children there to keep her kids busy.

"Where's the broom?" Meredith asked.

Curtis looked at her approvingly and nodded toward a closet in the corner. She dug out the broom and a dustpan and started sweeping slowly, glancing over at Curtis from time to time. She wanted to ask him what he was doing to find Gemma, wanted to tell him about her own failed search. She needed to ask again about Honey and whether she could be pressured to tell him more about the girl's whereabouts.

For the moment, there was something soothing about being in the same room with him and performing her domestic task. He mostly ignored her as she swept her way across the room, apparently taking it in stride that she would show up for no other reason than to sweep the floor of a city office. Sometimes though, as she glanced over at him, she caught his eye and then they both looked back down and focused again on their tasks.

It didn't take her long to sweep the humble office and as she emptied the dustpan into the garbage can, she bit her lip and readied herself to talk business. It occurred to her he could still be investigating her, waiting for her to say something that would give him a final reason to arrest her.

Trust him.

"Sometimes I mop the floor, too." Curtis didn't look up. "Gives it a nice shine."

Meredith looked at him sharply to see if he was kidding but Curtis just continued writing notes in a file. She sighed and returned to the closet to find the mop and a bucket.

"Water?" she asked.

"There's a hose around the back."

Maybe the building needs painting, too, she wondered as she walked around the back of the building with the bucket. *Or the plumbing needs adjustments? Maybe a new roof while I'm at it?* But she filled the bucket with water and obediently slid the mop around the floor, rinsing out black water into the bucket. She dumped the dirty water twice behind the building, refilled the bucket with clean water and returned to finish the job.

"How did this floor get so filthy?" she asked.

"I doubt it's been mopped in months," Curtis said with a smile, now watching her openly.

A muscle twitched in Meredith's jaw.

"You told me you mop the floor sometimes," she said indignantly.

"I guess I did once, years ago, when I was in high school and my mom sent me down here." He was looking at her with a mischievous grin. "Who knows if anyone's cleaned it since."

She glared at him a moment but couldn't resist his smile. Her annoyance faded and she smiled back.

His expression turned serious and he leaned back in his chair. "I'm guessing this isn't just a casual visit."

"I went looking for Gemma yesterday," she revealed.

"Meredith. You need to let me handle this."

She gave a huff at that.

"What are you doing to find her? I drove around, asking people, looking for the house she and Brian were at. What are *you* doing?"

"I have a name and a picture. It's gone out to every sheriff's office in Idaho. If she's still in the state, we'll find her."

Meredith swallowed. *Of course. Of course he's not going to drive around showing her picture to people on the street.*

"What about Honey?" she asked.

"She probably knows more than she's saying," he agreed. "That's her granddaughter. If Gemma's involved in Brian's murder, and Honey knew anything about it, she's going to have to answer for it."

Meredith was at a loss. They were close to having an answer, and the waiting was more frustrating than ever.

"In the meantime, I want you to go home and let me do my job," he said.

Meredith turned to go and then an idea occurred to her.

"Would Shorty know anything? He's Gemma's grandfather, right?"

Curtis snorted.

"Shorty? Gemma wouldn't go near him. You know the family's history now. Far as I know, Honey's never talked to him since he tried to kill her way back when. Can you blame her?"

"I think he knows Gemma's pregnant." Meredith recalled her visit to his house. "He put a play set in his yard."

Curtis stared at her. "You went to his house? You talked to him?"

"Weeks ago. With my kids. I didn't know who he was at the time, but he talked about a pregnant granddaughter."

Curtis stood up.

"I need to pay him a visit and hear what he knows about all this." Curtis grabbed his keys.

"I'm going too," Meredith said immediately.

He shook his head. "Not a chance."

"Who knew about Gemma?" she challenged. "Who told you about Shorty? I'm going."

Without a word, he walked out the door and she followed quickly behind. Curtis locked the door and they stepped briskly across the empty highway, past the grocery store and down two streets to Shorty's house. Again, the neighborhood looked like a ghost town, silent and still.

If possible, the house looked even more dilapidated than before. One roof shingle hung loosely over the door, swinging lightly in the breeze. Meredith stood to one side of the door and looked up at the shingle in concern as Curtis stood below it and knocked. *One good gust of wind, and it's coming down hard.*

"Sheriff Barney," Shorty sneered in greeting when he finally opened the door. A sour smell drifted out the door and Meredith wondered if it was coming off of the old man or from inside the house. "What can I do you for?"

"How're you doing Shorty? Haven't seen you out much lately," Curtis responded.

"The good lord's keeping me close these days," Shorty said. "Got bursitis, bronchitis, arthritis, and, excuse me Missy," he added with a nod toward Meredith, "but a bit of gastritis today."

He cackled at this last bit and then let out a belch. "See what I mean. Coming out from all ends."

Meredith smiled weakly. Curtis ignored the comments.

"Want to come out and chat for a bit?" he asked. "Nothing official, you know."

"I got nothing official to say to you anyway," Shorty retorted sharply. "You got no business here."

Meredith took a half step forward.

"Shorty," she began, again finding it hard to believe he and Honey had once been married. "We just want to ask you about Gemma."

At the mention of Gemma's name, Shorty stepped onto the front step, making Curtis move back. He closed the door behind him.

"Is she here?" he asked, looking around. "I told her enough's enough already. I got no money for her."

"Gemma's not here," Meredith responded quickly, giving Curtis a glance that said *I told you so*. "But she came by my house, your old house. I met her."

Meredith hesitated and then added, "She knew my husband, too."

Shorty waved a hand dismissively at Meredith.

"She has a bit of her grandmother in her. Fly in the Honey, I used to call it." He snorted. "Don't you worry. It all works out in the end."

With that, he stepped off the porch and headed toward the side of the house. Meredith and Curtis looked at each other, puzzled, and then followed. Shorty stumbled once as he rounded the corner of the house and Meredith realized he was drunk. She looked up at Curtis, concerned, but he simply shrugged.

In the back of the house, the play set looked as new

and shiny as ever, in contrast to Shorty's house and the rest of the neighborhood. Meredith saw a rag lying on the slide and it struck her that Shorty kept it polished and clean. The thought, and the hope it represented, depressed her.

Shorty settled into the same chair he was in the first time Meredith was there, when he frightened Jamie with his rant about the Garden of Eden. He rocked back in the chair and looked out at the play set. Meredith and Curtis stood to one side and watched him for a moment, but Shorty ignored them as though they had vanished.

"Shorty," Curtis started, "About Gemma…"

Shorty held up a hand.

"I ain't talking to a boy sheriff." Then he added with a sneer, "Barney."

Meredith put a hand on Curtis's arm and then stepped forward, close to the old man.

"Shorty," she said. "We need to find her. Do you know where she is?"

Shorty rocked forward in his chair.

"You know where her name came from?" he asked instead.

Meredith shook her head.

"Gem state," he answered. "Idaho's called the gem state and she's my little gem. She's my chance at redemption, for all my sins."

Meredith nodded, unsure of what he was saying but wanting to humor him. She remembered her mother, drunk for days, falling into reveries and talking nonsense. It frightened her as a child but not anymore.

"We want to talk to Gemma," she said.

"The snake whispered in Eve's ear and she got thrown out of the garden," he barked at her. "I told you about the snake."

Curtis shook his head and looped a finger near his head, and Meredith despaired at getting any information from Shorty. She tried one last time.

"I remember you telling us the story of the snake." Meredith spoke slowly, feeling her way carefully now so Shorty would continue talking. "Maybe we can go tell the story to Gemma."

A pickup truck roared suddenly to life in a driveway across the street, startling Meredith and Curtis, but Shorty wasn't aware of anything but his own reflections. Meredith looked over at the play set and experienced a pang of sympathy for Shorty. He had prepared for Gemma's child, his great grandchild, thinking he would have a family relationship at last. She and Shorty had that in common, a lack of family connections. She knew how lonely a place that could be.

"I told her." Shorty's voice lifted into a whine. "I told her the snake was evil."

Shorty struggled out of his chair to stand up. Meredith reached out to help, but Shorty ignored her hand. He staggered, almost falling against her, but caught himself just in time. He grabbed Meredith's arm and Curtis tensed up.

"There is redemption in defeating evil," he said, his fingers digging deeper into Meredith's arm. "When he came here with my Gemma, I recognized him. The snake hissed in my little girl's ear, so I stepped on it. It was God's plan."

Meredith stopped breathing. A terrible idea came to her.

"What snake?" she asked. "What snake did you

step on?"

She looked into Shorty's wide demented eyes, set into yellowed skin, and smelled the sickness in him. Her arm burned from his fingers digging into her flesh and she tried to pull away.

"He thought I was just taking a piss by the side of the road, an old man who can't hold it one more minute," Shorty hissed. "He didn't expect me to do it; that's what made it easy. I don't regret it."

"Who?" Meredith gasped out. "*Who* did you step on?"

"You know who," Shorty said. "You're free now, too."

Chapter 20

Jamie bounced in the seat in the grocery cart, shaking it and threatening to tip it over.

"You're out of there," Meredith ordered and lifted her wiggling five-year-old onto the tile floor.

"I want to ride," Jamie whined.

"You're a five-year-old now. Big girls walk."

Jamie sat on the floor in protest. Meredith turned away and faced the counter where deli boy waited with his usual sneer.

"I don't have all day." He tapped his fingers on the counter. "Are you ordering something or not?"

"Hard to remember my order, isn't it?" Meredith was determined not to let the kid rile her this time. *He's just a punk*, she thought. "Half turkey, half ham."

She turned back to Jamie.

"Get up. Now," she ordered.

Jamie wiggled her bottom on the floor, as though rooting it more firmly in place.

"That worked," muttered deli boy snidely before pulling the turkey and ham out of the counter case.

Meredith ignored him, not wanting to show how much he annoyed her. She pointedly looked at her grocery list and then dug into her purse and pulled out a pen.

"I guess we'll skip the cereal aisle today." She made a show out of scratching out 'cereal' on her list.

"I bet eggs are on sale. We can get lots of eggs instead."

Jamie looked up with a horrified expression.

"I don't like eggs," she complained, kicking one foot out in protest.

"Fried eggs," Meredith added. "With runny yolks."

Jamie glared up at her, but Meredith calmly studied her list. After a moment, Jamie got to her feet.

"The floor's too hard," she explained, and then stood quietly by the cart.

"I heard about Shorty and all," deli boy said, slapping the wrapped packages on the counter top.

Meredith tensed up as she grabbed the packages, waiting for his next rude comment. She just hoped it wouldn't be anything that would upset Jamie. Meredith didn't meet his eye and prayed it wouldn't be too bad.

"Guess it's tough," he added in a low tone.

Surprised, she acknowledged the comment with a nod, and turned the cart away. Could deli boy be softening up?

"Knowing you live in his house," deli boy continued.

Meredith turned back to him and faced him full on.

"My house," she said hotly. "I live in *my* house."

Meredith glared at him until deli boy dropped his eyes.

"Yeah." His tone was sulky.

She pushed the cart away quickly before he could say anything else.

"Merry and her little lambs!" a deep voice boomed out and she halted and turned around.

Crusty strode up holding a hand-basket full of crackers, peanuts, and canned soups. Meredith smiled up at him, glad to behold a friendly face.

"I'm not a lamb," Jamie shouted out with a laugh. "I'm a girl. I'm five now."

Crusty bent down, peered closely at Jamie and then stood tall again.

"You're right," he exclaimed. "Lambs don't talk, so you must be a girl."

He chuckled at this and turned to Meredith.

"And how are you doing?" he asked in a serious tone. "You getting through this okay?"

She shrugged.

"Well enough."

"Well enough is well enough for now," he said.

Jamie started bleating like a sheep and hopping around the grocery cart. Meredith looked back at her daughter and son. Atticus, who had just wakened, was blinking sleepily at his sister.

"You just take care of those little lambs of yours," Crusty said.

"We'll come back in soon." The words popped out before Meredith knew what she was saying, surprising herself. "To the hardware store. I'm planning on doing some more painting."

As soon as she gave voice to the idea, she knew it was true. Gradually, she'd made the decision to stay in Hay City and in her broken-down old house. At some point, it had started to become her home. She believed she could make it a good home, for herself and her children.

Crusty's face broke into a huge smile, as though this was the best news he'd heard in months.

"Maroon? Puce? A bit of atomic tangerine? I can give you a good deal."

Meredith laughed and shook her head.

"Maybe white."

"Too bad, too bad." He winked at her. "Going to Honey's tonight for dinner. Maybe breakfast too if she's lucky."

Meredith's smile faded at his comment and she watched him stride away. Did Crusty know what he was getting himself into with Honey?

As she worked her way through her grocery list—Choco Puffs ("*Huffs,* Mommy"), granola, tomatoes, cucumbers, and rice—she thought back to the day two weeks earlier, when Shorty confessed to Brian's murder.

The aftermath of that day left her head spinning. She'd been certain Gemma had killed Brian, and then had been equally certain it was Honey. Finding out it was Shorty in the end was a shock. *So many people with motives to kill Brian, and I guess that includes me, too.*

Curtis had quickly stepped forward, pried Shorty's fingers from her arm and then arrested him in order to get his confession on record.

It spewed out full tilt. Once started, Shorty wouldn't shut up about the evil snake and his own version of Adam and Eve and the Garden of Eden.

"Shot him in the head," Shorty said, as Meredith turned away in tears. "It's what you do with a snake. Got to shoot 'em in the head."

Later, Curtis told her Shorty's deranged motive was atonement for his earlier sins.

"The snake was luring my sweet grandbaby Gemma into evil," Shorty shouted and raged. "He held out temptation and she reached out and took it, just like that. She didn't know him for what he was. Not me, though. I recognized what he was inside."

Shorty related how one night after a bout of drinking, he walked along the highway for hours to get to the top of the hill, to pray for guidance in the matter. It was a matter of coincidence, or "divine intervention" Shorty claimed, how Brian came along, recognized the old man by the roadside, and stopped.

"Oh, he knew me all right," growled Shorty. "Gemma must have told him I have a stash set aside. He had a gun laying on the floor. Now, wasn't that an angel talking loud and clear?"

Meredith didn't know why Brian had his gun with him. Maybe he'd started taking it with him for safety while out driving at night in remote areas. Maybe he was planning something else. After all, there would be one more thing in the way of him and Gemma and the life insurance money. Meredith didn't dare let herself think maybe an angel had been watching out for her, too.

****

It was just a few days after she ran into Crusty at the grocery store that she decided to start a new home improvement project.

"Sure you don't want to wait for summer?" Crusty asked when Meredith told him her plan for building a chicken coop.

Meredith shook her head firmly.

"I need to hit something now," she said at the hardware store, making Crusty's bushy gray eyebrows rise almost to his hairline. "That reminds me. I need a hammer, too."

"You know," he mused. "I could use someone like you to give me some help around here, inventorying and organizing, stuff like that. You can bring the kids with you."

She stood back and stared at him for a moment.

"Just a couple of hours a day to start," he added when she didn't respond immediately. "Just until Jamie starts kindergarten in September and you have more time."

"Are you offering me a job?"

He stroked his beard.

"I guess so." He appeared puzzled by his own idea.

"Did Honey put you up to this?" Meredith challenged, not sure anymore how she felt about the older woman. She wondered how much Honey knew about Shorty, and whether Honey had any influence over her long-ago, first husband, feeding his ideas about redemption.

A slow smile crept onto Crusty's lips and broadened until his entire face was involved.

"I suppose she might've," he conceded, and then he waggled his eyebrows at her. "I think that woman could get me to do a lot of things."

Meredith nodded. Honey was a woman with a lot of influence. She considered Crusty's offer. Curtis had given her all of Brian's secret money stash back, telling her it was no longer part of an investigation. At some point, she would receive Brian's life insurance money. But while it all seemed a fortune, she had other plans for the money. In any case, she needed a job.

"Then you can tell Honey I accepted." She tried to make light of the matter, and swallowing before adding, "And that I'm grateful."

Crusty had insisted on sealing the deal with a free can of paint, the atomic tangerine, which he guaranteed would frighten away coyotes, bears, and the common cold.

****

Now, despite her best efforts, the chicken coop's wooden frame listed to the right. She drove another nail into the wood.

"Ow, ow, ow!" Meredith cried. "Damn it all to hell!"

It felt good to shout it out. Her finger still throbbed from the hammer hitting it, but her complaint to the world made her feel better. She looked at her reddening finger and stepped back from the structure before her. A chicken coop. Nothing that would put Honey out of business; just a home for Laf and maybe a friend or two of his. What could be easier than building a box on stilts?

"Merry, Merry, quite contrary."

Meredith stiffened.

Curtis popped his head into the shed, a concerned look on his face.

"Hey," Curtis called. "Everything okay in here?"

He doesn't know Brian used to say that to me, Meredith realized, and she turned toward him holding up her finger.

"Missed," she said.

He held up his hand, palm forward, and she noticed for the first time how his little finger didn't straighten all the way up.

"Snapped it chipping ice off the roof two years ago. My hands were so cold I didn't even realize it 'til the next morning."

"You should have worn gloves," Meredith said callously, annoyed at how he dismissed her pain so easily by comparing it to his own, more serious, injury.

He didn't take the bait. Instead, he moved closer to the chicken coop and frowned as he examined it.

"I think a couple of brackets on the corners will firm it up," he advised. "I'll bring some by tomorrow."

She sighed.

"Brackets?"

"Easier than it sounds," he said.

She looked out the shed door where Jamie was struggling to drag a rake across the driveway. The obstacle course of potholes had disappeared, filled with gravel, packed down and raked over by Curtis. Atticus chased after Jamie, and Meredith wondered how many rocks he had eaten that afternoon.

"They're going to have a half-brother or sister soon," Meredith said, thinking about Gemma's round stomach and how it must be growing quickly.

Curtis nodded gravely.

"Sounds like it. That's what Gemma says."

Meredith felt his eyes on her, watching for her reaction. After Shorty's arrest, Gemma had shown up at Honey's house, staying for a week before disappearing again. She knew she should be angry or outraged or something, but she couldn't muster up any emotion at all.

"How are they doing?" she asked flatly. "Gemma and Honey? What are they going to do now?"

"I suspect Gemma knew, and maybe Honey as well, but there's no way of knowing for sure. Shorty insists he never talked to them about his plan. I suspect he's worried someone's going to steal away his redemption."

Meredith sighed heavily. She'd made the decision

to stay in Hay City, in Honey's old house. There was no way she could avoid Honey forever in this small town, but surely their relationship would be changed now. It struck her that Jamie and Atticus would not only be related to Gemma's child, but also in a way to Honey.

I have the most dysfunctional family in the world.

She chewed her lip nervously before she spoke again.

"Brian tricked Gemma into signing this house over to him," she said. "I need to give her the money Brian owed her. Can you take it to Honey? So she can get it to Gemma?"

Curtis took a deep breath and let it out slowly.

"Honey misses you and the kids. She's sincere, I know. Could be best if you took the money there yourself."

Meredith watched as Jamie dropped the rake and sat cross-legged on the gravel driveway next to Atticus. The two of them were engrossed in something crawling on the ground. Her heart swelled with love as she looked at the two of them, their heads bent together.

Meredith wondered at how kids could lose themselves in something so small. Her own childhood had been filled with anxiety, yet she remembered being caught up in following a butterfly or digging in the mud for worms. Time, hunger, and worry would all disappear for a while. If she could conquer her own childhood challenges, surely her children could emerge from all of this okay.

Surely she could mend things with Honey. As a first step.

"Maybe someday," she mused out loud, and then looked up at Curtis. "Maybe someday I'll go visit

Gemma, wherever she is, and talk about things."

Someday, she'd have to talk to her kids about their father and how he really died. When they were ready, she wouldn't hide it from them; she would tell them the truth. The whole messy truth. Including the fact that their father had loved them. Her kids wouldn't grow up feeling lost, she vowed.

Curtis was watching her carefully, a sad smile in his eyes.

"Life is messy," he said. "It's all about how we handle it."

She startled at that, an echoing of her mother's mantra coming at her when she needed it most.

"I can handle it." She lifted her head high.

****

"The world balances things out," Honey was saying. "Shorty committed his crime against me. Now, he saved both you and my granddaughter from a similar fate."

Honey shook her head in disbelief. "It's a strange world indeed," she added.

Meredith didn't answer. She just took another bite of Honey's iced lemon cake, chewing into its sweet tartness. From her living room, she heard Jamie reading a story to Atticus, sounding out words from a book carefully and making up parts of the story when she didn't know the words.

My kids are going to be okay. It's all that matters. We're all going to be okay.

"Take me and Crusty, for instance," Honey continued. "Never in a million years did I think…I mean, well…that beard and all, you know. Quite a hairy beast, that man."

Honey gave a girlish giggle and then rose. She patted her generous hips with satisfaction. Meredith followed her with her eyes, watching as Honey refilled her coffee cup and added cream. Meredith called her the previous day after Curtis left, and Honey accepted her invitation for coffee and a chat. While Honey wasn't bashful about diving into the subject of Shorty's arrest, Meredith was reticent on pressing her about what she knew and when.

Honey was looking at her thoughtfully.

"You know what's been on my mind lately?" she asked. "I didn't want to say anything earlier, but I think you should know this."

Meredith held her breath. In the weeks since Shorty's arrest, she considered more and more whether Honey might have influenced Shorty in his actions to protect their granddaughter. Had Honey whispered the idea of redemption in Shorty's ear? Could it be possible Honey was going to confess this to her?

Do I really want to know this? Can I stand not knowing?

"I'm thinking about getting a few goats," Honey said. "Make my own cheese."

Meredith exhaled.

"I promise, though," continued Honey, "I won't offer any baby goats to Jamie to raise, even if she begs me. Not unless you say it's okay first."

"That would be wonderful," Meredith spoke in a rush. "About you having the goats, I mean, not about any goats coming over here. No goats here, okay?"

Honey nodded.

"You deserve a new start, Honey," Meredith added, thinking that, for now, she could stand not knowing the whole truth. "And someone to cook for, aside from us."

Honey gave a contented sigh and then nodded toward the window.

"Speaking of fresh starts," she said. "I don't like meddling, but he's a nice young man."

Meredith turned, looking out across her yard and beyond the driveway. A long plume of dust rose along the road from the highway that led to her house. The sheriff's truck was visible at the head of the plume, growing in size as it raced toward her home.

"Did you invite him here?" Meredith asked.

Honey waggled her head with a smile.

"Maybe, maybe not," she said. "Let an old lady keep her secrets."

Meredith took another sip of her coffee, warmth filling her inside. *Maybe I will*, she thought.

A word about the author...

Julie Howard is a former journalist and editor who has covered topics ranging from crime to cowboy poetry. She has published a number of short stories in several literary journals. *Crime and Paradise* is the first novel in her Wild Crime series. Julie lives in Idaho.

www.ingramcontent.com/pod-product-compliance
Lightning Source LLC
Chambersburg PA
CBHW060523260626
47161CB00003B/741
9781509216451